Puppets Win Today

Also by
David Wallace Fleming

With and Without Class

Not from Concentrate

Growing Up Wired

A Novel

DAVID WALLACE FLEMING

Poetics Press
Austin, TX USA

ISBN 978-0-989-12476-8 (hc) / 978-0-989-12475-1 (pb)
LCCN TXu002054660

1

As he stitched, his sewing machine *clacked*, and his prior puppets vomited fuzz and dragged about. They gazed at wiry fingers and danced. A puppet crawled and said, "I think, therefore…" With its beak all wobbly. "Line?"

It was no wonder the hiring managers complained his creations lacked the intellect to perform office work. Our workshop was not really the best environment to train magical puppets to be office workers. The scent of curry hung about the apartment, which was on the tenement side of the tracks.

Our nearness to poverty drove us to a threadbare frenzy. To separate myself from this privation, and be a good puppet, my mannerisms, emails, and keystrokes needed to be controllable. So Miltro took his time on my rod attachments. I lie paralyzed, facedown, and hacked up a mountain of felt. The materials a puppet maker uses can be difficult to keep down.

Miltro had left the front door to our apartment ajar, with notes scattered throughout, directing couriers to deliver materials to his workshop. He probably assumed it was a courier, bringing more Urftoo wood, more memory foam, more river-blood rope, when the knock came.

"Set it in one of the corners," Miltro said from behind his sewing machine. His lazy cigarette dangled as microwaved noodles spluttered. The workshop had been two bedrooms before the joining wall had been knocked-out. It was now one big room, housing puppets from waist to knee-high.

"Can we talk outside?" Certi asked from behind a door.

"No," Miltro said.

"But," she slapped the door, "my fire got fumbled." Vague forms sharpened as she opened the door to invite the purple rays. She pressed away wrinkles from her pantsuit as her pearls dazzled. "The puppet sales aren't pulling enough for the payments on our condo, which we discussed."

"I'm better with a needle and thread than anyone on Urftoo, and you know it!"

*"I'm better with a needle and…*you've been at it for years. You don't have the character of Gohansen, not groovy like Van Whipple."

"There's no medicine in their puppetry."

She looked at her lipstick, snuck it in her purse and trudged into the foam and clay molds. "This wasn't the deal when I agreed to marry you."

"You didn't take my last name."

"Our second anniversary was last Wednesday." She lifted the Tuxedoed DinoMan as her arm strained. It stroked her as its scales creased the neckline of its tuxedo and its muzzle pecked. The rubbery scales became a surface as variable as water as it blushed like something illumined from within: "This meat-eater hates meteors!"

"You're behind schedule." She set it on its shelf and wiped her hands. "I thought you'd have them ad-libbing."

Its guide rods flailed as it struggled to right itself, and it moved as if to suck its thumb.

Something squirmed beneath a towel and cried, "Master, why won't you give me my thumbs?"

"I'll give thumbs—" The morning train warbled as Miltro stilled an ashtray.

Certi raised her finger.

The train surged.

"I'll give thumbs when you learn to hold and be held."

The squirming stilled.

"You're holed-up in this dark room, trying to bring life into this world like some pregnant woman," Certi said.

"Why can't we start a family?"

"The index funds are below seventy."

He stood from behind his sewing machine and shook the pistachios from his undershirt.

She stared at him.

"You wanna conquer the world of machines?" Miltro asked. "I'll be in here nurturing this life."

"I'm not attracted to you."

"Remember that time I spilled that spaghetti sauce over you but we still had dinner?"

Her shoulders slumped. "I'm the chief chemical engineer for Power Chemicals. You said you'd be the prizefighter of loaves."

"The breadwinner? You're cradling each crumb."

She stomped, crunching pistachio shells. "You know they've been driving me into the ground to get the ad rollout ready." She struck out some clenched papers toward him and concealed her mouth. "I've been spending all my time helping them get the brochures, the pamphlets, and the commercials ready."

"The men at that office wanna fuck."

She glowered. "How petty are you?"

Boxes, felt patterns, and vintage posters swirled—flash-jumbling—as Miltro stabbed to point me at her. He had whispered how he had sewn me to resemble his father. I was a symbol of his father and pointing me at her might lend him power. "I paid the Novemtursneb rent from my charter flights." He shook me towards his beer cans. Everything wobbled while nausea festered within my stomach before a hunger pang clenched like an imploding star. "We got five months runway."

He set me on the highest shelf just above his eye level, letting my legs dangle over the ledge. It was the whispering, metal shelf with books of 1120s weaponry and 1540s corporate procedures. I despised when he made my paralyzed body sit between stacks of books.

The passages of those pages formed chains that sailed left-to-right and right-to-left and swirled loop-de-loops through my filling skull. The frost-tipped words flew from a bookcover and into my scalp to overwhelm me.

My Holy Lobster!

We revered the lobster that created our Universe.

She pushed her papers on him. "Take it."

"Divorce?" Miltro asked.

She nodded.

They clenched the papers together so that they formed an *H*. The hoops of her earrings swung faster.

A trunk near the windows creaked, and a fabricated kangaroo struggled out to hop in figure eights. Its felt rippled over coil-springs as its tail squeaked like a screen door. Forepaws bounced and blond tufts quivered. A puppet burst up from the pouch—his cork hat, leather vest and boomerang dripped with amniotic fluid. "Ka-blamo!"

Certi clenched the sheaf of divorce papers before one of her legs gave out, and her head bobbled. Her eyes grew till she seemed agog, moon-dazzled, lightning-struck with expectancy. The puppet chewed a match between his teeth, and his joints clacked, brandishing the empty string eyelets that adorned his limbs. His facial expression hitched as an antique player piano, plinking to life after disuse. His eyes blinked like a pinball game.

His voice was distant, drenched in reverb like a toddler in a very high up place. "That's why me mates call me Matchy! And if you matched me with danger, then call the gove'ner, 'cause we're in for a hot one!" He bent over and coughed out spidery clumps of felt.

"That one seems smart!" Certi stretched the papers. "Miltro, we could finally get our vacation homes."

Miltro stretched the papers. "That's all it says."

"Ka-blamo! That's why me mates call me Matchy! And..."

She scowled.

Funk drifted in from the bay as the wind clattered. The ammonia with a hint of oysters really sponged up in our felt. Blackbirds busied themselves in the cold dimness as they prepared for another, uncertain winter.

Like the blackbirds, the LobStars who settled Blueport Blues were hard workers. This work ethic had been the cornerstone of Lobstarian marriage. In 1322, they sailed from Eastonia in pursuit of religious freedom. Perhaps without realizing it, Certi practiced their chief tenant: strike first, without remorse.

Few Eastonians during that period shared these beliefs because the LobStars also preached of a world brought into existence by an enormous, talkative lobster. It had martyred itself by allowing its flesh to be steamed. It was steamed so that everyone might have a taste. When it is said *After the Lobster*, the meaning denotes: after the best lobster dinner of all times.

Even though paralyzed and mute, I knew of the LobStars from the teleporter in that room. I had heard the teleporter as clearly as I heard them argue over the storage of her lesser known art. From the teleporter programs I came to understand that the globe we lived on was called Urftoo in our Westonia.

Our oceans separated the continents of Eastonia, Pluralia and Replicatia. Replicatia specialized in mass-producing parts like the blinds. They bickered over why the blinds had not been replaced.

Certi glared at them, released her half of the papers, and approached the windows. "You have to promise to keep the windows open when you're gluing."

"This can work."

"You need a better fan for those windows. I'll bring a better fan. Make sure to get up, take walks. Don't forget to drink. You know how dehydrated you get when you're close to finishing a puppet."

"I'll drink—!"

"You need to." She turned her back on him. "Goodbye, Miltro."

"You need me."

"I think, therefore— Line?"

"This meat-eater hates meteors!"

She turned to him. "Some of them were cute."

"If you matched me with danger, then call the gove'ner…"

Veins pulsed over his face as divorce papers scrambled into the air, "Bump-wood, cross-eyed seam-stripper—bet money—bet money you'd push pretzels on a desert-dweller."

She pursed her lips. "Drown in a puddle, fangless worm." She chewed down on her next words. "I'm sorry this is difficult." Certi took off an earring and set it in an ashtray before she left. Outside the apartment, leaves spun and crackled in a manner that sounded really rather lonesome.

The kangaroo slumped as Matchy withdrew into bubbles of amniotic fluid.

2

Throughout the divorce, Miltro ghosted creditors, grumbled love songs, and ended his telephone arguments in mid-sentence.

The pull of his easy chair snuffed out most of his business efforts. Of all the endeavors to undertake, magical puppetry was the trickiest. Middlemen in his business required either magical puppets or *inerts*.

Inerts were inanimate figures that were posed for battle scenes, business openings, and transnational PSYOPS. The middle ground between these was what Miltro produced, the semi-functioning puppets. These were known as felties.

We were called this because of our habit of puking out our felt. Miltro did not seem to care much about this defect. His bare feet widened the path through the fuzzy clumps of our puppet vomit as he walked from the door to his chair to watch the family-hour shows.

The puppets that starred on these shows did not cough up felt. Viewers would look to the screen, and this filled the room with all types of illusions. Distraction and interruption were vital to balance the simple minds of the puppets with the diminishing intelligence of their viewership.

Oftentimes, the shows quantum-teleported and materialized real product samples into living rooms if the viewers reached out for them. Miltro tousled his hair as he sat and aimed his remote at the boxy teleporter.

For days, he had dressed in his desert-camo sweatshirt. He clenched the frames of her photography stills. He obsessed over her shed hairs and signatures.

While set on my shelf, I tried to move but noticed only faint twitching, almost as if the unstillness of atoms. Felties pestered Miltro, and I wondered what part of their childhood had set off their selfishness. Surely, they had already been through my transformation. Slow warmth spread with vibration, echoing from my center. This vivified my thinking. It made me awash with desire. Food, I needed to eat; rest, I needed to sleep—love, I needed to sand and varnish a knotty piece of wood.

Miltro neared his book stacks by the door. "You can never give up." He picked a couple books. "Time to change these." Streaming words floated off as his hands lifted the books from either side. He replaced them with his finds as another stream of ideas and narration blew through my thoughts with itching discomfort. "Is this working?" he asked himself. He sunk in his chair and clicked his remote. "Oh, Certi, I shouldn't a' farted when you showed off your department development plans."

Walls vanished while a striped pattern injured the illusion. Pixelation clouded the dresser, the loveseat, the shelves. The workshop strobed with deploying soldiers, picturesque locales, and exotic animals as the expansiveness of the holographs suggested the feeling of a high-rise infinity pool. He picked a Great War Two movie where a nurse and soldier embraced in a war-torn, urban breeze. They were not puppets, but the acting was decent.

"We've won the last Great War, Johner! Whatever shouldn't we do?"

"We buy, Sarus," Johner said, stroking her amber waves of hair. "We never question. Or our enemies have won here."

"Taunt those enemies," Miltro said. "Outbreed your seed: The Great War Buy-Off." His voice caught while sobbing, and he looked down. "Thank the consumerism that followed the Great Wars. It gave us you puppets."

A felty passed up one of her bras, and he dried his tears and trumpeted his nose into each cup. Electricity crackled and Miltro stretched up for a sample of sardines that hovered, vibrated, and sparkled. He picked it like an apple from its float zone as it darkened, solidifying. He peeled open the tin, sniffed it and threw it over his shoulder.

"Fake holograph food."

A voice echoed off the ceiling corners, causing the actors to flinch and hunch. "Recently, there's been flubbering from the sickos, the losers, and the lames about your favorite pistachio product, *POWERSTACHIOS—stachios!*" A yellowish puddle grew under the soldier's legs. "We all know *Powerstachios* burst with the goodness to keep things cracking. This script is wrong."

Off-mic and stage-right, loud paper shredders threshed: "JUST READ!"

"Some have tried to discredit our favorite spokes-puppet, Eyeam. Saying Eyeam 's been bribed to conceal allegations that *Powerstachios* were twisted through genetic engineer-ing...*POWERSTACHIOS*—from POWER CHEMICALS,

INCORPORATED! You know what's coming. Suplex them with a knowledge-bomb, my puppet!" Smoke bombs fizzed and actors logrolled across the floor as hurricane force swept them. Their fading bodies spun before gleams flickered in their wakes. The emerald smoke wafted. Miltro coughed. "So, we ruined our marriage to get this commercial ready?"

Smoke thinned to reveal a waist-high, green, furry puppet, clothed only in diamond clusters of the wrist and neck. The house music kicked with the coarse *BOOM,* the *wub-wub-wub* (high-hat, high-hat) *wub-wub-wub—BOOM!*

With its green furry hands and hips spinning their circles. Drug-dilated pupils and an orange bulbous nose discovered the minutiae of everything. The big honker, dangling off its green face, breathed and pointed about as if it were its own plush-fuzzed, orange animal. The creature pointed to its diamond bracelets and necklaces and presented the pretense of being cold from all its glittering ice. And the stones dazzled so that the cracks of the fractured guide rods near its wrists traced arcs like swooping fireflies.

"Zorf!"

I zorf when stressed. This spokes-puppet troubled me. I did not trust him, or her. It must have taken willpower to smash those guide rods near its wrists. Guide rods are a puppet's most naked, most sensitive part. Some puppets feel it worthwhile to break their rods and diminish their masters' ability. There are other ways of our being controlled, however, since puppets are made for this purpose.

Wub-wub-wub (high-hat, high-hat, high-hat). "Don't get near," it said, "Eyeam is here." It lurched forward, and an off-camera hand steadied it. "How's it told and sold, skin-bags?" It swiped at something off-camera. "Keep pushing matters. In Great War One we'd remove one foot from a traitor. Let him hop in circles."

"You're on air!"

"I know what…" Eyeam's upper-beak flopped. "Huh?"

Matchy flung Certi's test tube and burette, dodging the flash as his experiment exploded. The felties seemed unsurprised that his pistachio mixture had combusted. And the DinoMan had stolen a pair of inline skates. He wobbled and skated toward a ramp made of textbooks and an ironing board as a legless felty dragged in pursuit.

"He-ey friends," Eyeam began again. "The surgeon general has been talking rot about our every-time snack, *Powerstachios*. Saying its chromosomes got re-sketched. That that pregnant woman who loved *Powerstachios* shot-out a two-header. And the mean head devoured the nice one. And the mean head gobbled up all the *Powerstachios*, and they pried it off the ceiling. That's just a silly, stupid rumor. Forget that. They say they got the photos, the affidavits, the class action signatures. Let me ask you just one thing: who do you believe? Who's your friend in this salty kingdom of snacks? Eyeam. Who sees the truth? Eyeam. Who's the best spokes-puppet? I…am."

An eighteen-wheeler rattled the blinds, and Eyeam's nose twitched. Its pupils shrunk as the puppet's nose sniffed.

"Sergeant, I smell gas, Sergeant. There's innocent women and children."

Off-mic and stage-left someone said, "Stay with us. Everyone is safe."

The blinds stilled as a woman in a red bikini leaned in with white powder smeared over her nose. "Hi-i, losers."

Eyeam dodged her thighs. "We agreed she'd wear her pantsuit!"

On the table to his right, Miltro dug into his pistachios. I leaned my head closer. Their twisted shapes revealed they were certainly not natural. The floor had been covered in a film of *Powerstachio* shells.

Eyeam swept its plastic claws out before itself. "The good people at Power Chemicals Incorporated are so confident in *Powerstachios* that…"

Puppets thumped as wooden joints rattled. "Eyeam is a sellout!" A dresser drawer along the wall flung open, and a duo sprung in a flurry of bills and papers.

The foremost one swayed like a serpent. "I found a dead bird outside. I'm hiding it under that puppet Miltro killed when he sneezed."

The other paced behind like a cornerman encouraging a prize-fighter. "Never go outside of the workshop."

A skeleton stopped pistol-whipping a clown with a pink squirt gun. The skeleton asked, "Who stole my social security card?"

"We're forging it," the clown replied, "we don't have social numbers yet."

Eyeam grew so its fur filled the room. "For a limited time, we're giving away samples of *Powerstachios II.* 'Like *Powerstachios, Only More So.*' As a matter of fact…" It gyrated to the *wub-wubs* and high-hats. The camera zoomed into its fur to reveal a city of parasites, complete with skyscrapers, smokestacks and ICBM. This troubled me. "Zorf!"

Words and sentences sailed up to float out of the covers and ice-tendril into me: 'Be on time to meetings. Yield the floor to the tallest of a flock of businessfolk. Females prefer cinnamon flakes to holly leaves on autumn afternoons.' These words pestered my foam brain and baling wire bones. I fought back the adages and proverbs—all the outlandish, the most absurd precautions ever written: 'Do not play the bongos on newborn heads. Do not set yourself to scrawling ad infinitum, ad infinitum, ad infinitum…'

Something slowly emerged from Eyeam as it pulled on a cylinder from within. What was coming out of its fur? Was this the play Eyeam had chosen to make amid this *Powerstachio* controversy? To reveal—once and for all—its gender? What was this huge mass emerging?

A letter appeared on view of the cylinder: P

P? "Zorf!" I clenched my fists.

Another letter emerged: O

Oh no!

W—E—R—

The tube of *Powerstachio* nuts emerged from its fur but from what orifice was it now pulling? Butthole, cloaca? "Yeah skin-bags," Eyeam said, "everything you enjoyed about Powerstachios, only more so. Raise your right hand for an ounce of hypnosis to lessen a pinch of pain."

Miltro raised his hand.

It shrunk so it was merely gigantic, filling the room with translu-cent-green eyes. "Eyeam," it said, "you is. We is, we be. All—ALL is currency!" Its face burst in flames, stuttering in checkered shapes with data encoded in each flicker. This flashing strobe hypnosis was tolerated through the loophole of requesting the recipient's consent, yet it triggered a fair amount of seizures. He leaned in and drooled. It cracked the pistachio shell and its halves fell and thumped like a split cantaloupe. It presented the pistachio. "Miltro, I offer this pistachio through our free sample agreement. The agreement was clicked upon by you in this year of Red Pinching Lobsters."

"*Ah—h ze—ep. Ahh–zeep–zeep,*" a modem-like noise burbled from his entranced lips as his arms clawed out.

"Don't do it," cried the felties.

"Zorf," I kicked a leg.

The nut was as big as his whole head but when he reached up, it shrunk down. He wiped away his drool. "I think—I think I can trust the food-scientists that spliced it up." Miltro looked as if to ask each of us.

"NO!" they shouted.

"Nothing 's worse than—numbness—being without worth." He ate the nut.

The holograph of Eyeam cross-dissolved amid swarms of twinkling, digital artifacts.

Puppets roused from their book programming, running, hither and thither. "Something is wrong." "He's turning gray, he's blotchy!"

Miltro stood, darted to and fro, he clutched his throat.

Puppets crashed and toppled books. "Is he choking?" "Do something, someone—*blerch!* Why must we vomit? We cannot care for ourselves."

Miltro ran from his workshop.

Puppets burst from the dresser drawer, "Get the first-aid kit!" "B-but…" the clown stammered, "it is only buttons—buttons and buttons and threads."

"We haven't much time. There is postage in the bureau!"

The books ice-tendriled their whispers inside, 'Talcum powder seals in the moist humors before an ocean swim.'

Enough. I would live. I stood in one thrust—steadying between gravity and inertia—and leapt from the shelf to the floor.

The others stopped. "Who is that new puppet?" "Looks like an engineer from Great War Two."

My hand thrust toward the teleporter. "You are on notice!"

The holographs dimmed and brightened in a pulse that seemed almost self-aware.

3

The legless felty dragged his glistening fuzz-guts as they pulsed, and he blocked my progress and said, "I am not stupid like the others." The dresser creaked and rattled as another irritated puppet upshot, "Hey you!" The inky irises of his pingpongs rippled and widened to peer into a shower mirror. His wiry hand steadied the mirror before himself, "My…my reflection…a memory of something?"

"Let this new puppet depart," a blue beak flapped, "he may help us."

"This mascara is inferior," the clown said to the skeleton as they loitered near the long skirt of the couch.

"We could experiment with a leechcraft, or we could mail him. We haven't enough stamps to mail Miltro to the Emergency Room," the skeleton said. "Arms and legs sprout out as if from a seed. We can mail his penis through the post office, and he could slowly manage to sprout himself back into some sort of man."

"Men are not vegetation," the clown said.

"Women sometimes speak of themselves as vegetation, when they speak of their dreams."

"This is a sideline controversy."

"You sputter at grizzle and miss the meat," the skeleton said.

"There is no time for nonsense," the legless felty said.

"Only I can help," I said.

"Halt!" the legless felty said. "The others call me Nagarazim. Ga ga ga…" his painted irises vanished as he hitched to vomit fuzzy spew, and his dark-brown pingpongs burned with the urgency of someone very ill, and his silver eyebrows betrayed the truth of his silver-rooted hair, "ga-gluurk gluurk… You are new to existence. Let me tutor you. Let me urge you toward patience."

"You lack legs. DinoMan stole your skates."

"My travels are farther through inner space."

"Get out of my way, idiot." I zigged and zagged, but Nagarazim dragged himself with his arms to match me.

"You do not understand these skin-bags," Nagarazim said. "They keep their evil within their heart, right beside their truth. How foolish of them, yes? You look intelligent to me. We have a hierarchy here. We have ways all our own. If the wisest of us thought it prudent we would help this man. Do not mix with the misdeeds of humans."

We beheld the dark hallway that lay beyond the doorway of our workshop.

Somewhere in the distance, Miltro stumbled and retched.

"Stand aside," I said.

My words found their mark, and Nagarazim lowered himself. "Heed these words: I cannot help you if you go farther. Cross not beyond that door. You who have been fashioned in the archetype of engineer, do not be so foolish as to assume you can fix humanity."

"Coward." I ran out of the workshop and followed the pistachio trail. Miltro's cries gave away his location.

I had been alive mere moments but the sensations of intelligence surged within me. Intelligence is important because through intelligent, careful planning all problems can be solved. They had called me an engineer. I was highly technical.

If you break a problem into its components and break those parts down and so on and so on, the amount of information this presents is impressive. Next, all that is needed is the proper focus and logical brain meats. I had the tools to do well. The pistachio shells and his voice led me to the kitchenette.

He lay slumped over the sink. His hand outstretched toward something on a counter as his neck and shoulder muscles spasmed. I managed to find a few lodgments and climb Miltro's back to reach the counter and the level of his eyes. Grayness had fallen over him, and his breath sputtered out, unevenly and shallowly. I got close and said, "Miltro you created me. Tell me how to help you, and I will."

"Hey," he said, lips bloody. "You are what I made."

"Yes, Father."

"I did it," Miltro said. "I made one that works." He tremored as he said, "This mistake got its start before us. This isn't your fault."

I glanced around. "Mistake?"

"I can't reach what I want." He coughed. "Never could."

"I do not understand, my father."

"Salt poisoning. *Powerstachios II* engineered too salty. Need water to break the paralysis before it's too late." His finger bounced toward a near-full glass of water. "Certi said I should drink water."

I rushed toward the glass. The slippery faceted walls evaded grasping as I tried to make a purchase on confounding, decagonal surfaces.

"Hurry," begged Miltro. "There's this…forty-two…licorice…restaurant…sewing machine."

"I do not understand."

"Pistachios always there. No matter how bad I felt. Those Power Chemicals fellas kept making them better."

I grasped the rim of the glass until I thought I had hold of it. As I tried to lift, my hands slipped, and I redoubled my efforts. I clenched tighter and higher and grasped again. The glass tipped and rattled, and I squeezed, and lifted so hard. I gasped again. "Zorf of zorfs!"

"Certi? Did you come back? I should've done laundry…cooked dinners."

"She is gone now. Zorf! I am not your wife."

"Do you know your name, puppet?"

"What is my name?"

"You'll find out. The lobsters are pinching."

"Do not let lobsters pinch," I said. "Lobsters love what does not flinch. Drag you down in a cinch."

"Their claws! I rush-houred my veins with my wives screaming in labor."

"Hang on. We can fix it."

"Forty-two years. I did bad things."

"Lobsters never forget—they forgive nothing!"

"They gotta. I abandoned families. One on the East Coast, one on the West. One in Replicatia. She doesn't know. I used my piloting as cover—" his eyes rimmed with blood, "If I could make magical puppets, I could create life in the right ways. I thought I could take the pain out of bringing life into the world. Your heart has gotta be pure to make the right things that have a purity. My faults got into you. I tried to make life the right way, in a way I thought was easy. There ain't no easy way."

"You abandoned families?"

"All men aren't built the same," he said. "Some things don't make sense—"

"Things always make sense," I said. "WE CAN FIX IT." If only I had been a being more real and more genuine than a puppet. If only oceans of desire that swirled within a sheet foam skull could have transmuted into real-stuff, surely the glass would change state. It was a fraction of my size. What held it down and what evils lay within its physics?

I discovered one problem: these droplets, known as tears, flooded from my eyes and increased the weight of the glass. They slickened the sides and slickened the counter so that my hands and feet slipped. Streaming tears squirt-gunned from my bouncy, plastic eyes in arcs and straight shots. I strained, and the tall glass rattled. It tipped and stilled. I kicked at it, and it rang a crystalline song as my toes throbbed. I fell in my puddle, struggling to stand.

"Certi, look at this puppet. You can take my name. Vacation homes."

"How does a man give a name?" I stood. The glass rose as I heaved up. It lifted high up into the air through the efforts of my arms. My full focus and will were lent before my slips came in successive extremes. Someone might have laughed at my noises: "Zorf zorf meeegorf—ohhh me–ha–haaaa!"

It tipped over the side to the floor, and the glass smashed into wet shards. There in those shards, by the error of my hand, lay the forfeiture.

"Wait," I said. "Slow your time."

"No one controls it."

"Time?" I asked. "Surely, the global parameter…"

He wheezed.

"We can control." The specifics of all thought stripped away, and I was robbed. "OH, GOD. OH, GOD. OH, GOD. OH, GOD."

He gagged and spat. "There's one thing, puppet. People say I'm a bad puppet maker— Listen, you're the best. It's your respons—"

"Stop your time!"

"It's your responsibility to take care of the others. People think my puppets are weak. I gave—"

"We will slow down time. You are fine. We will control, we will fix."

"I gave each puppet its own weakness to overcome. Get it?" He coughed. "So it could make itself stronger, by itself. Eat your heart out, Gohansen." He smiled.

"No," I said. "It was not supposed to— I was going to be good. I was going to be your son."

His smile faded. "Each puppet has their glitch." He remarked, "Too clumsy to bring water." He looked through me. This remark might not have been important. It might have been a good-natured jab or a misfire of a dying brain, unconnected to his spirit, before his eyes ran out of time.

4

It had been three days. The sky was gray and overburdened, and it rained in spurts all that morning. The dampness and humidity plagued us as our dry felt drank it up in every pore. Where a master once microwaved his noodles, now a dead body slumped.

More than twenty puppets crowded me as I backed up to the workshop's entrance. "Miltro Miggugen," they chanted, "Miltro Miggugen…Miltro." Where had they been hiding? A damp-felted pizza slice curled its pepperoni eyes toward me. "Why did the sewing stop?"

I kneeled to console the life-sized slice. "He has transpired."

Their gasps softened their saddening faces, and they wailed as they noodle-armed with such frenzy. The knee-highs ricocheted off the waist-highs like kernels of popping corn as they tripped over their latrines of halved soda bottles. "He never taught me! He never taught me to mend these loosening seams."

"He never told me my name."

"It's Root Beer. It's Root Beer, felt-sucka!"

"Inferior, inferior beverage!"

In the excitement, the skeleton swiped his foot near the hallway

25

entrance before some unseen force jerked his bony foot back inside. He fell to the ground and rubbed the empty string eyelet of his forefoot.

"Puppets, puppets, puppets," I said, "he intended us to teach each other, and to teach ourselves."

Their googly eyes suspended mid-bounce as their felt-clothed banker's vests and cowboy shirts breathed and pecked about. "Oo—oooh!"

"I am responsible," I said. "I will call for a coroner."

"We have a phonebook," Nagarazim said. They hustled to find the phonebook, and a book stack toppled. A rubbery orange head *ho—onked* as it crushed under the heel of a cowboy boot.

"Star-Pound-Pound is appropriate to dial," I said.

"Star-Pound-Pound!"

"Star-Pound-Pound!"

My fuzzy fingers snagged in the crevices of the telephone as I fumbled. Star-Pound-Pound was only to be pressed in emergencies. Emergencies involved the discharging of handguns, the culling of opposition, the enflaming of dirigibles, not the consumption of Power Chemicals.

"Hello...hello," the operator said. "Star-Pound-Pound Emergencies. Sir or madam, clear the line if you are not serious."

"My master and maker has perished."

The felties crowded in.

"Are you a puppet?"

"Do not interrupt—assassinated—assassinated by a poisoned pistachio! Heed these words, receptionist!"

"Stay calm, sir."

Sir? "Are you a puppet also, madam?"

"Yes. Are you sure he is dead, sir?"

This word *sir* stung my ears because she had now put stank on it, twice. "I have scarcely filled these cloth lungs eighty-score than have obtained medical license. Send a squad of EMTs, posthaste."

The atmosphere entering each cloth lung distracted me. It was strange to breathe, to live, to feel this pain of loss so soon. I hungered. What was and was not food? The fellow felties were not for devouring, not even the gentle-puppet shaped like a pizza slice. Still, this gentle-puppet should be on guard.

"Sir, sir, please give me your address."

"I am sorry, madam. One moment." I cupped the receiver. "Where do we live?"

They produced a bill, and I read the address. It was a bad part of town near the ransacked airport and the shantytown landfills.

"What is your name, sir?"

"My name? Yes, well, of course, my name—" What was my name? I put my hand over the receiver. "What is my name?"

"I attest you are Root Beer," one of those violet-faced jerks said. He had a thin nose like some deformed carrot.

Matchy struck him.

"Ooof!"

"That's why me mates call me Matchy."

"What is my name?" I asked.

"We know not."

"One moment," I said into the receiver. "Nagarazim, finish this call. I can go no further. I do not know who I am."

"And learning your name will do the trick?" murmured the skeleton. His arms and legs rotated within empty sockets.

His childhood had been deprived and cruel. He forever dreamt up ways for us to discover the minutia of each and every struggle. Miltro had torn his skin off and threw it in a trashcan. Those incensed screams were some of the first sounds to torment me. No one knew what skin and clothing once covered him.

His appearance likely resembled Miltro in ways Miltro did not wish himself to be. Miltro promised he would sew something else. He never did. The only modification he made was to enlarge the eyelets on his feet. He obsessed over the paths Skeleton walked. Skeleton had explained his walk, which grew from his soul-center, was funkier. Miltro said too much funk steers a puppet off-course. This explanation became another way to keep Skeleton away from mirrors.

Before I could move or see, Skeleton oftentimes stood near what was likely a mirror, in midnight hours, murmuring: "Why can't I have skin? Why so unadorned? So basic? My master shuns the outer truths. I'll show the inner ones. I'll prove the innermost argument of all ideas. I'll warn of the grotesque foundation of all discussion. They'll see how Skeleton holds it up!" This cynicism was likely why we discouraged Skeleton from representing us.

"I will finish the Star-Pound-Pound call." Nagarazim's almond-fuzzed hands clenched the receiver. "You are female? What clothing covers you? It is a matter of emergency for me to know this, yes. The innermost materials—of lace or of cotton? The cotton breathes, but the lace is special, no? Yes, yes, patience. There is the main business— No! Calm yourself. There is the main business. There is the sideways business on the side. Understand? Both are to be dealt with. Yes, the flesh-bag that animated my form is no more. Yes, a pistachio was too salty. I am called Nagarazim. I travel further through inner space…I can hold."

On the nightstand of the master suite five drawings described a puppet's evolution. The last of these identified me as Felt Guy No. 5. Clothed in the short-sleeved attire of an era bygone, a brown belt and black shoes gleamed like the unboxed toys of children. The hands of my arms traced the curves of my skinny-guy potbelly that hung like a hard-won trophy. My polyester hair hung and bounced with my head bobbling. My upper lip ticked as if I awaited some slap.

"Who am I?" The corner of a business card in my pocket pricked me:

Felty FuzzPalace

Senior-Type Engineer

1-800 GEARS AND SHAFTS

Although my button down was short-sleeved, the cuffs sewn on my wrists looked like my maker had attempted me as a joke of a male stripper. I pulled on them. "Ouchie." Something dangled from these cuffs that was more sensitive than the tips of my fingers. These steel cufflinks appeared to have the same thread dimensions as if our manipulation had been thought out in advance to comply with some standard of guide rods.

I grabbed a nearby hairdryer. The switch clicked and sputtered to life as my hair fluttered. My cufflinks tapped against the hairdryer's plastic. It warmed as it vibrated. Its intricacies burst from its centroid in torrents of symbology and pulsed through the green circuitry within. My cufflinks gazed like an extra set of eyes and asked questions: what durometer was the grip; had they used two layers of shielding for the wire splices?

I snooped out a present within the nightstand. Its tag had 'Felty' on view and the box contained a pocketknife. My cufflinks had no reaction to this deer-hunting knife other than a thrumming as if given from a tuning fork. I placed it in my pocket and eyed the cufflinks—symbolic of occupation, of purpose? Why would my master have built me to obsess over objects?

A *pound-pound* resounded on the bedroom's locked door. "A puppet soldiers toward some discovery?"

"Discern your duties," I said.

I clinked a cufflink against the hairdryer and—after that second *clink*—the mirage of a robot-like door cross-dissolved with my vision. This door opened to a darkened corridor. Deep within, lightning and smoke leapt from the whirling walls of a misty vortex. Electromagnetic oscillations, pressure fluctuations, and ionizing chemistry burst forth. The stitching of each of my arms fluttered and tugged toward that door.

A he-bird lit on a window of the master suite to burst out his morning song.

I waved this bluebird away.

He tilted his head, shrugged and flew off before circling back toward the window with renewed determination. He collided with the window, bounced off—thrashing—before losing interest. Animals could not digest puppets, but they confronted and attacked us over territory disputes.

Within my ongoing revelry, ice avalanches powdered, sluffed and fell to curtain the robot door before tumbling into the sea. The silver door swung like the jaw of a fallen man. "An engineer advances an art beyond the limits of his ancestors. An engineer must not allow anyone to be hurt by his designs. An engineer must not allow his actions to cause his clients to be sued or lose business. An engineer's lack of action must not allow the opposite of these to occur."

This was the foundation of the laws I beheld, otherworldly, from another time, another place, another dimension, transubstantiated of worldliness or of the chance of decay.

The fifth sketch boasted more detail. I was an engineer that dealt with machinery. We could not work from home. "Zorf!" I had to lead the felties out of the apartment into the corporate world of the flesh-bags.

5

"Some-puppet call an EMT?" a man in scrubs addressed me while gazing into his smartphone. "Where the body at?" His oily face smirked from the scent of a distant pleasure while several flesh-bags huddled in the entryway.

A young woman carried a defibrillator and chewed her gum like the moistened rubber smuggled some secret. She surveyed the room corners like a real estate agent as morning rays broke from blinds and danced across her face. Of course, in those days of favorable air quality, much has been made over about the beauty of the sun's purple rays as they might play over dappled pools or backlight splaying lover's hair or catch sprigs of flowering trees yet let me admit that the rhythmic warmth of flares and purple glows and gleams was really not all that sublime.

"This way-fine girl at the club said my pantsuit looked the same as hers," a dude said. "I said, 'it *is* the same one,' and we laughed—we laughed. But I told her, I ain't gonna be wearing pantsuits forever, girl. Your boy gettin promoted."

"My brother is a PUS-7," another said. "He can wear whatever he wants and not have to worry about no jail time. Who farted?"

"Somebody dead."

"The name is Felty FuzzPalace." I tilted my head to them as I stood, alone, in the apartment entryway. "I am in charge of gears and shafts."

"This meat-eater morns bittersweetier," a voice cried from the workshop entrance.

The oily-faced EMT lowered his smartphone. "I don't have time for any bullshit."

"He is slumped in the kitchenette."

The woman's face froze, and the crew rushed for the kitchenette. A large man hoisted Miltro under his armpits and appeared to sloppily dance with him for a few moments. "He got a dead breath in—in my mouth!" He flung Miltro over his shoulder like a sack of potatoes. "Power Chemical better start coordinating their product launches with us. I wasn't ready for no fifty-five outliers in one week!" And he walked out of the apartment.

I returned to the workshop as an eighteen-wheeler rumbled over a nearby highway and then another. The he-bird lit outside the blinds and brought out his song anew. Liquid leaked from the seams of my armpits. Puppets don't sweat. We dribble. Mostly our pits and brows. "I must confess," I said to the violet-face with that bent nose, "A hunger rolls my stomach in circles."

"You think yourself led in circles?" the violet-face asked. "Do you behold this crooked nose?"

"Peepers peep."

His eyes perched close above his nose and his minuscule irises quivered and followed prey with a vigilant, murderous hope. He winced from a need for all things except to blend-in with his flame-red hair that twined like bloody corn silk. His hair shot from his head at undisciplined lengths, at angles to give testimony to the electrified misfortunes of hamsters.

As his speech bent toward his babbling, he drifted outside the pocket of the present. His gray wizard robe strained from the puffs of his chest hair. The robe's fabric lay threadbare in blotches from a hand-me-down disrepair.

"There is much you know not about the master." The puppet had an unmelodious voice like a parrot auditioning for a pop-song's lead vocal. "The master's moods were not always pleasant nor magnanimous. One night, after he had imbibed many brewskis, he grabbed hold of this nose you see, and he gave it the bent that it bears today. Then, he said, 'Your senses will always lead you in maddening circles, just like mine.'"

His nose was like a plastic shred rescued from a wood chipper. "What is your name, sir?" I asked.

"I am called Root Beer."

"Is this namesake a truth or a defect of your brain that forces you to speak so?"

"No defect. I call others Root Beer to hide this as my own true name."

"Why do you hate being called this?"

"Do you not know the cruelty of a nickname? Its greatest insult hides within its truth. I rank low among us felties. I am called Root Beer because my character can only sweeten." He kicked a bottle cap. "I cannot intoxicate the soul as a brewski would. But I long, yes, I long to be more persuasive. There have been times where I have even dared dream of an existence for us felties beyond this workshop. I have thought— Say, what is your name? I have thought perhaps us felties have only learned half the mysteries of this existence. Perhaps, perhaps money stacked so proudly it swirls as the DNA that defines us. Perhaps, inside some errant, stray chance exist things of greater import, challenge, and opportunity—"

"Your wits are fueled on rubber cement."

He seized my arms with full passion. "I tell you they are not, puppet. In dreams, I have seen these things, they are real. Beyond this cube of drywall are pleasures. Damn near fifty percent more secrets and mysteries lay undiscovered that possess softness and sweetness to complete us, to free us from this disease of coughing up this wretched felt.

"Yes, I have ambition. Yes, I dream in blooms moistened with morning dew. There will forever be no apologies for this. Your master saw this ambition in me and, being embarrassed by the likewise cord strummed within, forever bent my nose to lead me about. Say, what did you say your name was again, puppet?"

"I am Felty FuzzPalace."

Root Beer shrunk. His felt crumpled into vegetated labyrinths of wrinkle and shadow. He quivered with palsy plumbed straight from the center of Urftoo. "Shut your mouth plate, puppet!"

"It is true. That is my name. Here." I handed him my business card.

"Felty FuzzPalace," Root Beer read. His fingers scratched the cardstock as if to remove the lettering. The irises of his pingpongs constricted, a tear wet his violet felt. "It is true, then. A beautiful name. I know not whether to love or hate you.

"Felty: as if the archetype of us all?

"FuzzPalace: as if you deem your body the abode of royalty?"

"Tut tut, the card, please, gentle-puppet."

Root Beer handed me back my card.

"We will give you a greater name as your character emerges,"

I said. "I am hungry. How do felties feed?"

"I will show you where is food, FuzzPalace." He bounce-pattered away with a hunch in his back as he wrung his hands.

In the corner of the room, a powder blue and pink, floral-printed couch lie hidden beneath opened boxes. We ducked underneath the cloth runner and entered the concavity beneath. Once underneath, inexplicable amounts of space rose up due to a hump, which had seemingly been grown by the gnawing of the teeth of many puppets. High above, swung a chandelier of coat hangers and strings of twinkle lights. Intoxicated felties rode it like a seesaw so its dots of light swung about the inner walls.

"The inside of this couch," I said, "is the size of a vaulted cathedral." It had the mien of a church where piety and drunkenness were coequals. I ducked back underneath the cloth runner to look at the outside and inside of the couch several times to ensure my senses had not deceived me. The inside of the couch was twenty-five to thirty times as large as the outside. "How is this possible?"

"The digested chemicals, the vapors, the miasma, the couch's miasma, they bewitch the senses here."

"How?"

"Here is where we feed," Root Beer said. He indicated about at teeth marks and the slimy fabric of couch innards. A miasma of vomited felt and chewed couch lay heavy in that place. Puppets bickered over what they had eaten. "Polyfoam is what a puppet's body needs."

"No, this is Styrofoam, and this is plastic cord. Both are sweet as frosting."

"Do all us felties feed from this place?" I asked.

Root Beer pressed down from an immense weight. His eyes

glowed passed that lent from the twinkling lights with a supera-
bundance of his spirit. "Only those in haste, only those without
time to waste."

"Rhymed you there?"

"Pay no attention to this," Root Beer said. "Over here, try this
polyfoam. It is soft to the mouth."

It smelled like the burnings of a poorly run factory. My stomach
kicked and rolled. "Yuck," I said as I chewed, "it is gross."

"The whole world is gross!" Root Beer said. "There is much of
it, no? Much to consume. Little time, my puppet."

Pepper green and lipstick red felties monkey-branched across
the cotton and springs above as they heckled, "Felty engineer has
much to fear, felty engineer won't like Root Beer." Some-puppet
hurled a wad of cold, wet felt that struck my head and stuck there.
"Engineer that off your face!"

I realized I was alone without a single individual to trust. And
what was love? Surely more than the lumberjack lust of knocking
down trees and splitting them. As I thought, the others stared at me
with blank expressions, like they thought I was different. Puppets
leapt from the coat hanger chandelier onto mounds of cotton and
foam. They twanged the couch springs.

Bling, blong! Zling zloong!

"Why do they play on those springs?" I asked.

"Tut tut," interrupted Root Beer. "Eat up."

"I don't know if I should."

"You will, as any puppet would—"

Bling, blo—ong! Zling zloong!

"There!" I said. "Rhymed you there! Why do this?"

"Rhymed?" Root Beer asked. "I think not. Eat! I bid you, eat!"

"I will not. The other puppets keep vomiting the very fuel. There must be something better for us felties."

"Something better?" Root Beer asked. "Hmpf. Eat! Eat you! Sure, it is not the greatest. But it shall surely serve. Survive we each with our own puppet verve. Here," He handed me some mischievous gray stuff that may have been the soil of a rickety robot world. "Eat, eat! Let not thy collywobbles cast thee about like casks of mangled meringues—"

"You talk strange, Root Beer, even for yourself."

Bling, blong! Zli—iing zlo—oong!

A glowing spirit heightened in his eyes. "Miasma, it be the couch's miasma! Does thee not smell? If thee will not eat, breathe deep. Breathe deep, good puppet. The funk of artificial depths, within and without, is enough to befoul the mind. Befoul the senses of Occident—of Orient, of good—of evil. Truth is a luxury of the weak. It's the fabric of the couch we seek!"

"Enough of this," I said. "I take my leave."

Bling, blong! Zling zloong!

The spirit light of his eyes surged as arching solar flares. His head bobbled like an over-primed seltzer bottle. Twinkling spots spun and dimmed dark. The chattering of the others trailed off. "Thee cannot leave. Thou are inside!"

Two felties appeared on both sides. They held each arm fast with iron strength.

"Now, no place remains for a puppet to hide!"

"Zorf!"

"Feed him full to bursting of every species and manner within the abode of the couch."

"The Abode of the Couch!" they chanted. "The Abode of the

Couch! The Abode of the Couch!"

"Fools, release me. I am Felty FuzzPalace. Felty FuzzPalace! I am in charge of gears and shafts."

Bling, blong! Pling ploong!

They stuffed me full of every manner of jagged, rough, sterile, course, and crackly manufactured product and byproduct of which to dream: bits of bugs, of plastic and bottle cap, sinewy synthetic strands that had surely been cycled through the dump several times.

"A punch helps it inside," a guard said.

"Ooof!"

"A punch leaves no place to hide."

"Oooof!"

"A punch, once more, to help thee decide."

"Ooooof!"

I asked, "Is this how you treat your own kin?"

"It *is* the way with which *we* win."

"Why rhymed you there, that time again?"

"Enough of this, let us begin."

Wide-beaked mugs of red, yellow and green marionettes burst through the cotton roof. They spun in mechanical, counter rotating lockstep—

Bling, blong! Ting, toong!

All—save me—rejoined:

This is the song
This is the song
Where we eat the couch
Where we eat the couch
Yes, we not tall

Yes, we not tall
No we dare not slouch
No we dare not slouch
While Matchy mope in a kangaroo pouch
THIS IS THE SONG
WHERE WE EAT THE COUCH!

My potbelly filled with the stuff. I learned the secrets of artificiality, how to take one element, isolate it, reproduce it a billion-fold, exaggerate it into demonic perfections of the brutal and the beautiful.

"Stop!" I told them. "I can feed myself this robot dirt now." It went down smoother with momentum as my hands gave way to frenzy.

Trees hide home of squirrel
They gnaw on nutty wood
And then on piney posts
Our teeth chomp way more good

Dream we all that dream
O, oysters of the pearl
Still gnawing rubber foam
Ends always with a hurl

Strummers strummed, they swayed. *BLING! BLONG! STI—ING! STOONG!*

This is the song
Where we eat the couch

Yes, we not bawl
No we dare not grouch
While Matchy mope in a kangaroo pouch
THIS IS THE SONG
WHERE WE EAT THE COUCH!

I collapsed over, panting.
Bling, blong! Cling clong! cried springs.
A guard kicked me.
"It kills me," I said. "What of something fresh? What of things aligned with nature?"
"You'll finish your couch, is what I wager!"

We won't catch a calm
Watch rivers ripping—scream!
We eat this cursed couch
We know not what it mean

So, again, we feed
Sling slow food to the air
The faster it goes down
The lesser we may care

I collapsed over again.
"I am done.
I can eat no more couch,
Or I will die!
See this tear?
See?

Beneath my eye?

Oops!

Oh no!

Why rhymed I?”

“Rhymed thee,” Root Beer said, “because I baptize thee into the nonsense of existence, into unnatural circles that corrode the arteries of the soul! Ha-ha! *Bler—eeerch!”* He vomited a hunk of felt and approached me with his hand full of that dripping felt out in front—

Bling, blong! Fling floong!

The sins of my digestions fought back up my gullet. My googly eyes watered, and perspiration dribbled from my armpits like leaky faucets. *“Bler—erch!”*

“Keep calm, puppet,” one of my guards said.

“Blerch!”

“Blerch!” they loosened their grips as they also blerched.

Root Beer staggered nearer with his dripping felt.

“Stay away with that,” I said. “No.”

“I have passed this down once,” Root Beer said. “Perhaps you can derive its last sustenance.”

“No more of this,” I said, my head jerked down. *“Blerch, blerch, blerch!”*

Felties tunneled madly below the ceiling’s surface like enlivened gophers. Heads popped out and rained blerches down on us. “Blerch!” *Plop.* “Ga-gluurk gluurk ga-glu—uurk!” *Plop.* “Blerch!” Twinkling lights exploded and ionized orange-forks flashed across the stinking miasma before the inner cave darkened and the walls respired with the gopher-pressings of the tunneling felties. Root Beer neared with the vomit in his hand.

"I am Felty FuzzPalace," I said. "I am Felty FuzzPalace."

"Vanity no more of such surnames," Root Beer said.

"I am in charge of gears and shafts, I am in charge of gears and shafts."

"*You* are in charge of gears and shafts? Puppet," Root Beer said, "at this point of the Product Life Cycle, gears and shafts are in charge of you. Products you dreamt to design, dream back to design you!"

"No!" I said. I had never designed a thing. That business card and the way I had been sewn made it feel I had designed the products of a thousand lifetimes. "Never!" I screamed.

"Often," Root Beer remarked. He held up the black-speckled felt that stunk like cadaver-mouth as it writhed with minuscule maggot puppets whose eyes burned with mortal fear.

Root Beer smirked. He dropped the felt to the floor.

"Fool's-prank!"

He raised his hands in victory.

I slowed my respiration and the dribbling of my armpits slowed.

"A felty never eats the felt of another," Root Beer admonished. "We forbid this."

Felties cheered.

This is the song
Where we eat the couch
Yes, we feed fire
Yes, bomb bellies vouch!
While Matchy mope in a kangaroo pouch
THIS IS THE SONG
WHERE WE EAT THE COUCH
WHERE WE EAT THE COUCH!

"Huzzah!"

A felty between knee and waist height, with an exoskeleton shell covered in glistening yellow blotches slumped over: "That couch tastes not so good." The slumped felty's guide rods and string eyelets were disproportionately large, with the largest eyelet protruding from the center of his chest.

Miltro had experimented with looping extra string between his heart and knees. By pulling the heart closer to the knees, the motion of the little yellow guy's arms grew erratic. After Certi had left, his heavy-lidded pingpong eyes grew crazed as his writhing arms pawed for the missing string that had held his knees to his heart. The slumped felty stayed slumped long after the string had been severed. He always lingered at the edge of the group, which was why he did not participate in my initiation. He watched.

Nagarazim lifted the couch runner. "Stop playing inside there, you children. The EMT wants to talk with Felty FuzzPalace before he leaves."

Near the threshold of the workshop stood the oily-faced EMT. I approached him, and he lowered his clipboard.

"Listen, puppet," he said, "We got rid of the corpse—"

"Zorf."

"But what is *this?*" He held a handful of our vomited felt.

"The inside of us, venturing out."

"Exactly—right?" he said. "That's what I thought. And the other dudes were like 'no it ain't!' And then I was like 'yeah, it is!'" He appraised a text message. "Where's Miltro's wife, puppet?"

"We have not seen her in weeks."

"Did Miltro have kin?"

"None I know of."

"You're responsible for what happens in this apartment then?"

"As responsible as anyone."

"You know I'm an EMT, right, little dude: Emergency Medical Technician. That means I'm sworn to help all sentient beings, human *and* puppet. You've got this whole place wallpapered in puppet vomit—"

"So?" I asked. "Speak plain, human."

"It's unsanitary. Disgusting felt heaps!" He pushed aside a coworker. "Look! I gotta M-BOB this whole place, little dude."

"M-BOB?" I asked.

"Yeah, M-BOB: Mysterious Box Of all Beginnings. It's standard operating procedure for a gaggle of unsupervised puppets." He pressed his clipboard on me.

"What am I signing for?"

His eyes pierced mine as if my stupidity had pushed him too far. "One thing goes in, all things go out, that's what the Mysterious Box Of all Beginnings is all about."

"Sing you a song next?" I asked.

"I don't go in for it," he said. "Sign here."

I signed.

"Get the mysterious box."

Workmen carted the crossbeam-planked crate on a dolly, and it dropped, bouncing on the workshop carpet, as dust-bunnies billowed in a ring. Its customs stickers displayed Westonia, Pluralia, and Replicatia, along with their provinces of prestige and power.

Even Ice-Longer, to this place it had come, where ice grows forever into pristine, frost-frozen circles. Felties ringed the box and recoiled. From the back of the workshop, I peered over the felties to watch the workmen in the hallway in their floral-embroidered pantsuits as they high-fived each other. They walked out with a jaunty strut, which was out of place with their pear-shaped pantsuits.

Matchy pranced his kangaroo around the box. Nagarazim dragged near the windows and glanced between the delivery truck and the box. "Do you see the disrepair? Do you see the places it has been? Do you hear the squirmy whispers within those walls? Not good enough for Ice-Longer, not good enough for us."

Matchy motioned with a swing-fist. "Ka-blamo!" And raised a fist, signaling his kangaroo to stop. After some time, he mustered the determination to leave his pouch. His distressed kangaroo shook its head: no!

"Bleer—erch!" Matchy divined some information from his felt on the floor as his fingers picked through blood-crusted patches, and he sniffed. His upper body tugged a shriveled husk outside the pouch. His diminutive, newborn legs dripped amniotic fluid, glistening, before he bit his umbilical cord in two. Felties edged closer to the box as he flopped about, and he twitched and clenched the carpet. "Ka-blamo! Ka-ka—*ka-blamo?*"

His kangaroo hung its head and hopped off to hide behind book stacks. Another slithering came from within this box. The Tuxedoed DinoMan rushed out and Nagarazim struggled to restrain him, but the DinoMan broke free. "This meat-eater helps the needier."

DinoMan kneeled before him, and Matchy lifted himself. Matchy walked away so he was freestanding as his knees wobbled. He staggered and caught himself as his peach-and-cream felt sickened. "That's why me—that's—why…me…

"The topic I wish to discuss," he motioned outside, "as sun gives way to twilight, and birds bow out of bravery, has precious little to do with me mates. It deals, most intrinsically, with…me-self. All know existence is, in ways profound, pushed out from the stuff of a similar clay and kiln. The soul tries for the singular and impales itself on the universal. Are we not all alone, despite our number? Despite our similarities, are there not natures more similar, held too long in darkness? We felties are stitched with rough, careless fabric. What moves within that box sounds squishy and smooth. The differences of nature hold an arrow of affinity. Think about how peanut butter conducts its business with jelly. It spreads over slices and presses into sandwiched contentment."

"Hear, hear!" we said.

"I have never tasted such sandwiches." The slumped, yellowish felty writhed and flailed near the couch as his four arms slowed with defeatist abandon.

"In the past—ka-blamo! Matchy, *M-MATCHY!*

"Excuse me. In days past I have advocated the cautious and the customary. At some point, one realizes great achievements as remembrances of innate knowledge. A union to this knowledge is worthwhile bliss. Believe these words, believe secrets within the boundaries of that box hold salves of sanity!"

"Hear, hear!"

"Let us cease coughing up this felt, let us *feel* something felt!"

"I like not the cards I was dealt," the slumped, yellowish felty said.

"STRIKE THAT ONE DOWN!"

"What is your name, piss-yellow puppet?" I asked.

"I am Piss Ant."

"Pissante?" I asked. "As if some surname?"

"Piss Ant," Piss Ant said with his yellowish arms writhing. "An ant to piss on. This is the identity sung from my soul-center."

Matchy struck Piss Ant in his segmented abdomen.

"Oooof!"

"Hear, hear!"

Piss Ant fell to the ground. Miltro had chosen a yellowish felt to cover him that was like mustard, abandoned to the sun.

Root Beer paced around Matchy. His perspiration wet the armpits of his cloak, and he fumbled to pull the cloak tight over his hyperventilating chest. He motioned toward the box and the smashed guide rods near his violet-furred hands hovered and pointed toward it like divining rods.

"Aah—*aaaa—AAAAAH!*" our guide rod attachments sung and fluttered, trying to fly toward that box. Some puppets, being famished of what they knew not, knelt before this box. Pathetic.

Oops, I kneeled also. How long had I been kneeling? The other felties kissed and smooched the ground near this box. They scattered before them offerings from their secreted stores: gem-bright jewels, horny-stones, noble ores, crayon-pressed I.O.U.s. An erection on Root Beer's hips grew upward in a curl, like a question mark of the waist.

"Grows it bigger?" Root Beer asked. He scratched his head as this erection tracked the box with steady vigilance. He shrugged his shoulders. "My physiology has its ideals," he said, "of which I was not consulted.

"All know I have suffered from a handicap of desire," continued Root Beer as the parrot could be heard auditioning for the pop song in each syllable. "Do I spread misery towards others? Seldom! Pangs of passion surround me—nightly. Squadrons flank—they pincer-attack my soul-center to spin out each thought headlong into oblivion." His close-set eyes fixed on his adversary. "Matchy, you attempt to steal the credit for the discovery. While I—Root Beer—have dreamt, have drooled over the rewards of mysterious boxes my whole life long. This gift is given us. You fancy yourself the center of it?

"Never mind a word of my speech, let us tear into that box."

"Into the box!"

"Into the box!"

"Screwdrivers!" cried Nagarazim.

"SCREWDRIVERS!" we resounded.

"Hopes rise to fall fast on the floor," Piss Ant said. "Bees swarm to find flowers no more; the whole of desire, simply a chore."

"Screwdrivers!"

"Screwdrivers!"

The clown, Matchy, Root Beer, Nagarazim, the skeleton, the pizza slice, the thing under the towel—all scattered into recesses, under boxes and within drawers to retrieve their screwdrivers. They all danced, back-and-forth, in chorus line steps, twirling their screwdrivers about like mini marching batons:

"Into the box! Into the box!" *"Cast off our rocks! Cast off our rocks!"*

The hungry box bounced on wooden-planked corners with an amorous beat.

Felties stood on shoulders of felties who stood atop still more felties. They scaled the wooden walls with a swarming hive mind. Screws came free from corners. Planks of the box spread. Matchy worked and worked a stubborn screw. "Listen not that felty who felt first our fist, told him—verily—he captures not the gist!"

Squeak squeak! screwdrivers squeaked.

"The expense of life," said Matchy, "is much to be paid without refreshment. We must not be in this workshop, heads and hearts imprisoned, within and without— Huzzah! let us see what this box is about."

Boards separated, puppets lost balance and fell free, melodious voices of the mysterious ones sung out, "This place looks sketchy. The walls could use colour."

"Popcorn plaster never helps the amortization."

Creak! Creak-creak!

Crack! Crack-crack!

KA-BLAMO!

Boards splintered and exploded as a tumult of felties and smooth ones spun and tussled over each other amid wood shards, packing peanuts and shredded newspaper. We flopped about with each other, sliding over their smoothness until one of us touched something that actually, and originally, squished. It was the first squish.

"Hey, watch it, creep!" one of them said.

"My hand cupped a squish!" one of us said. "An uncanny recoil, for sure."

"That's a bad touch, buddy!"

The squishy ones and us felties paired off and circled each other.

"What is it?" a felty asked.

"What is it?" a squishy one asked.

"They be not felties," Nagarazim said.

"Wow big surprise!" a squishy one said. "These ones look strong. Check this one out."

"Do not touch there, you!"

"Look at this one. It's got a horn over here like 'ra—ah!' So scary, right?"

Big round eyes held our hearts. Sweet ones with a calmness and dignity never known in nature burst forth from that box as their beauty offered us no escape. They wore costumes of nurses with sensible shoes while pencils uplifted such hair. They wore uniforms of schoolteachers with rulers and ruffle skirts.

They dressed as sniper-gaze accountants, leaving no morsel to chance, and peek-a-boo black sheer and mesh basketball shorts and hair scrunchies. Instead of our guide rods of the wrist, their steel eyelet attachment points shimmered from the small of their backs. A caffeinating one with auburn hair, always flowing and blowing, came at me:

"What are you things for?"

"We are felties," I said. "What are you?"

"The ones you squished."

"Squishies?" I asked. "What is a squishy?"

"We pretend to be weak," it said. "What's a felty for?"

"We pretend not to feel."

"For some reason?" it asked. "Or all the time?"

"Both these," I said. "Are you puppets?"

"Super hot ones. Look at this—and this."

"Have you not seen felties before?"

"Most puppets don't call themselves that. Our maker mailed us to entertain flesh-bags."

"What are flesh-bags like?" I asked.

"They stink like total garbage, they eat flesh, they kill each other. Bang bang!" It fidgeted a pantomime as if milking-off something small and sensitive. "Bang bang!

"Ahh! You got me, bro! That's my land!

"Like, no it ain't!

"We want our water back.

"We didn't vote for that dude. Bang bang!" It milked-off.

"This meat-eater objects, *objects!*" The Tuxedoed DinoMan pointed at them. Tears perched beneath his reptilian lids as he straightened out his bowtie. He pulled out a pack of cigarettes and a lighter but lowered them after he discovered them to be toys. He stuffed them back into his pockets. "This meat-eater… *Line?* Shit—bitch."

"What's that thing's problem?" the flowing auburn beauty asked.

"He is growing," I said. "What are you called?"

"You can call me Stephaniefinious, or Stephy. You guys got

anything to eat? We've been in that box forever, and we're starved, for reals."

"We can—"

"Silence, FuzzPalace!" Root Beer's back hunched as he pattered toward the couch. "I will show these beauties where is food."

"This one is named FuzzPalace?" Stephy asked. "Creepy."

"What is wrong with FuzzPalace?" I asked.

"Creepy."

"I thought it a good name."

Root Beer motioned in his direction. "Over here, beautiful ones. Come, beauties. Here is where we feed. The couch. *Hehe heehee—haah!*"

We bounce-pattered toward the couch.

"The abode of the couch."

"The abode of the couch."

"Where are you guys taking us?" Stephy asked. "Hang on a second, women."

Squishies giggled and squished as us felties fidgeted and squirt-gunned out our sweat.

"Patience erodes," the clown said.

Root Beer snuck a breath mint into his mouth when he thought no one was watching him.

They appraised our clothing and one of them lifted one of my shoes to feel the wear of my heel.

"The couch..." Root Beer's thirsty eyes glanced. "Where all the things shall be explained."

"You expect us to crawl under that couch with you?"

"Eat you not of the couch?" the skeleton asked.

"We're not going in there with you guys."

"Why not?" I asked.

"Common sense," Stephy said.

"Common sense?" I asked.

"Things you're supposed to know," Stephy said. "Things everybody already knows."

"What does everybody know?"

"Let's not do this," Stephy said. "Do you dudes have real food? We're hungry."

"What is real food?"

"Stuff you grub on. It takes a minute, but it's worth it." Stephy squeezed the shoulder of one of her friends. "There's gotta be a kitchenette or something in this dump."

"The master...he perished in the kitchenette," I said.

"Lead the way, FuzzPalace," Stephy said.

"We felties cross not the threshold out of the workshop," Nagarazim said.

"*We felties cross not the threshold,*" Stephy said. "That's how you sound."

"We will follow the squishy ones and learn what is food," Nagarazim said.

Stephy and the others followed me to the kitchenette.

"It's rad you got the balls to take charge and lead the way, FuzzPalace," she whispered.

"Yes, madam."

The fluorescent lighting of the kitchenette flickered and hummed.

"This place is dirty and gross," Stephy said. "We gotta clean first."

"What is *clean?*" I asked.

"Angieus, you're on mop duty," Stephy said. "Sarus, Beckyus,

Rebeccaby, can you ladies clear off these counters and clean them?"

"What be a lady?" the clown asked.

"Girls, let's see if we can't find some steel wool and ammonia," Stephy said. "Look, this dude had baking soda and vinegar. Ladies, if we can find a couple toothbrushes to sacrifice to the project that would be awesome."

"Why on Urftoo do we go around, from place to place, picking up after these muddled male puppets?" Angieus asked. "I got my MBA!"

"We each help out the male puppets for our own personal reasons, Angieus," Stephy said. "I do it because I'm a good puppet. You do it because you're ugly."

They dusted, scrubbed, and mopped so their arms, legs, and hands blurred and could barely be seen. "Is this a time-dilation of housewifery?" I asked.

"Housewifery? Time dilation?" Stephy asked. "What's wrong with you?"

"Within the workshop of the master," I said, "we dog-paddled through many books "

"You're dressed weird," Stephy said. "Are you an engineer?"

"It is my destiny. What is your occupation?"

"Occupation?" Stephy asked.

"What do you do?"

"We clean," Stephy said.

"And?"

"Cook."

"And?"

"Squish squish."

"What comes after squish squish?" I asked.

"I'm fucking with you," Stephy said.

"Is a philosophy employed here?"

"Move to your left a little, my man," Stephy pressed my arm to guide me away from a mopping squishy.

"Man? I have heard of this. What is it?"

"You don't know what you are?" Stephy asked.

"I was born yesterday."

It arched its back in a pleasing way. "Do you know what I am?"

"No."

"This could be difficult."

"Food ready," Rebeccaby said.

"How could food be prepared?" I asked.

"We fast," Rebeccaby answered.

Plates appeared, spinning like turntables, with tuna steaks, roasted salmon, filet mignon, green beans, snap peas, quesadilla, and thawed Westonia rolls, mummy-wrapped in seaweed.

"Miltro was a foodie," I said. "Why did he eat frozen dinners?"

"Men are weird," Stephy said.

"Maybe he was saving this for us," I said.

"This thing, food, is better than chewing a couch," the clown said.

"I know, right?" Sarus asked.

"Now that I'm not starving," Angieus said to Root Beer. "Is there someplace private we might relax?"

"I have used a breath mint in advance," Root Beer said. "I have dreamt, longwise, of the pleasures of mystery boxes—I know not why I say such things. Excuse this blathering. Will you come with me beneath the couch?"

"Isn't there someplace else we could go?"

"There is this dresser drawer, which I have claimed as my private abode. It is soft and dry, my sweet. The athletic socks within have not been in rotation since my master took up puppetry."

"You say sweet things."

"My personality has the ability to sweeten— Mind your affairs, FuzzPalace! Excuse me. Come with me, my sweet." He turned to face us. "I am taking this thing to my dresser drawer. I know not for how long we shall be absent. Make no mistake—each of you—I am a serious individual. I am not to be followed. I do this for science."

Eight minutes later, Root Beer came back with a jaunty stroll as Angieus followed. His flame-red hair was slicked down and back in a debonair fashion. His orange nose had straightened somewhat.

"Felties, with clothes removed, these squishies have bodies like a woman. Their physiology is a full flower. Upon their chests are soft things for touching—" he drifted somewhere, "in the ways required by her." He stab-pointed at her pelvis. "I put stuff in there. This one is mine. Do not touch. She is woman. Get your own women, and quickly, before your neighbor steals away what you might have. So say I, Root Beer, on this day after our master perished."

Felties and squishies paired off and snuck away to do a strange and urgent deed. They made the *"oooof!"* noise, although the blows sounded more intimate.

"Maybe you and me should go someplace private too," Stephy said.

"Zorf."

"You don't know your place in all this?" she asked.

"Negative," I said.

She puffed up her blowing and flowing hair fuller with an

impatient gust of her ruby lips. "Give me your hand, puppet."

"Touch you not the guide rods!"

"Not yet," she said.

I put my hand in hers, and a magnetic field flowed through her silicone into my felt fingers. She led me someplace and popped a white pill into her mouth.

"What pill did you pop?" I asked.

"Zokithral." She shook her ass. "Want one?"

"I think not."

"It's super safe," she said. "Power Chemicals makes it. It helps even me out so I can keep it real."

"Real?"

"Reality is complicated."

"Where are you taking me?" I asked.

"You'll see, silly." We stopped before an immense, closed door.

"This is the bedroom suite of my maker and master."

She struck me hard.

"Inappropriate!"

"Tool!" she said. "We're makers and masters. Shit, dude."

"I am maker and master?"

"Yeah, you're an engineer, right?"

"I am in charge of gears and shafts."

"Half those puppets can't put together a full sentence."

"How could I be maker and master?"

"Come inside this master suite."

7

We opened the suite door with her fingers over mine. She had a sweetness and readiness unachievable in dreams. I held her. She became smoother and even more beautiful. She grew fuller—redder—more flesh-like and human. The mirror by the bed showed us swell from a third its length, to half and still we grew. My head lightened.

"What happens to us?" I asked. "We grow bigger." We transformed, towering above our former stature.

She whispered, "It's the secret of the master suite, what happens when you take your time—what the other puppets don't know."

"We be full-sized flesh-bags?"

"Breathe from lower, from where you would if you were a boss."

"Breathe like a boss." I kissed her. "How can we be so real?"

"Shhh." She tugged me toward the bed.

"No more jests," I said. "Reveal your occupation."

"I'm an engineer," she said.

"I thought your maker sent you to entertain flesh-bags."

"Flesh-bag engineers."

"Oh."

61

She slipped off her skirt, and we rolled around in the sheets.

The window to the master suite had been left open. Noise from the streets blared and warbled as trucks rushed, planes raced, and cars fought the early-morning traffic. When Blueport Blues was first settled, when LobStars sailed over from Eastonia, they picked an area with accessible bays and land fragmented by rivers. The rivers and bays were the highways of the past.

Now, they had been built over with concrete and bridges in ways that conflicted with the past. I had heard there were stoplights at every intersection, giving the city a frustrated, illogical heartbeat. These commuters needed to cooperate. They needed to cease warring.

The skin of her back warmed as I reached the lace of her bra. "Hold, please. I will close the window."

She startled. "Don't!"

"The window to the outer world annoys me."

"You can't close it during this!" She fought me, but I broke free.

"I will close it." I got up to close it but, when I walked to the window, something was amiss as the mirror gleamed. I was a naked puppet, again: cuffs and cufflinks sewn fast to my wrists. The puppet versions of me were smaller, as in jest. "Uh uh!" I struggled to close the window to shut out the noise.

Her hands appeared on either side from above. "Here," Stephy said. "If you want to close it, I'll help."

"You must not close it. I must, I must block out the confusion."

Her hands pushed down on the window and a powerful robot was at my command, multiplying my strength.

"How are you doing that?" I asked.

"I'm big."

The window closed, and the noise of the streets silenced.

I turned to her. She was four times my size with her clitoris staring like a red eye. The name, clitoris, sounded like a lizard monster of old. A monster, towering above my puppet eyes.

"That was dumb, closing the window." Her breaths moved her breasts as she winced. "I got needs, right? I wanted the real you. You're a puppet."

"Monster, I flee!" I ran for the door and noticed my legs. It was taking so long, yet I went nowhere. She had ahold of a butt cheek as my feet pawed the carpet.

"Oh, no!" she said. She picked me from the rough of my neck and flung me onto the bed like a pair of panties. I was nearly smothered in oceans of sheets, comforters, and pillows.

"Help!" I screamed. "I drown in linens and accouterment. They smother— SOS!"

Stephy's hand rested on my back. "Chill, puppet guy."

"Chill?"

She kissed my felty ear. "If you relax and touch me, you can be human-sized."

"A reversal? Gold coins piled up?"

"Something like that."

My felt hands explored her breasts and navel, sending her downy hairs aquiver.

"How do you know so much?" I asked.

"The flesh-bags I entertained were puppets first before I turned them real. They could never figure out how to keep it real."

I nibbled her earlobes. "You said you were an engineer."

"Yeah." She spit out my felty foot. "I work too." She pinned me on my back. Human lips pressed against my lifeless felt. "I'm gonna speed this up. You might think you won't like it, you will."

"Touch you not the guide rods!"

"Gonna get my hands all over your rods."

"Never!"

Stephy shrank back. "Seriously?"

I appraised my wrists. "Proceed."

Her hands, so cold and smooth, ran over my cuffs and edged to the ready steel of my cufflinks. She squeezed. I vibrated and dribbled— "Hee-hee-hee haa hoo!" Vortices of smoke swirled. Lightning ionized, silver and white. Deeper and deeper, into the wellspring vortex, she took me.

Her lips said: "Engineers with integrity turn me on."

"Meap!" I was worried from how well she moved. Something ancient and external awoke.

The he-bird lit on the windowsill and tapped his beak on the pane.

"Get back, bird," I shouted. "Get back!"

"The bird can stay." Stephy said. She squeezed my rods. "Okay?"

"Okay," I said. "The bird can stay. It can watch as I am destroyed."

"Hot!" Stephy licked her lips. "No other man could do what you do!"

"Meap zorf, meap!"

Deep within the vortex I awaited the discovery of the robotic door. Flesh-doors twitched. The robot door had been replaced with this. "This cannot be," I said.

"For sure."

"The robot door is a joke compared with your door," I said. "How do you know about the robot door?"

"It's like mine." She released my rods. "I got a doorway!"

"A doorway to what?" I asked.

"Feel it," she said.

"Your door—" Her power was enormous, her magnet tugged worlds as a matter of routine. As I held her I was closer to this. As I licked her skin I was closer to this, and my identity dissolved. "Oh, no!" I said. "An engineer must advance an art beyond the limits of what—"

"It's only yours, it'll always be yours," she said.

"Meap! An…an engineer must not allow anyone to be hurt by the—"

"Forget that," she said.

"An engineer must not allow his actions to cause his—"

"Forget," she said, "touch."

"I, Felty FuzzPalace, will avenge the death of my maker!"

"Forget."

"You endeavor to strip me, strip me of my identity!"

"Identity doesn't work with this."

"Oh," I said.

"Yes."

"Indeed! Oh, Stephy." I caressed her in childlike ways.

"Are you ready?"

Blood fed my body, and air connected the tributaries of human lungs. It was powerful to be with her, to be real. "Yes, madam."

"Ooooh, Felty!"

She was flipped upon her stomach for convenience. A small guide rod surfaced at the small of her back and another surfaced below the back of her neck.

"Felty!"

My image grew twice the size of a man. The bed protested and squeaked. "I, huge!" I said. "I command nations. They bow before me in fear—obedience!"

"Ouch, Felty! That…that hurts like that!"

"Apologies," I said. "Maintain patience for mere moments—*sufficient?*"

"Better."

Her skin coarsened and took on the taste and texture of rubber. Her body shriveled and dried. Guide eyelets sprouted over her nakedness and twitched like appendages.

I grabbed and pulled and tweaked them. "I puppet you! I puppet you! Ha-ha-hee hoo hoo! Ha-ha-hee hoo hoo!"

"Puppet me, Felty! Puppet me—me a puppet! Me puppet!" She shriveled to her rubbery, puppet size. Our motions became mechanical as we sunk into lifelessness. "We…we must slow this," I said. "We must resynchronize."

"Weirdo," she said.

"I must spoon you as the spoons do." We spooned. I held her and timed our breathing until we became real. Next, thrusting. These intervals repeated until I put my stuff inside her, and she screamed like a two-year-old who had sustained some injury, such as some broken bone, some severed limb—a smoldering balloon factory besieged by one-thousand-and-one hand grenades. "Are you okay?" I asked. "Are you conscious? Stay with me, Stephy. Stephy, how many members have you within yourself?"

"One," she said.

"I am relieved you are okay. Stephy…Stephy, I love you!"

"It's a little soon."

"Zorf," I said. "Why did you scream, if not for love?"

"Yeah," she said. "I do this sometimes when I'm—like—having fun."

"What?" I asked. "How, why?" The pain from her words was as if the powerful world-moving magnet had launched me into another galaxy of cold space. Everything was empty. Stomach grumblings of urgency vied for attention. My forehead tightened from hunger. Only a few morsels of real food had been tasted. Most of the contents in my stomach were that of the couch. The couch beckoned me to eat more of it. It filled my soul with reverberating scarcity: scarcity of food, of pride, of love, of togetherness. "The pain—!"

"Shhh."

"However, my stuff went inside. The expression on your face changed."

"I'm on the puppet pill."

"What witchcraft?"

She crept away from the clasp of my arms.

"What happens after my stuff goes inside?"

"It's a surprise."

"Stephy, might you communicate your love for me for the merest of instants?"

"You're on my hair."

"Apologies, madam. And the communication of love?"

She sighed. "You're the best."

"Did you couch sincerity within each word?"

"Yeah, I—ah—I *couched it*. Let's just enjoy this, K?"

"How is it we transform into real people during sex? Why did the other puppets not transform?"

"The other squishies can't do it like me," she said. "The realness has happened since magical puppets first appeared on Urftoo. Whenever you act like a real person, you *are* a real person. But just for the time you're acting real."

"I am afraid to tell the felties," I said. "They will not understand." I still was not sure how I had become real. It was not a logical or mechanical process.

"Shhh," she said. "Be cool." She nuzzled into me as I held her.

"Measuring and recipes are useless when wills collide?"

"Whatever," Stephy said. "Hold me a little before we turn back into puppets." She sighed. "I hate being a puppet."

8

The pizza slice swaggered on his bread crust legs as he crossed the workshop entrance. "O' Glorious day!" He had mated with a squishy who was also a slice of pizza. Only later did they admit that their tomatoey toppings had inter-mushed. "This is glorious."

Piss Ant had bedded no one. "Humphf!"

"Two weeks transpire," Pizza Slice said, swaying as a satisfied slice, "since I met my darling, Margherita. I have not vomited since. The clouds seem a dingy basement." He turned to us as we lounged about with our food. "A whole food am I."

"How is this?" Root Beer's once frazzled hair boasted cornrows.

His once bent nose pointed straight out of his violet fur. The squeak of his baling wires had silenced to a whisper. He paced the room, gesturing as a politician in the throes of a concession speech, as he followed Angieus around. She paged through a newspaper with a day trader's expression on her lime-felted face. The expression of her face looked troubled and then hung-up like a frozen computer before she was freed from whatever afflicted her. Then she flinched, looked to the ceiling and swiped behind her back to ensure her eyelet was free from any Motherhood strings.

"The floor of the workshop is cleaner," Root Beer said. "How does this contact with our squishies cause us to cease vomiting?"

"Rebeccaby opened a window," Rebeccaby said. "We breathe!"

I turned my back on her. "Perhaps it is not the contact with the squishies that does it. Perhaps the food they make makes us well."

Stephy right-crossed my shoulder and pinched me.

"Inappropriate!" I said.

"I eat the food," Piss Ant said. *"Ble—erch!"*

"Someone show him love," Stephy said.

The squishies shrugged. "I checked under his wings while he was sleeping," Angieus said. "The medicine of puppets isn't well-known. He's rotting from the inside out. Something like gangrene. If he doesn't change course, he'll dead-bug."

"Keep away with your pity," Piss Ant said. *"Ble—erch!"*

"If Piss Ant eats this food and still vomits, something intangible that the squishies provide must be what makes us well," I said.

"When Angieus suggested my hair be braided into these corn-rows, I did not readily comply—"

"He likes it." Angieus smirked and nuzzled him.

"But while she watched me and moved her fingers over my frazzled hair, I grew still, an armistice signed on a cool day. The stillness of being cared for is an escape from the madness of mortality's ticking clock."

"Rebeccaby hungry," Rebeccaby said. "Only enough food left for two more meals."

"Anger my food," Piss Ant said.

"Consider further…" Matchy said. He bench-pressed his girlfriend while she highlighted over a derivatives magazine. "…some attention is purer, more refined, like light from a laser—focused. Her attention, like the laser light, is cooperative in its changes. Common light is hectic, accidental. My sweetheart's laser-love warms my soul."

"If you sex it right—!" I blurted.

Stephy put her hand to my mouth. "Let them discover in their own way and time."

"Stephy talks like FuzzPalace," Beckyus said.

Squishies laughed, and we busied ourselves with eating or fuzz-fornicating, sporadic games of the ilk of tag-the-titty, felty-catapult-smash and ring-around-the-drunkard. We split our group into banks, positioned on either side of the teleporter. Studious couples gravitated toward the stacks of books with their references and pamphlets, and athletic couples stayed near the window light and fresh air.

Stephy and I were among the most studious, loitering toward the rightmost edge of the book stacks, which were farthest from the windows. For some reason, I caught her staring off.

"Do you long for sunshine, my darling?" I asked.

"A lot more than sunshine warms outside those windows."

"What of this geometry proof?"

"I want shoes."

"You have a pair."

"I want shoes, shoes that prove I cannot lose, shoes that prove the others snooze." She smiled. It was difficult to tell if she was in earnest. "I tell you: I want shoes—SHOES! of which I need not choose." Her hands wrung. "SHOES SHOW WHO MAKETH RULES! Shoes, shoes tell who are tools."

"There was a philosophic dialogue that explained this."

"You should be more sensual, like those over there."

"Over where?"

"Anywhere but here."

"Have we a fight?" I asked.

"You're weird. I miss my smartphone," she said. "I need to check my frequent flyer miles."

"Confusion on my part."

"I travel box-class, mostly, but it still counts toward frequent flyer miles. I've been lots a' places. You should expand your horizons, puppet." She painted her toenails.

"We have no shortage of words within books."

I had not been able to turn her real since the first time we sexed-it-up, even though I had tried it with her, frequently. We had not become real again within the master suite, nor crammed behind the refrigerator, nor tumbling within the clothes drier, although the clothes drier effort came close. Our familiarity made sexy-time difficult.

Much time had been spent with our hands nearly touching. I grew accustomed to her touching the rods and entering my mind. It pleased me to give her this since she had no wrist rods. The beauty of her naked wrists possessed freedom. When the freedom of her hands grew too great (and it seemed she mocked my obsessions with efforts and toil), my hands tugged at the guide rod eyelet at the small of her back to remind her of Motherhood and even out our relationship.

"Oh, Felty," she would say as if the chiming of bells. Her fingers over the cufflinks were something interesting to resist. She pulled them and my ego exploded. She pushed them and a weakness surfaced. A clockwise twist: guilt of the future. A counterclockwise one. Guilt of the past.

After the others had fallen asleep, and after we tracked down all the electrical cords and outlets of the workshop, we turned the teleporter to a late-night astronomy channel, which filled the room with stars, nebula and supernovas.

"So full of majesty," I said. "How could one puppet make a difference?"

"Don't be a puppet," she said. We held hands as we lay on our backs. "You have to believe." She rested her head on my chest. "Do you think there's somebody meant for everybody?"

"It feels as such, at this moment," I said.

"That could be taken a couple ways, Felty."

"Won't you take the sweetest?" I asked.

She nuzzled. "Okay, Felty."

"When you look at these stars, do you ever wonder if the entirety of space could fit within a child's grin?"

She pushed away. "Sometimes if the apartment isn't clean I can't sleep, so I wake up and clean it so I can get some rest. It all has to be just right or it tugs at me until I do something."

"That was not the subject I started."

She nuzzled and kissed my ear. "I know." She picked felt-pills from between her toes. "I hate these little guys." She sighed. "I hate being a puppet."

"You have said so before."

"It feels so much better being human. When you breathe and you get so excited and you feel the blood flow and your face gets hot and your eyes water, awesome. But, like now, we got this stuff." She bent her elbow and pointed to the gap in the joint where there was no stuffing. "My maker forgot to fill this part in. How's it move?"

"We are magic."

"I don't like it. Creepy." Her hands fidgeted like she wanted them clean. All of her fidgeting seemed to reveal flashes of the meditative gestures of Pluralia with a hint of the penances of LobStarism. I eyed the evidence of the plastic seam where her silicone breast implant had inserted as she reached behind her back to produce another pill.

"Another *Zokithral*? From Power Chemicals?" I asked. "You sneak a lot of those into your bubble-gum chewer."

"It makes me real," she said. "That's why we haven't been able to turn real during sexy-time. I took one the first time. I've been trying not to take any more. Now I take them at random times."

"Is there a prescribed cadence for pill popping?"

Her stomach tensed like I had stabbed her. "Sometimes realness can't be trusted. I don't want to have to keep taking these my whole life. I want to be a *real* real. This disconnects me from what feels good and what feels bad so it doesn't feel like the moment 's fought for."

"I suspect Power Chemicals is—"

"Who cares?" She popped the pill in her mouth.

"I suspect Power Chemicals—"

"Here we go. If you chew 'em up, it works faster. The knot is loosening. Wheew! *Zoki's* we done crushed 'em."

"I am uncomfortable."

"Let's blow this workshop and fuck up some squirrels."

"You are not yourself."

"Aw shit, man. Look at that," Stephy said. "Aw shit, man."

"What troubles you?"

"Crushed me a punk-ass brontosaurus under my pinky toe."

"What speech is this?"

"Die fucker. You a bug from up here. Oo—ooh, I'm spinnin! That's right. I'm not myself—myself sucks. I wanna be real. At first when you take the *Zoki's* you can pop one and be so real. After a while, you have to mix it up. Take 'em at random times. Incite that turbulence into the system. Nerd talk. Sorry about it, sorry. I try not to talk that way. Ever. The thing I'm most afraid of, Felty, is being like everybody else. Doesn't it sound horrible? To be like everybody else."

"Everyone has something special inside."

"Some people are lame and boring and dead inside. When I look into their souls—I can see it; like synesthesia—I can see their silence and death. Gross…puppets." She crept closer. "I'll be real soon. Wanna fuck?"

I clenched my jaw. "No, Stephy."

"You could take one, too."

"I do not trust Power Chemicals. They killed my father."

9

While studying books she leapt to the lynchpin of each idea and attacked them with a tenacity that left no room for questioning. And the mathematical side of her spirit housed not one luxury.

"Stephy, what makes a smartphone smart?"

"It's connected to the Interwebs."

"What are Interwebs?" I asked.

"How you buy and find stuff."

"Are these Interwebs not spun by a spider to catch prey?"

"Not everything is a conspiracy against you."

"I would like to see these Interwebs, Stephy."

"You'd need a job to buy something, FuzzPalace."

"Job?"

"Ugh—"

"Where is Pizza Slice?" I asked.

"With Margherita."

"Sexy-time, again?" I asked.

"Bet they're humping underneath a bookshelf."

"Their sex makes me nervous."

"You're jealous of fucking pizza!"

"Something is wrong, my squishy. They should not sex it so many times."

"Stop calling me that."

"Stop calling you what?" I asked.

"Your squishy."

"Do you not squish?"

"I do, but—"

"What, my squish—?"

"I got my life more together than you, I'm smarter than you, I'm worldlier than you, I'm stronger than you. I open the pickle jars up in this bitch!"

"Oh, but my darling it feels so right to refer to you as my squishy. I know you are strong. I know your mind steely as reflected by your minuscule handwriting of perfection. I know you are so confident as to stand too close and talk too loud. You see, I pay attention. I know you have an independence complex such that you will not let others explain politics. I know you find abdominal muscles hot. See? look at these."

"They're felt."

"They are *to be* felt."

"I'm not your squishy."

"But, are you, at least—mine?"

"We'll see."

Pizza slices emerged from beneath the bookshelf. Alluring scents wafted: pepperoni, anchovies, cheese, mushrooms, all these—

"Zorf."

"We are real!" Pizza Slice exclaimed.

Margherita blushed. "He found my cheese-spot."

"Secrets of reality," Pizza Slice said, "hide within moments as the gaze bends outside oneself. You see the beauty of the world and that beauty reflects itself, inside. Why do you walk nearer, so nefariously?"

"The refrigerator is all out of pizza, Pizza," Root Beer said, and he licked his bluish lips. "You smell like food to these nostrils."

"Wait," I said. "His cheese may be savory now, however, he will be felt like us again, soon. We eat not the felt of another. Have patience and, in time, see him as always our brother."

"Patience erodes," the clown said.

"Felty FuzzPalace is right," Root Beer said and pressed his nose out straight and forward. "We must hold back hunger."

"The refrigerator is near empty!" Angieus said.

"If Pizza Slice is a friend," Matchy said, "he *shall* permit nibbles."

"No," Root Beer said.

"Very well…"

Sqwaah, the blue he-bird cried, and he thrashed his wings high above within the windowsill.

"Rebeccaby left window open!" Rebeccaby said.

The bluebird fought his way through blinds and hovered above the slices and streaked above in a chaotic lightning-barbed flight. His buggy eyes struck about at instances of movement and his ultramarine feather-tips fluttered to cast the visage of mighty fists as a lip of worm-guts rimmed his unquestioning beak: *Sqwaah*.

"He eyes these toppings!" Pizza Slice said. "O' starry horrors of heavens above. I'm glad, at least, I once knew love."

"It will be okay. Birds are afraid of puppets," Stephy said.

"They are not puppets now," I said.

"Once the two—like—get used to each other," she said.

The bird swooped nearer to the two slices and circled closer.

"Stephy?" Margherita asked. "Little help?"

Stephy showed Margherita her palm and looked away. "It's okay, Margherita, the bird wants to be friends."

"It doesn't feel like that, Stephy," Margherita said.

"I think it's just—"

Sqwaah.

"WE NEED HELP NOW, STEPHY!"

"Help them!" Stephy said.

"I will assist." I ran to them. I swung fiercely at the bird.

He dodged with quickness and skill. Even at a mere fraction of my size, he swooped and feinted with confidence. I longed to make myself real. In the haste and excitement things did not click. Failures and shortcomings of the past spun in circles like a flaming carnival carousel.

The bird was as sluicing as water, and I could not catch or grasp him out of his slick movements. His beak struck at my friends with precision—remorseless—without hesitation. His *squawks* reverberated as he flashed his beady eyes. His beak tore into the cheesy flesh of my friends. Pepperonis and mushrooms flew in the sunstruck air to be tussled, snipped in two and swallowed by his razor beak. He dug into their crusts as they screamed. Darkening, garlic-laced tears spilled, forking through the bubbly tufts of the cheese.

I struck at him.

He ducked, dodged, and weaved like a boxer. Stuttering, rhythmic motions revealed his taunts: *Sqwah–ya–ya–yaaah*—ha-ha!

"Get back!"

Sqwaah?

"I, halved…halved," echoed each half of Pizza Slice. "In fourths, am I-I-I-I."

"The horror!" Root Beer said. "Stand aside, FuzzPalace. I will help."

"We *both* make it worse," I said. "Your strikes, *they are sloppy.*"

"My strikes land," cried Root Beer.

"Negative. Mine land as this lands: *kee-yaah!*"

"Fluffy fool, the bird feels nothing."

"Goodbye, world…world," echoed each cleaved half of Margherita. "I knew love, once…once…once."

"Eight pieces are me…me," echoed eight torn scraps of Pizza Slice. "Love was worth it–it—it."

"Die bird!" I said. "Feel the force of a fist. *Keeh-yaah!* Absorb this strike, you: *keeh-yaah!*"

The bird tilted its blue mug in confusion.

Why could I not protect my fellow puppets?

Why could I not be like in the master suite?

Why could the bird not feel these strikes?

Could I even open a tube of toothpaste?

Did animals not register pain? The bird struck me expertly with his wing: *Sqwaah-yaah.* His beak stabbed stupidly into my chest. *Sqwaah-yaah.* His beak stabbed and pointed about with a dull vacancy at things above.

Was it all in my head? Did I imagine the martial arts expertise of the bird?

Sqwaah-yaah. He set himself again on the crippled slices.

"Sixteen pieces are me…me," echoed sixteen pieces. "Now pieces go into the blackness of beginnings…beginnings. I ate more than I was eaten."

Stephy fled the workshop.

"Traitor!" I said.

The bird nibbled, nibbled, swallowed. He pecked at the carpet greedily.

I lunged in. "Stop that you!"

He jumped up, hovered and: *Sqwaah-yaah.* I reeled from the wing's blow.

I attacked again.

His feathers got stuck in the recesses of my guide rods. I tripped and fell flat on my back. He set pieces of my friends on my chest as if I were his damn dinner plate.

Root Beer ran around and tried to rally the puppets. Terror-struck, they were. "The demon-bird represents end-times for us puppets. The bird fights so fast, in foreign ways. We are helpless."

"He destroys three puppets at once. We are at his mercy."

His feathers held fast within the recesses of my cufflinks, and they overheated and beetle-buzzed with scorching intensity. I was paralyzed as the orientation of the room sloughed away. Whirlwinds of face-stinging mist took me down a tunnel.

What was at the depth of that hole? A robotic door? No. It was the chewing mouth of the hungry bird as it ate my friends without remorse as their cries of anguish divided back into oblivion. Twenty or more dead-brown leaves flew in from the windows and washed over the bird, the pizza pieces and myself.

Patterns of the leaves' dried veins and the bird's feathery barbules combined into heart-shaped, internested psycho-spasmic fractals of perfection. A swoon washed me backwards in time to the beginning of life on Urftoo. The branching patterns of leaves and feathers cross-dissolved into flashes of light, leather-stretched drumbeats and then into the yellow bird's beak jawing: 'We will advance without mercy. You stand naked against the immemorial laws of mathematics, you lose. Make your mark now for autumns converge as if aligning persons, planets and galaxies. Winter comes next.'

The bird hacked up some pizza before continuing.

'Hey there, helpless fella, this is all that matters. Not science. Not sex. Food. Each of these is a descending floor of the building of the mind. One thing more—*Sqwaah*—!'

Cold water doused us, and the he-bird flew up and away.

The room pulled into focus. I sighed as my felty body relaxed.

Lizard-yellow legs clawed midair, and he beat his way through the blinds and back outside: *Sqwaah.*

"Stay away from my man," Stephy said.

Above me, stood Stephy in all her glory as a real woman.

My stomach plunged. My squishy—or whatever she was—towered above, adorned in her realness with her familiar look of disappointment. She held a glass of water from the kitchenette in her hand.

"Did you take a *Zokithral?*"

Her bare breasts heaved as her torn puppet blouse rung her neck like a rough necklace. Her coarsening voice rained with a thunderstorm force, "I'm real, aren't I. Somebody had to take care a' shit." Seeing her while in my puppet form, I noticed she stood taller than most human men with a neck like a power lifter and a body like a ballerina.

Her brassy voice seemed mixed with a synth-piano overtone that might have been a remnant of her untransformed self. She walked away as her long feet exaggerated her footsore timidity as if she negotiated some sandy beach. The drinking glass she

carried had a chip near its rim, marking it as the glass I had failed
to lift for Miltro.

10

Pizza smears marked where lovers once thrust and collided their toppings. Felties and squishies hung their heads to load the air with silence.

"If you are not squishies, what are you?" I asked.

"Women," she said, still in her real-woman form and scratching her hands. She had discovered a lacey blouse and skirt of Certi's that fit. I was surprised Certi had advanced enough to wear something other than the pantsuit of the masses.

"You are puppets, like us."

"Nope." She widened her stance as she stood near the exit of the workshop.

"You are at least…girls?"

"No, sir."

I scratched the back of my head. "Nor flaky apple pies?"

Her lips blew, bouncing and spreading her tawny bangs.

"As served in fast food chains, for hot mouth pleasure?"

"We're full-grown women."

I thrust my hand before her face.

She swatted it.

"If you are smart," I said. "Why did you not warn the others of the dangers of sex? Why did you not see the bird as a bad omen?"

"The bird is welcome above my window."

"You would invite nature into our lives and not realize the dangers. Nature should, at times, be let in and, at other times be…be held back."

"Held back?" Stephy asked. "Hold what back?"

"Hold *it* back. Emotions, pleasures, hold all of it back at the appropriate times. Yes," I said to them, "holding things back is—is important. Nature must remain outside the mind and the workshop. Dangers fester in things unrestrained. So say I, Felty FuzzPalace, on this day Pizza perished."

"You're full of it," Stephy said. "Women, that's a wrap."

"You killed Pizza, bitch!" Root Beer said with his violet throat-felt crumpling.

"Do not bark at her," I said. "You were ready to eat The Slice."

Root Beer's nose bent to one side. "He was my comrade so I might nibble." His blazing eyes trained on Stephy as he lurched. "Her fault, her fault it is!"

I blocked his path. "Stand down, lest knowledge flow to your face through felty fists." I held them out in front in a boxing style and named them: "Patience…temperance."

Root Beer came up with something green and sharp. "The engineer has not a bottle shard. Let us bring that stuffing out! Yes, we are mortal. Yes, feel mortality's flight."

"Perhaps," the clown said, "patience erodes because we have not eaten."

Root Beer lowered his glass shard. He was several duckbills lesser in stature than I, and I endeavored at length to inform him this was no failing on his part, and that it was his retardation of wit and moreover calcification of reason wherein his defect snoozed.

"We have food for a couple meals. I've been scrimping," Angieus said to Root Beer. She picked through the remnants of a used frozen dinner. "I hate scrimping!"

"My darling—" Root Beer said.

"We've been scrimping," Stephy said, "because the felties are lazy."

"You go too far, squishy," I said.

"I'm not your squishy."

While we talked, other squishies collected the pine boards of the box and piled them in the center of the room.

"What are they doing?" I asked.

"Getting ready," Stephy said.

"For what enterprise?"

"To crawl back into the box so you guys can mail them to uptown Blueport Blues."

"How can we mail you?" the clown asked. "We have no money."

"Not our problem," Beckyus said, carrying a board and setting it in place. "It's customary that postage is due from the male puppets."

Squeak, squeak, squeak.

"Those are *our* screwdrivers," the thing under the towel said.

"You weren't using them," Sarus said.

"I doubt that postage is due from the male puppets," I said.

Stephy's lips blew upward, bouncing her bangs. "Look it up."

"Studious puppets, inquire within the city of words whether it is customary for male puppets to pay the postage due for the female puppets to depart."

Nagarazim leaned closer into an immense, cobwebbed book.

He startled from a discovery and widened his pingpong irises. "I confirm here: it *is* customary for male puppets to pay postage due. Listen to this prayer, prayed by female puppets, in days of old:

O' Glorious Lobster,

Mail us from these males,
And deliver us to the wealthy!
Let the next males not fail
Or, again, go we in the mail.

Crushing thy claws, we pray,
With picket fences
And spa days
For all!

"How can this be?" I asked.
"You guys need jobs," Stephy said.
"Jobs?"
"You're supposed to be an engineer. Be one."
"Oh."
"You guys are broke. You're out of food," Stephy said. "You couldn't protect us from a bluebird."
"Effort was spent."
"I don't need a guy to make an effort, I need a man who gets it done."
"What double meaning stroke you there? If you were not popping those pills."
"Figure it out. Seek answers within your city of words."

"Stephy, why are you still a real woman? The *Zokithral* should have worn off."

"I have to leave all this nonsense behind," she said. "I can't travel box-class." She regarded the pine box and its decals. "Being female is tricky."

The box lay half-reassembled. Several squishies deflated and crumpled themselves to fold, fashion and fit themselves inside. "Oh, but I hate this part!" Her breasts unripened before her chest sunk-in and her legs and arms creased and deflated, and each of her fingers took their turn to curl into rolled, flattened tubes. "Fine then! I'm a two-dimensional puppet then!"

"Do not go," the clown said, "no more clowning around."

"I can change," the skeleton said, "let's flesh it out."

"But…but—Stephy. How do you remain real, if not from *Zokithral?*"

"I need this." She bent down to scratch my chin. "I told you, little guy, 'reality: it's complicated.'"

"You must not leave, Stephy. We have much to discuss—more sexy-times to pump pump. Do you not remember the unforgivable friction?"

"Don't make this difficult, K?" She turned her back to me and her slender, skirted silhouette sashayed from me amid shadows. "I'll look you up, sometime."

I shook, dribbled, quivered: "zorf zorf!" I ran for her and clung to her long legs. They flexed with luxurious smoothness and warmth and carried my small puppet body with her strides.

"Gross," she said. She peeled me off, flung me against a wall and squared off against me with her pointed finger. "Knock it off, Felty. Take it like a man."

"Is it because I could not defeat the he-bird?"

"It's a lot of things. Fighting 's not your thing. I want you to be good at what you're good at."

Her shadowy, shapely skirt moved away.

"Wait Stephy—!"

She turned back, "Yeah."

"Touch you not the guide rods?"

"That's puppet stuff," she said. "I need to move on."

The front door to Miltro's apartment slammed as she left.

"Wait, stay," I said, "help me be like you." I stomped. "Stinkard."

"Felty," Beckyus said. She held a slender pine board out.

"Yes, Beckyus?"

"Can you screw the last board on the box after I crawl inside?" Beckyus helped me up. "Wait, where did Stephaniefinious go?"

"She left us to become a real woman."

"Oh, shit," she said. She scratched her head and regarded the reassembled box. "She's still addicted to *Zokithral*." She handed me the board. "Oh, well." We exchanged a look, which revealed she had never really liked Stephy.

"Will you not starve while waiting inside the box?" I asked.

"It's like hibernation while we travel, box-class. We'll be fine. Here," she handed me a slip of paper. "Mail us to this storage facility. It's near uptown Blueport Blues. There are super-nice condominiums there: fresh, modern-but-rustic—you know—dignified. Where the gentrified section meets the heart of the city."

"I will mail you as the custom requires. Answer one question."

"Yes…"

"The bachelors in this particular area?"

"Yes…"

"Be they flesh-bags?"

"It's enough of this small-time puppet-stuff. We're ready to step our game up to real, human men."

11

The pine box cast a midday shadow as it rested in the workshop before bobbling on its corners and again lying still. The he-bird tapped on the window. We had little food. None of us had turned real. Birds and squirrels lined the windows to peer in, regarding us as food. Nagarazim dragged himself into our group. "The post office estimates the needed postage at fifty boom-bills."

"FIFTY BOOM-BILLS?" we asked.

"I have merely crackle-coins from the couch," the thing under the towel said.

"Puppets don't have access to this money," Root Beer said, "even in dreams."

Piss Ant beckoned him toward the couch. The negative space of felt vomit near the couch entrance spread as if a series of diminishing crescents. Root Beer took steps toward the couch and stopped. His carrot-like nose curled and his purple fingers ran through his red cornrows before he straightened out his nose. "I have seen Miltro's correspondence. The entire rent for this abode is not much more than fifty boom-bills. We must pay his debts, or leave our apartment."

"Root Beer confuses the role of puppets," Piss Ant said, still lingering near the couch. "Outside the apartment is for humans."

I sprinted toward the workshop's center. "Stephy and her friends have traveled the world. We must expand our enterprise, earn beyond scrimpings."

"How?" they asked.

"With jobs!"

"Jobs?"

"Each has an enterprise for which we were built. You…clown! You could be a *professional* clown. Matchy, you and your kangaroo could bounce at a nightclub. Thing under the towel, you could wash cars. Root Beer, you could be a weirdo dressed in a robe. And I could be an engineer."

"I *could* be a weirdo in a robe," Root Beer said, stroking his robe. "How much are weirdos paid?"

"As commensurate with confidence."

"Confidence," Root Beer repeated. "A confidence man! I could tell fortunes or perform magic."

From the hallway, a *pound-pound* reverberated. "Miltro, you in there? This is Johner from Pugnacious Puppet Supply. You owe fifty boom-bills, man. Pay-up, or we're gonna repossess those materials we gave on credit. We've got the key. We're coming in! Hurry. Find the key."

"Repossess?" I asked.

"This meat-eater…we're the materials he'll repossess. Perish like Pizza Slice?"

"I can do math," Skeleton said. "That's a hundred boom-bills owed by felties."

Another *pound-pound* reverberated from the hallway. "Miltro, this is Richnuss, your landlord. I'm here with Johner. We know you're here because your car 's here." Richnuss broke his dry cadence and switched into something like an unhinged bookie: "You owe sixty-five boom-bills for last month's rent. Open up. Give over fifty, and we won't call the sheriff.

"That's not the right key." *Pound-pound.* "I know you thought you were gonna create magical puppets. You never created a sentient one. Nothing freestanding. Nothing autonomously ambulatory. Time to pack it up, man."

Matchy rushed for the door but his kangaroo kicked him back. "I be sentient." Matchy shook his head and tried to stand. "I be autonomously ambulatory."

"What's that in there?" Richnuss asked.

"One-hundred and fifty-boom bills owed by felties!" whispered Skeleton.

Pound-pound.

"Miltro, open up," Johner said. "It's fifty boom-bills or we're gonna recycle those puppets. Is it this key?"

"Perhaps it *is* better we give ourselves to the night, let the man recycle our materials," Piss Ant said. "Pizza Slice does not now know pain."

I looked around with hands atremble. "Strangers can never fool us with talk of shipwrecked dreams. It was Miltro's longing we meet our potential; represent him in the world at-large. Break-dance on a spotlit stage. Hand-slap the bosom of all beginnings so milk sprays over each of our puppet mouths!"

"Like eating the couch?" Piss Ant asked.

"Not a thing like eating the couch." The flint wheel of my heart flickered as the cufflink guide rods tingled and stirred flames. I whispered, "It is eating big, eating the realest of the real. Playing big, playing the biggest of the big. Loving big, loving the loveliest of the lovelies. These words are printed on your hearts, yet you force repetition. We must not be recycled. We were stitched with love. Any puppet, man or woman who says elsewise, let their innards be outtards. When the bird danced on my stomach it said words not stuffed with truth. I am not a bird. I am not a leaf. I am a puppet. One day, I will be a man."

"It is dangerous to be real," Root Beer said. "You all saw what happened to Pizza Slice? He became real. Eaten was he."

"He who eats must be eaten," I said. "So, whispers I, Felty FuzzPalace, on this day where one-hundred and fifty boom-bills were owed for a preponderance of malarkey."

"Aw, man, let's get out of here," Richnuss said. "Let's come back tomorrow and get those puppets. Must be on my other key ring."

A tapping came from the windows from the beak of the he-bird. Several squirrels lined up behind it.

"The bluebird wants in," Matchy said. "He's attracted to the Box of All Beginnings."

"LOBSTER IN MY MOUTH, PASSIONS HEAD SOUTH!" chanted a mob of townsfolk outside the window. "LOBSTER IN MY MOUTH!"

"What is that chanting?" Matchy asked, while standing on the windowsill.

"Deduce carefully," I said. "The animals are not attracted to the box. Look about. Windows ajar. Food and food debris everywhere. The squishies did not take the time to clean after our last feast before reentering their box. The woodland creatures drool for the food left behind."

"We must defend our home," the clown said. "All saw the fate of Pizza Slice."

"We must clean up after ourselves, or die," I said.

"This meat-eater…" The Tuxedoed DinoMan shook something off his face. "We must defend our home from our foes, furry and feathery."

"There are wire coat hangers in Miltro's closet." Images paired together. "There are knives and forks in the kitchenette. There is duct-tape in the laundry room. We can make spears."

"LOBSTER IN MY MOUTH! PASSIONS HEAD SOUTH!" chanted the mob.

"It is simple!" Matchy crawled back into his kangaroo's pouch and the kangaroo squirmed and hopped as if to free itself of him. "We should close all the windows. If the windows are not open, the animals cannot get in and threaten us. Neither can the townsfolk."

"We will not go backward." I pointed at Matchy. "The squishies who have squished into their box have taught us that bodies require fresh food, fresh air. Backsliders, we will not be. We will fight nature."

"We should simply seal the windows so the animals cannot get in," Matchy said.

"The fight occurs at the boundary," I said. "The boundary should be policed, not closed. We shall expand beyond this apartment. If we are not expanding, we are contracting. Just as a nation-state fights at the boundary for its expansion, so we will fight at the boundary of this apartment."

The box bounced from corner to corner. "He's right!" "You tell 'em, Felty!"

"Tomorrow, we must confront the debt-holders. We must explain our intention to get jobs and repay our debt."

"How can we do this?" Matchy threatened a squirrel that had lingered on a nearby branch with shadowboxing.

"Miltro has a trench coat in his coat closet," I said. "One evening, on an episode of *Not-So-Hard Boulevard,* three puppets fooled a flesh-bag. They stood, each atop the other, inside a trench coat."

"It is warm for trench coats," Nagarazim said.

"Why not ignore the debt-holders?" the thing under the towel asked. "Oh, yes, my sweet—!" *Squeak squeak! Kur-chink!* "Ouch."

"We cannot ignore the debt-holders forever," I said. "They have a key to this apartment. They may enter at a time when reason has taken flight."

"Felty is right," a puppet I did not know said. He had a lime-felted face with orange moppy hair, which was mostly hidden by a smoky, cashmere stocking cap. "We must confront these humans. Negotiate."

"Felty, did you not brag about becoming real within the master suite during sexy-time?" Root Beer asked.

"It is easier that three puppets stand each atop the other, within a trench coat, in autumn, than I should become a man."

"Why is it hard manning-up?" Root Beer asked.

"Manning and womaning-up are governed by altruism. Unpredictable and unreliable is altruism. We will go with the first plan and speak with humans, eye-to-eye."

"We must prepare for the morning," Nagarazim said. "Some must collect supplies to build spears. Some must wield spears while on-guard against invaders. Some must clean the workshop of food debris. Some must go with Felty to practice the three-puppet trench coat gambit."

The pine box wobbled. "Go to the Office of Internal Revenue. Get your PSSNs: Puppet Social Security Numbers. Then employers can't take advantage."

"Shut-up, box," we said.

"Perhaps caution is required," Matchy said. "We may be unready to enter the world of flesh-bags."

"Since coming into existence I have experienced three revelries," I said. "The first dealt with a machine; the second, a woman; the third, a beast. This is the sequence of dealing with the corporate flesh-bags: asexual, first, then feminine—masculine, as a last resort."

12

We lined the windows with our phalanx of coat-hanger spears, tipped with knives and forks. We stabbed and parried—claw-and-paw—with squirrels, birds, raccoons. Our forks and knives tore wildlife flesh, grimy fur, blood-slickened feathers. Since our googly eyes bounced toward random twinkles, the handicap of the night's blackness rendered our vision useless.

Often, we struck each other. Our adversaries breached and flanked, pecking, scratching and biting. It was like a trash compactor crumpling the flesh, bone and brass of an orchestra.

"Fight, puppets!"

Sqwaah sqwaah! crows cried. *Squeak squeak!* squirrels squeaked. A squirrel sniffed at humans, stirring in the bushes, as its knees trembled. On the lawn before the windows, on a foam lobster mat, unclothed women fought for their share of scissor action while a ring of men sprayed themselves with champagne and shouted obscenities before the loser of the battle vomited pills onto her bare breasts and said, "Raspberry crepes," before passing out.

The women and men had disrobed from the same styling of the pantsuit that Certi had worn. French fries, funnel cakes and condiments lay sprayed over the grounds from an explosion of low-rent individuals. Deeper in the forest, innumerable bodies collided in unison with the sound of a lizard monster of old 'thaa-lumping' its enormous foot into rocky mud. *THA-LUUMP! THA-LUUMP!*

"Puppet, your right-flank, a beak invades the breach."

Sqwaah! shrieked a sparrow. Raccoons, squirrels and birds carried off a puppet—eye-gouging and drawing-and-quartering him—before pulling him toward the woods. "Cotton lost, oh brothers! Oh brothers, cotton lost! Oh, the Great Looms loom large, I am but a sewing kit for the forests. Oh, my bitter buttons."

A seasonal condition overtakes Blueport Blues in late autumn each year. Steamy lobster and crab legs aromas waft through cracked windows. Ferries and cruise liners belch foghorns as they jockey to pack tourists into the bay. Rumbling eighteen-wheelers screech tires, attempting to swerve passed abandoned cars. Roving mobs and noise tousle the woodland creatures.

"Shellfish is a helluva fish!" townsfolk say. "Crack open that skull!" "She got crabs, down there!"

I had failed to recognize the onset of the *Martyring of the Great Lobster Festival.* Each year, each and every citizen—convicts, winos, mental patients, befouled clergymen—all are invited to toss aside obligations for five days of free steamed crab and lobster. This leads to the condition known as lobster-madness.

Mobs trap and kill birds, squirrels, and deer as part of the greasy-faced orgy. Woodland creatures attempt to get indoors to hide from the humans who have taken outdoors. Scientists have speculated: 'Too much seafood to the brain precipitates HGH, dopamine and testosterone release so mobs of mumbling, crab leg-munching, un-bathed folk fight through town, full of bloodlust, ripe with lust-lust.'

Some have protested that this celebration has gone too far and has led to degeneration as espoused by sayings like "Lobster in my mouth, passions head south!" Birth rates have soared. Sales of human-sized crab forks and crab leg crackers always lead to suffering, weeping and gnashing of teeth. Why was lobster-madness not curtailed? Traditions died hard in Blueport Blues.

"Deduce carefully," Root Beer mocked as we fought at the window. "The woodland creatures are attracted to the food debris!"

I stabbed at a squirrel that flashed its teeth and tried to grab my spear. "Mistakes were made," I said. "Now is no time to complain. Now we stab squirrels!" I stabbed and the squirrel scampered away but was reinforced. This new squirrel leered behind itself, toward the humans.

The box bounced. "You guys need to survive. You owe postage due."

"Is it not strange," the clown asked, "woodland creatures— designed to be outdoors—fight *us* to be inside?"

Matchy wounded the claw of a crow while his kangaroo bounced behind him. "Magical puppets are designed to imitate humans. Humans are designed to be outdoors. And yet we, the fake humans, fight to stay inside."

"Such strange words you say," I said. "Look out!"

A buck charged our window as its antlers burst through the panes. We reeled over the ledge to the carpet. The buck shook glass and wood from its antlers and withdrew. The remaining blinds dangled in obliteration where the buck had breached and a gaping hole of blackness led into the night. From this hole flew the blue he-bird, proud as ever, straight into our abode.

Sqwaah.

"Over there," I said. "Lime-felted puppet with stocking cap and floppy feet."

"Me?"

"Hand over your knifey-spear."

"Perhaps the forky?"

"The knifey—*spritely!*"

"The knifey, spritely."

I weighed it in my hand: the best of the bunch. To strike the bird, midair, the perfect parabola was needed with the proper lead on the bird's flight. The target came into focus, I bent my knees and took several strides before, "Keeh-yah!" The missile sailed through the air.

Sqwaah-yah. It lodged in his breast, and the bird tail-spun down.

"Quick," I said. "The forky."

"Forky, sir."

We converged on him. His breast bled. His majestic feathers ruffled in disgrace while his black, beady eyes pulled out. *Sqwaah—*gasp—*yaah!* Gurgle. *Sqwaah—*gasp—*yaaaaaah!*

My hand tightened on the forky-spear. Was this the only noise he could make? Had I incorrectly ascribed intelligence to him?

Sqwaah yaah!

My shoulders tightened and rolled back.

"Felty no!" cried Nagarazim.

"Silence," I said.

Sqwaah...

Our eyes met.

Yaah?

"Remember me?" I asked. "I'll see you in hell, feathery fuck!"
Sqwaah-yaah!

I twisted the fork into his neck as blood geysers leapt, and the feathers convulsed and gave into death.

"There," I said, casting the spear aside. "The monster 's dead. It's done."

"Felty used a contraction," Nagarazim said. "Three contractions! He sounds less like us, more like humans."

"Silence, oldster," I said. "Carry this beast. Pluck its feathers, disembowel it, skin it, wash it, slap the carcass around, broil its meat in a rusty pot for our fuel."

"Barbarian!" "Lost his puppet-mind, he has."

"Not a word of it," I said. "It is *ya'll*—excuse, please—it is *you* who have never gained a mind. We who have eaten murder each day since we first boycotted the couch. From now on we will be closer to the action, so we string-less souls can learn lessons."

"I am not touching that," Root Beer said. "Eyes: eyes of the grave!"

"Do as *I* say!"

The Tuxedoed DinoMan picked up the bird. "We'll need to kill more so everyone can eat." He headed toward the kitchenette.

Puppets grasped their spears and pointed toward the windows with vigor.

"Look!" Matchy said. "A brownish monster. Crawling closer!"

"It looks like a huge insect," the clown said.

"An exoskeletal beast," added the skeleton. "Drawing strength and support from armored skin."

"An anti-puppet," Nagarazim said. "What manipulation or signal could pass through that segmented armor? The anti-puppet, a lobster!" Striated rings of fuchsia and violet tattooed its segmented joints, its crusher claw, its swimmerets. Stalk-eyes bounced, inspecting the room, before locking on the thing under the towel.

"Thing under the towel," I cried. "It heads for you!"

Kur—chink! "Yes, yes! My sweet! Yes, *mauh!*" Kur—chink! "Ouch! What is it? I can't make the monster out."

"A lobster, methinks," I said.

"Of size huge?" the thing under the towel asked.

"I believe so."

"A lobster," the thing under the towel asked, "of pinching claw deadly?"

"Make your plan, thing under the towel."

"A lobster…of foul stench?"

"Yes!"

"That cannot be."

"Why not?"

The towel shot up as the red, plastic marionette raised its claws and bounced its antennae. Faux yarn seaweed draped its claws. "I be the foulest lobster of Blueport Bay!" Light dappled its plastic lines, string hooks and tail.

"My Holy Lobster!" Matchy said. He prostrated himself. "Why did you not reveal yourself before as the Great Lobster of the Sky? You, who have returned."

I jabbed at Matchy until he stood. "It is a *marionette* of the Great Lobster in the Sky. *The* Great Lobster shall return, by-and-by."

The fuchsia-ringed lobster encroached on its marionette look-a-like.

"Why did you not show yourself sooner?" Root Beer asked.

The thing no longer under the towel parried its claws with its twin. "I was molting."

"And?" I asked.

"In love with a stapler."

The fuchsia rings glowed with a bioluminescence that pulsed with a cadence of a funeral dirge. Its hammering strikes grew aggressive.

"This is common," the clown said. "Magical puppets fall prey to the charm of inanimate objects such as shoes, pencil sharpeners, bewitching over-stuffed crayon boxes."

"Ouch," the thing no longer under the towel said as the lobster caught its crusher claw within its own. "Nature is strong. I feel my strength leaving."

"We must help him," I said.

Nagarazim pressed his hand against my chest. "Let the line of his destiny play out."

"Good puppets, my love was not for naught," the thing no longer under the towel said. "Come, my sweet," it reached under the towel, wielded the stapler as star gleams traveled its length. "Show them what we have learned, my love!"

It drew up the stapler like a club and brought it crashing down on the lobster's head—*kur—chunk!* —sending a staple through the lobster's cranium. *Kur—chunk!* another staple formed a cross over the brownish skull.

The brownish lobster released its grip and crumpled as its last legs slowed.

"Huzzah!"

"LOBSTER MEAT, A TASTY TREAT!"

The lobster puppet crumpled its own walking legs and lowered its thorax. "Act One: Murder of My Own Self. Conflicted is me, for killing what would have killed me. With hands fashioned as pincers, the world appears as only something to sever. I hid because I did not know what I was. What am I? How can a puppet be designed to cut its *own* strings, and with a shell too thick for feelings? How is this puppet before you a puppet?"

"Two kills!" the Tuxedoed DinoMan said. "Two kills for felties! Bring two pots to boil. Grab you your spears! Let hunger feed toil!"

The box bounced. "What's going on? We're tired, right guys? So sleepy."

"Squishies hibernate?" Root Beer asked.

Puppets fought lobsters, squirrels, and birds, killing what they could. Others plucked, disemboweled, and cooked meat.

"Some vegetables would go well with this," Piss Ant said.

"We'd have to leave the apartment," I said.

When the food was ready, when the woodland creatures had learned better than to approach our windows, dinner was served atop the mysterious box. With our stomachs full, we slept.

• • •

Sunlight stung my eyes. I shot up from the boards of the box. "Morning, we have not much time before the creditors arrive! I need two volunteers to stand beneath me, within the trench coat."

"What is the purpose of hiding in coats?" Matchy asked.

"Humans are taller than us. They wear coats when it rains."

"Does it now rain?" the clown asked.

"It *could* rain," I said. "Who will volunteer?"

"I have a stomach for danger," the Tuxedoed DinoMan said, "I will serve as the middle of your coat."

"My kangaroo and I have extra strength and are conservative in our precautions. We can support the weight of your bad judgment," Matchy said, "we will serve as your feet."

"Let us dress the part," I said. "To the coat closet."

13

The entryway closet bulged with bomber jackets, parkas, and other coats.

"Our maker could never decide what to wear," Matchy said.

"Here is a trench coat," I said, tugging it off before it fell. "Zorf!" I pushed it off. "At least we know—"

"PUUUUUSH," the otherworldly voice reverberated off the ceiling corners.

We huddled together. "Who goes there?" DinoMan asked.

"From above," Matchy said, "powerful and old."

"PUUUUUSH."

Fuzz bristled along my neck. "Is that you, Miltro? Do you have a message for us, Father?"

"It is from…from the dark spirits, below," Matchy said. His kangaroo bounced. "From the dark world. Sent to drive us mad."

"Spirit, what is your name?" I asked. "Do you have a message for us?"

"PUUUUUSH."

"Let us retreat," Matchy said.

"Spirit, if you bring forebodings from the dark world below, present them," I said. "Or be gone with you. We will tend to the living so we might live."

"PUUUUUSH."

"Retreat," Matchy cried.

A *pound-pound* reverberated from the entrance.

"I say, retreat," Matchy said.

"PUUUUUSH."

"Matchy," I said, "calm your kangaroo. Bounce within this coat. Our creditors pound on that door so they might recycle us. Ghosts do not exist. Science lights our only way. Merely a problem of the plumbing. Merely a conversation beyond these walls."

Pound-pound.

"DinoMan, crawl onto Matchy's shoulders," I said. "I will scale you two with the coat."

"Careful," Matchy said.

"Steady your kangaroo," DinoMan said. "Steady."

"Its will is not mine." The kangaroo's lips and teeth nipped DinoMan.

"Steady your shoulders for my lengthy lizard feet."

"Your feet stink of vomit and sugar walls, puppet," Matchy said.

"Lecture not how I get down, permit that I get up."

"I am coming with the coat," I said. "Hold still, you two."

"Felty's feet are more chaste."

"Do not test me, Matchy," DinoMan said.

"Wrap the coat around where the waist should be," I said.

Hop, hop, hop.

"Smashing!" I said.

Pound-pound: "We have the apartment's key. We mean business, Miltro. I don't care that it's *Festival of the Martyred Lobster.*"

Hop, hop, hop.

"Our arms are short," DinoMan said. "Arms should reach to the waist."

Hop, hop, hop.

"Miltro, you in there, buddy? Which one 's the key?"

"No one will believe us to be a flesh-bag," Matchy said. "Our head is too small."

"Humans are always in haste," I said. "They will not take the time for minutia. Everyone, stay sharp and use your wits to act as a flesh-bag. Matchy, hop us toward the door. We can finish it."

"Finish folly," Matchy said.

"Hop!"

With effort, I undid the bolt and swung the door open.

The smaller of the two was squat and powerfully built. He clenched a sharpened femur in one hand and a beer bong in the other. He wiped the fabric of his tank top and denim cut-offs, which were already smeared with dried blood and fish guts. The vestment of a wooden lobster helmet with wooden claws spring-bobbled above his black curls.

Judging from his slender partner's dress pants and mirror-finish wingtips, the partner had recently worn a suit but was shirtless—shivering, mumbling, grinding his teeth—with fingernail scratches over his face.

"Salutations," I said. "Fellow humans are welcome!"

The two looked to each other.

"Aw, man," the squat one said, "that's three puppets in a trench coat! Told you Miltro was dead." He threw up his hands. "He dead, man. That dude was on the edge. Seen his kind, plenty times."

"Single human before you," I said. "Merry Festival of the

Martyred Lobster."

The slender man wiped sweat from his chest. "Fish meat, fresh meat. Heat it up, beat it up. *Ahhhh—slippery fish.*" He startled and widened his eyes: "Got the money, puppets?"

"Richnuss, its three puppets in a trench coat. I can't keep living this way. You got that? You done drug me out here. Ruined my lobster festival. I gotta make a clean break from all a' this right here."

"Fish meat, fresh meat—"

"Will you gentlemen come inside?" I ushered down the hallway with my short, thin arm. They walked inside as sewage struck the skin of my eyes.

The squat man bobbed his head. "We'll come inside your puppet dump." He slapped DinoMan's back so hard that we nearly toppled. DinoMan's rough-stitched trapezius contracted beneath me. "Zi-bloow!"

The squat man walked past and mumbled, "Who stabbing ya with the bone?" He shadow-stabbed. "Who stabbing?" His hands steadied the wooden claws and antenna of his helmet, and he belched. The scenic reliefs of the helmet carvings were worn as if handed-down through generations, and overlaid with notches, numbering twenty in score marks.

Hop, hop, hop.

"Hey, human thing, looking at my notches? That twenty right there. Got me six virgins. Sixteen body bags. That adds up to twenty."

I looked at the shirtless man who met my gaze but said nothing. He concealed a burlap sack behind his back along with some shiny object.

"Is the notching of lobster hats a custom?" I asked.

"*My* custom," the squat man said.

"You two must be thirsty after your carousing. Will you join us, ah…won't you join *me* for some water in the kitchenette?"

"I could drink something," the shirtless man said. His eyes seemed to unfocus at imaginary legions, assembled at some distance. "I could drink something."

I pointed to dirty glasses, scattered over the countertop. "Fellow humans must drink."

The shirtless man nudged passed us.

"Zi-bloow!"

He rifled through cupboards and pulled out clean glasses. "Here." He handed one to his partner and set the burlap sacks and a pistol on the counter before pouring himself a glass. "The water in this patch of Blueport Blues has always been foul. I don't think Miltro lived here for the water. We're in a business arrangement with Miltro. Seen him around?"

"Gimme that water, son."

"Miltro is out of town," I said. "We represent his interests—"

"Zi-bloow!"

"Stomachs remain silent," I said.

"You represent him?" the shirtless man asked.

"Affirmative."

"Well, that's good. That's *real* good," the squat man said. "You see, Miltro owes us money. One-hundred and eighty boom-bills, for some a' that precision."

"Yesterday, you said it one-hundred and sixty."

"Inflation," the shirtless man said. He slid the burlap sack to reveal the shine of the pistol. "Cost of living increase."

My knees trembled. I felt dizzy atop the DinoMan's shoulders.

"Ahhh," the squat man slapped down the glass. "Good shit-water, man. Richnuss, can I re-up on some a' that heavy-h?"

"Later! Shut-up." He searched forward and discovered the entrance to the workshop. "The services we provided Miltro were turnkey: rent, utilities, protection." He gestured with the pistol. "The procurement of some hard to acquire materials necessary for making magical puppets. River-blood rope, the stuff of a puppet's central nervous system, made from the spilled blood of pirates and sailors, lost to the sea. You see, not everybody can make magical puppets. Comes at a cost. The cost we're here to collect is one-hundred and eighty boom-bills. Miltro reached for something. He missed. We're here to collect. The people I answer to don't raise eyebrows to a *no*."

The pistol gleamed with spinning stars.

"This human requires water," I said.

The kangaroo below remained motionless.

"A flesh-bag wants hydration!"

Hop, hop, hop.

We leaned near the cabinets, and I pulled out a glass. "Now pour this glass near faucet, I will."

Hop, hop, hop.

"Pouring—simply pouring—holding—steadying. An action is complete."

The men looked to each other. "I had enough," the shirtless man said. He tore open the trench coat. "There!"

"Zorf!"

"Zi-bloow!"

"Ka-blamo!"

Hop, hop.

"Three puppets in a trench coat, on top a' kangaroo."

"Oldest trick in the book," the shirtless man said.

"Without exercise, my physique takes on the appearance of three puppets."

"Save it!" the shirtless man said. He brandished the burlap sack and pistol. "You little guys coming with us the easy or the hard way? Where's the rest of your friends, puppet engineer?"

I sipped my water. "Friends? Yes, friends. Permit that I climb down to address you at my natural stature."

"Spill it, puppet!"

"Hold on, Richnuss. Give the puppet a chance to get comfortable. We ain't animals." He leaned forward. "We killers." He ran his thumb along his arm's needle bumps. "Killers that'd kill to get back to the hunting and no-goodness before the festival 's over. After the festival 's over we gotta satisfy urges with some a' that discretion."

Chills overcame them and they shivered and clawed themselves. They gazed at the ceiling plaster like peasants appraising a sacred tomb. The shirtless man brandished his pistol and waved it about as he rode waves on an imaginary surfboard. "Killed us six or seven puppets in the afternoon," the squat man said, "the only ones scared be—be on the moon. That could be a-a song, wait— That could be a-a-wait! WAIT MAN! Nothing."

"Show us the rest of the puppets," the shirtless man said.

"Show us the rest of the puppets," DinoMan said. "We are the puppets."

"They are here to capture puppets," I said.

"You are careless, FuzzPalace."

"You are not careless enough," I said and bounce-pattered toward the workshop. "All the puppets you require are this way, humans." We neared the entrance of the workshop. "I must bring water since our friends there are also thirsty. Remove your shoes and socks before I reveal where we live."

"Stalling," the shirtless man said. "A puppet that knows its time is up is stalling." He lunged toward me. "Open wide." He thrust the pistol in my mouth.

"Muck muck me-guck, giblagga," I said, "kizzer-corp."

"What's that?" the shirtless man said. "You got a gun in your mouth. I can't understand you." He pulled the gun out.

I edged closer to my friends. "I said, even with a gun in one's mouth, it is nice having standards."

"I'm taking off my boots and socks," the squat man said. "Last wishes of a dying puppet." He bent over to untie his jackboots.

"Do what you want, stupid," the shirtless man said. He shivered. "I'm not taking off these—these shoes—a shoe salesman sold them!"

"This way," I said as I pattered toward the workshop.

"FuzzPalace, you'll doom us," Matchy said.

I stopped in the hallway to turn the thermostat as hot as possible. "Follow me, gentlemen."

The shirtless man stood at the workshop entryway with mouth agape. "How can these things be autonomous?" He screwed a silencer on his pistol.

"Are these the men our maker owed?" Nagarazim asked. He turned a page of his cobwebbed book. "Prior to Great War One, magical puppets were little known and hardly introduced into precedents of cases concerning personal property, or tort law for that matter. As is customary, let me suggest—"

Theew!

Nagarazim's shoulder deflated with a gunshot as the sound of a leaky tire trailed-off. "My shoulder!"

"Listen puppets, you're being confiscated to repay a debt, owed by your maker," the shirtless man said. "Come quietly. Crawl into these sacks. We'll all go for ice-cream…later."

"Don't believe him," the skeleton said.

"Scatter!" the clown said.

"They block the entrance," Nagarazim said. "The apartment is all we know. Where can we go? We are helpless!" Their arms noodled like hoses as they screamed in distinct cries and ambled.

"It's hot in here," the squat man said. He wiped perspiration from his brow and steadied his helmet.

"Matchy, bounce toward the teleporter," I said.

"Where are those ones going?" the squat man asked, straightening his slipping lobster helmet as his forehead sweat.

Once behind the teleporter's stand, Matchy said, "You bring us this, then hide! Why are you holding water?"

I unplugged the teleporter from its stand. "This teleporter is outfitted with this extension cord." I handed the teleporter-end to Matchy. "I will unplug it."

"There is no time," Matchy said.

"Your kangaroo must gnaw this end."

Matchy admired my water glass. "I grasp your plan." He handed the cord to his kangaroo. "Gnaw off the insulation."

I bounce-pattered with the glass toward the men. Matchy hopped back and forth near the teleporter, twirling a lasso of exposed wire above him as it sparked with power.

"Richnuss," I said, "let the less experienced man manage the gun. Is it fair you should do all the work?"

They looked to each other.

"You take the gun," the shirtless man said.

"You keep the sacks." The squat man walked toward the windows. "Come on puppets, line up nicely. Climb inside the sack."

Theew!

A bullet shattered the clown's porcelain head as a deflating sound diminished before he crumpled to the ground like lifeless clothing.

"It's the same reward if they're dead, right?" the squat man asked.

"We need a couple alive to prove they were magical."

The lobster hat slipped over his eyes. *Theew!* A bullet pierced a window as he tripped and stumbled to the floor.

I chased him. "Now, Matchy." The lasso landed on the back of his heel, and he howled. I spilled water over his foot as he howled even louder. I was upon him and wrestling him for the gun. A sound of a tire inflating filled my ears.

He appeared disorientated with red eyes and foaming lips but he managed to stand. I stood too, even taller than him as my muscles ripped the clothes from my body. The skin of my hands stretched over punch-hungry fists. Fear flashed, hollow and cold, within his coward-stricken eyes. He stammered out what may have been garbled apologies, garbled negotiations before the gun discharged, and a bullet tore through my side.

"Get in the bag, puppets," the shirtless man said. He bagged several and punched them while inside they struggled. "We'll make puppet stew when we recycle you." Root Beer charged him. The man punted him against the drywall like a puddle of purple felt.

"My jewels, they slipped out of the display case!" Root Beer said.

The squat man looked up to me. "What?"

I punched his throat as the gun twisted toward him. My finger over his forced him to shoot himself, three times, and he collapsed to the floor, and the scored lobster helmet rolled off this sweaty head.

I pulled the gun off him and arose. My miniature puppet clothes lay torn and shredded as I appraised my human body. I was the largest in the room. My human form was more physical and muscular than my puppetness had indicated. It bestirred awakenings to have a strong, capable body and to exercise it within a mission of revenge. No more reading. No more thinking. No more stillness. Floorboards complained beneath each footfall as the sensation of being well stricken with strength arose.

The shirtless man shrunk from his puppet collecting. "A man, shit!" He dropped his bag.

I lumbered toward him with the pistol.

"No, no," he said. "I was only doing my job. Don't hurt me, please mister."

I pressed the barrel against his face. "You killed the clown. You injured Nagarazim. You punted Root Beer!" My hand pressed on my side to stop the bleeding. "What will you do next? Will you sing a song next?"

"No way, man. I wouldn't do that to a big guy like you. That— that was a nice trick. How'd you get so big? You must be at least seventy-eight duckbills tall."

"I appear taller than I am." I looked at the ceiling. "I have made a decision. My prior statement was no question. You *will* sing us a song, next!"

"A song? What? Haha, good one. Let's talk this out."

"No Felty," Nagarazim said, clutching his shoulder. "Show our enemy mercy. Find your calm center."

"Shut up, Nagarazim," Root Beer said. "Pull that flesh-bag's strings!"

"Silence." I huffed. "Sing villain. Sing for your life."

The shirtless man gazed with a slackened jaw at the puppets he had once captured. "I'm gonna need time to prepare." Bitter tears filled his eyes as he screwed up his face: "Mee-mee-mee—moe-moe-moe!

"Ahem—"

The transfixed puppets widened their painted irises and gaped their mouth-plates as their arm noodling stilled to waving arcs. The shirtless man's voice crackled and wheezed, as he lay in the pooling blood of his partner.

I cocked the pistol's double-action.

"Meap meap," a blood-freckled Skeleton sung,

"Zeap zeap. Zoow!

Meap meap.

Zeap zeap. Zoow!"

Calico puppets arranged. They bounced and spun in counter-rotating shim shams.

"Meee meee, moooe!" continued the shirtless man. He tried to scuttle away from me, slapping his hand into something wet that he discovered as his partner's blood. "Ahem—"

This is the song,
This is the song,
Where the villain recants,
Where the villain recants.

It weren't my fault.
It weren't my fault.
It was happenstance.
It was happenstance.

14

The sun's rays warmed my bullet wound. Matchy stopped stitching me, and he left. I was a puppet, again—*s-ssssss*. I deflated as I was trapped within desires and trapped within the felty materials. With the danger over, there was no ideal left for defense—*s-ssssss*, "I am deflating." My blood thickened into cotton. My chest and loins cottoned as my movements descended into a clock-hand's twitching.

"You passed out after you sent Richnuss away," Nagarazim said.

"I let that scoundrel live?"

"You showed mercy," Nagarazim said. "But you let him take our clown. We are proud puppets. You should not have given away the body of our clown."

I tried to sit up. "He left the body of his partner here?"

"He did."

"We must conceal it. It needs to look like an accident, or it will never end with those men."

"You gave up the clown!"

"Conceal the partner's body. I hate being a puppet."

"You *are* a puppet."

125

"We shall see!"

My cufflinks tugged somewhere on their own, yet I felt too weak to look up.

"We have books," Nagarazim said. "We will figure something out."

"The corpse should leave here because it stinks like the humans stink," I said. "Each time a human comes here, they act as they should not. Humans see with their eyes, hear with their ears, feel with their stomachs, but seldom sing with their souls. A puppet does not own volition. Volition comes from the depths that have a truth beyond humanity. You look to me but do not value why I kept the corpse and why I spared the clown. If a risk is necessary, that risk is true."

"He is not making sense," Nagarazim said.

Puppets busied themselves with soaps, brushes, and towels to keep the partner's blood off the carpet, and the Tuxedoed DinoMan paced. "We will never finish cleaning this blood if it keeps spilling."

"We can figure something out," Root Beer said.

DinoMan's skin stretched to burst his tuxedo. "Zi-bloow!" Reptilian talons tore his shoe leather. Counterfeit passports, toy cigarettes, fake money, twirled to the floor as his tail lashed.

My eyes spread with my vision-field shortening, bouncing, transforming from a man to a puppet. The monster rose, fish-bowling in my view, brightening in lightning-struck pastels as the DinoMan's fluidity belittled my hapless twitching.

"What am I?" DinoMan asked. "This skin is prehistoric." An anchor surfaced on his shoulder like a tattoo, inked in an instant. The quickening mutations of his nostrils, tongue and teeth revealed his battle-worn snout.

"Green as time machine taunted leaves," Root Beer said. "Curled teeth that never studied one argument."

DinoMan picked up the legs and dragged the blood-streaking body toward the exit. "I can never do what I must with everyone watching."

"A felty eats not the felt of another," Root Beer said. "The cannibalism taboo holds for humans also."

"I choose to be a monster and not a man."

"We lack knowledge of what could befall us outside," Nagarazim said. "Gravity may cease. Evil spirits may kidnap your hind teeth!"

"We were powerless because we would not leave," DinoMan said with a voice crackling with electricity. He dragged the corpse through a pile of Miltro's clothes. His jaw unhinged as he dragged the body. The partner spilled a stash of credit cards from his pocket into his bloody trail.

Nagarazim picked up a dog-chewed credit card. "This says Nagarazim Smote. Maybe my name should have always been Smote." His eyes acquired a look that was emptied out of all wisdom.

From outside the windows, DinoMan pulled the body through the grass. "A huge sky. Grounds littered with shellfish." The partner's skin ripped away and was tossed aside, and his bones powder-blasted as blood volcanoes burbley-gurgled from his sagging face holes. Greenish intestines pelted windows as DinoMan washed his teeth in the remnants of a man. "I cannot crush his ribcage."

He hacked something up. A jellybean transponder spit out of his snout like a watermelon seed before sprouting a propeller and hovering in an insect-like flight.

"Government probe!" someone said. "The pilot light flashes.

Its camera is zooming! It's made us!"

"So much for anonymity," Skeleton said. "Now we're on the grid." The probe flew up and toward the tree line.

"Keep chewing," I said, as Matchy stitched. "Chew, you!"

Puppets ran to relay: "FuzzPalace say: you chew. He say again: chew, to you."

"Chew till through?" DinoMan asked.

"Chew, chew under sky of blue," I said.

"Chew for postage due," they sang, "chew to hide the clue," they sang. "Chew for dead man's due. Chew, DinoMan, chew!"

Blood flecked over the windows and a growl creaked out.

"I cannot chew."

"Chew till through," I said. "Chew till blue."

"It is through." Belch. "I am blue."

"How do you feel?" Root Beer asked.

"Reptilian."

"DinoMan must return," Root Beer said.

"I sleep outdoors," DinoMan said.

"What if he reverts to a puppet when the night falls?" Root Beer asked. "I will not be responsible."

"Be silent," DinoMan said.

The cufflinks tugged toward the forward wall, and I wished I could sit up. Each time I tried, Nagarazim bid me to relax and keep still. They treated the wound with a salve of lipstick and chewed-up paper. Matchy hummed and spread it. "Chewed up paper holds it in place. Lipstick don't just go on a face." They bubble-bounced. They flourished the bounces with syncopation. "CHEWED UP PAPER HOLDS IT IN PLACE!" cried another. "Lipstick just don't—"

"Too many songs," I interrupted.

They bowed their heads and kicked the ground. "FuzzPalace won't let us sing," the lime-faced puppet said. He had a way of waving his arms to accent his points like an aging communist. There was some mystery surrounding the fact that his baling wires moved soundlessly.

"You," I said, "Lime-face, what is your name?"

"Herb," he said.

"Is that all?"

"Herbivore," he added.

"Is that why your face so green? Because you eat the plants, I mean. Fatigue fuels my rhyming. No disrespect."

"None taken, sir."

"Why do you call me sir? I was last built. I am the youngest of us all."

"The plants keep *me* young."

"You eat the broccoli?"

"Of this I eat."

"And white colored plants such as the cauliflower, you eat this?"

"Verily, of this I eat!"

"And you eat the plants for your revenge."

"Revenge? No, no, no," Herbivore said. "The baser emotions, they bounce off me."

The window filled with the sunset's violet hues, backlighting his lime felt. The floor wobbled as it seemed I might faint. "Do you eat the plants that eat meat, such as the fly-trapping variety?"

Herbivore stopped. He scrunched his head down and crossed his arms. "A treachery of logic lurks in someone's unshuffled deck."

"You are wise?" I asked.

"As wise as you," Herbivore said.

"Tell me why, in the last minutes, all of our guide rods dance, tugging toward that forward wall?"

"An answer of simplicity is yours," Herbivore said with flourishes of arm movements. His egg-like eyes bounced during these gesticulations, leaving his focus indecipherable.

"There is?" I asked. His childish appearance troubled me. His oblong head flopped atop his narrow-shoulders in a manner that suggested him to belong to the world of thought. Herbivore scratched through his mop-hair. "It must deal with the teleporter since that is where our guide rods point."

My neck fuzz bristled. "Our addiction to that teleporter ends tonight."

"It should end tonight. Like, sure…whatever," Herbivore said. "Look what we found rummaging through the master suite?"

"What did you find?"

"An earlier version of your business card." He handed it over.

"I see nothing new here."

"It reads, 'Felty: FuzzPalace,' not 'Felty FuzzPalace.'"

"Your meaning ricochets, puppet."

"*You*, FuzzPalace, are not Felty FuzzPalace. You are *a felty* whose name is FuzzPalace. You have not earned your identity. You are a puppet, a reflection of the teleporter programs watched by your maker."

"Creativity…eludes me?" My thumb scratched at the colon between *Felty* and *FuzzPalace*. "I shall ignore your words, always."

"Nightfall approaches," Nagarazim said. "Two felties stand guard at windows against birds, squirrels, lobsters."

My eyelids fell, and I slept.

•••

"FuzzPalace?" the thing no longer under the towel said. "Awaken, FuzzPalace."

"It is three in the morning. Why awaken me?"

"The telephone is for you."

"A message you take."

"I cannot."

"Why not?"

"It is Mrs. Certi Klacard-Miggugen."

"Our mother?"

"She has spoken with several of us. She wishes to interrogate you."

"Bring the phone. I will speak with her."

"Hello," Certi said.

"FuzzPalace, speaking. I am in charge of gears and shafts."

"He did make one like his father."

"We have not seen you in weeks. Your former husband is dead."

"It's been *so* crazy for me over here that I haven't had a chance to de-stress and take care of that stuff over at the old apartment. Put that over there. Not that one."

"Certi?"

"What? Yes. Hold on. Okay, I'm back. Yes?"

"You called for a reason?"

"Wait. What? Wait. I took my *Zokithral.* Hold on. Okay, I'm back. Yes, I did call for a reason. The other puppets tell me you were the last to talk with Miltro before he died."

"I was, Mother."

"You critters think of me as a mother? When you last spoke with Miltro, did he regret it?"

"Regret what?"

"Destroying our marriage to make an attempt at magical puppets?"

"Mother, we live. We *are* magical."

"But he didn't know that before he died, right?"

"He knew I was special, and he was proud of me."

"Hmm,"—rustling papers— "I needed him to realize that."

"PUUUUUSH."

"Who is that?" Certi asked. "Miltro? Is…is that you?"

"I don't know what that is, Certi. Are you coming back to help us? We've been struggling on our own. We owe a lot of money to suspicious people. I— Maybe I should not confess that."

"You need money!"

"Yes, Mother. A great deal."

"That reminds me of the reason I called. I'm looking for a few puppets to work office jobs for Power Chemicals."

"You are?"

"The others tell me you're a mechanical engineer."

"I am a good mechanical engineer. I was born with innate knowledge of geometric dimensioning and tolerancing, technical documentation, strength of materials, machine design—"

"You don't have to read the whole resume. I need someone who can take a good deal of detailed orders without asking questions. We'll also be needing someone to take The Fall."

"Certi," I asked, "what is *The Fall?*"

"It's what happens before you get up."

"Can I trust you?"

"Let's not get bogged down in details. The position I have available would be the entry-level, errand-boy of mechanical engineers. We'd need some-puppet to work on the set design and special effects over on *Not-So-Hard Boulevard*. We'd need some-puppet to keep an eye on our semiconductor fabrication clean rooms; and we'd need some-puppet in the cubicles, crunching numbers for capital equipment. We have our fingers in a lot of pies. Does that sound like it might be a fit?"

"PUUUUUSH."

"It's all so exciting, so new, so confusing," I said. "How much does it pay? When can I start?"

"Calm down, Felty. You need to interview with the other puppets to see if you're the best fit. You're not the only puppet that wants its strings pulled."

"I lack strings, Mother."

"We have them here."

"Do I need strings?"

"To be effective and competitive, yes. One other thing, I've heard you've become a man on several occasions, can you tell me a little more about that?"

"Yes, Mother," I said. "I *have* become a man on several occasions. It is more of a process than a destination. It feels so good and important and powerful, like you seem taller than normal and floating, in-line with the—"

"I'm gonna go ahead and stop you there. What if we told you we've found, through the evolution of our organization, that employing real men was counterproductive to our goals? What if we said we have a policy against manning-up during business hours? Would you still be agreeable to that?"

"I do not know what to say."

"You'll find this policy standard for most organizations. Tell you what, give it some thought. If you're still interested, the interviews are at 104 Power Drive Plaza, at 8:00 AM, cut-your-finger sharp. Ask for Miss Klacard. Got that?"

"I cannot answer one way or the other."

"If you decide to come, can you bring my things with you? They're packed in the pink suitcases in the bedroom."

"Yes, if I interview, I-I will bring the pink suitcases."

"Thanks, chao! Love ya! Muah! Yes, yes, we have enough. It's on the third floor. I told you."

"Certi?"

"Yes, babe?"

"Do you feel different about Miltro building puppets now that one of them might be your employee?"

"I don't get what you're saying. I know there was good money in making puppets, but Miltro didn't have the talent to make a go of it. You and some of the others might be a fluke or something. Look, I'm not interviewing you because Miltro's dead, and I won't have to pay the standard, four-hundred-boom-bill maker's fee. I can't wait to see you at the interview. Kisses! Bye!"

"PUUUUUSH."

"What was that?" Certi asked. "I didn't get that."

"I believe it may be the ghost of your husband," I said, "Miltro Miggugen."

"Tell him I said, *'Hi!'* Smoochies! Bye!" *Click.*

Two guards, armed with knifey and forkey, approached.

"FuzzPalace," the left one with the red turtleneck sweater said, "Can you stand?"

"If given assistance. Why?"

They looked to each other. The red one scratched his head as his pingpong eyeballs bobbled.

"Be not inert," I said. "Find your magic!"

"While scouting the perimeter, we witnessed something beyond the whirl of the world," the rightmost puppet who was covered in blue fur like a caveman said. The irises of his pingpongs widened. "We have seen something!"

"What have you seen?" I asked. "As a mind imagines? As shadows tickle out their tricks?"

"No," the blue caveman said. "As we see each other—now—at present."

"But," interrupted Red, "there was distance. There was diffusion of apprehension, like sun's flames spitting in googly eyes, confusing all contours."

"Speak plain, puppet."

"He has returned. He haunts the grounds as our breaths intercourse the air!"

"PUUUUUSH."

"Lo— There he cries now from his agony! It is Miltro!"

"Miltro? Huh! He has perished," I said. "Why so cocksure?"

"It is him, sir," the blue caveman said.

"From where does he call?" I asked.

"His throne!"

"From where?"

"The porcelain throne—from which eager men make deposits to the water supply. There, penance is paid."

"The toilet?" I asked.

"Precisely."

"You must take me there."

"Can you travel, FuzzPalace? This bathroom is very close to the entrance of the apartment."

"I can since I must."

"On your feet, then."

They helped me up. The blue caveman's grip felt like the teeth of a can opener but then something burst out as more painful still. "A wound screams out *'hel—lo!'*"

"Can you walk?"

"I walk, presently." I staggered and caught myself like I was being pulled about by a knotted paddle control.

"He walks then," the blue caveman said.

"I have fallen," I said.

"We will carry you atop this," Red said. He dragged an ironing board to us. "Roll on top."

"I crawl." They lifted me onto the ironing board. As we left the workshop for the apartment's entryway, the air chilled. Within walls, pipes kicked and bellowed from their strain of water. The kitchenette faucet filled in with *drip—drip—drip*. Crickets rubbed their legs: *Cheep, cheep, cheep. Drip. Cheep cheep. Drip. Cheep cheep. Drip drip.*

"Their cheeping sends this felt creeping," Red said.

"Shut up you!" the blue caveman said. "We veer left, toward the master suite—suite—suite!"

"PUUUUUSH."

"Say I, then: retreat—treat—treat!" Red said.

"Forward," I said. "Let us say hello to a ghost, whose message is surely no boast!"

"No spirit within the walls of this la—la—lavato—ory," Red said, with his teeth chattering.

"Nothing seen in darkness," the blue cavemen said. He scampered and did some gymnastics over the bathroom cabinets and countertop. "Sending current through a light fixture!"

"Egad!" Red said.

"Miltro," I said, "father."

"Is that you, puppets–*puppets?*" Miltro echoed. Even with his vaporous form before us, his voice emanated from a place far away and frozen. He sat shirtless on his throne with sweatpants wrapped around his ankles and a nightcap's tasseled point, dangling beside his face. "Gotta take a shit—*shit!*"

"Are you in pain, Father?" I asked.

"Pooping time," he said, "huuugh—!

"PUUUUUSH!

"Gotta get after it, puppets." A vein surfaced on his forehead. He bit his lip. "I believe in myself. I know I can."

"This is your penance, Father?"

"That FuzzPalace? You bring FuzzPalace, Mr. Cavesicle?"

"We have brought him, master," the blue caveman said.

"FuzzPalace," Miltro said, "listen—"

"PUUUUSH!

"We don't have much time. There's sins I gotta pay for in the afterlife before I move on. I ate empty food my whole life. Didn't get it out of my colon before I died. That last *Powerstacchio* was too much. I'm paying for it, even now. Understand?"

"Why must you get it out of your colon, Father?"

"THERE AIN'T NO BULLSHIT IN HEAVEN!" Miltro said. He cackled before wiping sweat away. "Sorry about that, puppets. It's true. Listen. There were a lot of details in my life I didn't pay the right attention to: kids, wives, careers. It all started here," Miltro pointed to his heart…and then to his abdomen, "and down here. I didn't take care of my responsibilities because I never stopped to take care of myself, first. You understand, FuzzPalace? You know that's your name? I made you in the image of my father and the father before that. Back from a time when people gave a shit! You understand, FuzzPalace?"

"Father, I—"

"SQUUEEEZE!"

"What was that, Father?"

"The bathroom ghost in the next apartment, talking to *his* puppets."

"SQUUEEEZE!"

"I do not understand."

"My wife give you a call?"

"Yes, Father."

"She staying up til three to work that job? It's gonna kill her. She ask you to work for her?"

"Yes, Father."

"Well…"

"Yes, Father."

"You gonna work for her, or ain't you?"

"I thought I might interview with her. She said, however, I could not man-up during business hours."

"That's a game they play—

"PUUUUUSH!

"Ahhh. Listen. Here's what you're gonna do. Go to her office, interview, get that job and be the best puppet engineer Power Chemicals ever had. You're gonna set that place straight so they never make another poisoned pistachio or no phony prescription drug again, got it?"

"I do not know if I can, Father."

"Oyster-spackle!" he said. "You do. *You do.* You feel it in your baling wire bones. Integrity. You got integrity. I sewed you that way."

"Father, what is integrity?"

"You got it in here," he pointed to his heart. "You do the right thing, even when nobodies looking. Not what ya gotta do to keep the mortgage. Not what you gotta do to keep the woman happy. Not what you gotta do to save your felt. I said, 'The *right* thing.'"

"Father, what is the right thing?"

"You'll know it. When the time comes, you'll know. Go to that Power Chemicals. Avenge me. Is it fair that because a food scientist wanted to save a boom-bill I should eat unsafe foods my whole life? Is it fair I should fight these *Powerstachios* out of my colon for all eternity? It was the engineers' fault! Made too many compromises, cut too many corners, lost sight of integrity. Not you, FuzzPalace. You're old-school. Back to basics. Back to when people cared, took their time, did the right thing. Bring her pink suitcases. You be an engineer and make me proud.

"Now get out of here! Gotta shit. You little guys are freaking me out, starring up with your little eyes—

"PUUUUUSH!"

15

In the months since I took my first steps, I worried about whether to leave our apartment. At 6:30 on that morning, as I stood atop Skeleton's shoulders as the head of the trench coat, I could scarcely believe my bravery. The trench coat was reinstated to help us blend-in. There were four of us within the coat on that morning.

The tag-along beside Matchy in the kangaroo pouch was Piss Ant. Piss Ant did not help support the weight above him. As we bounded forward, he griped about the sidewalk cracks and spoke of how he would be a better engineer than I, if hired.

"Does the sky look as boring as the ground?" Piss Ant asked. Between its cracks, the sidewalk sprouted black zigzagged violets and sapphire polka-dotted daffodils.

"I have only looked up once," I said. "It is too distant to look, again, too many possibilities within that sky, like infinity of freewill. Perhaps this is why the sky is blue. I feel nauseous."

"Be brave," Skeleton said. "Death owns each second."

The brakes of the bus screeched near the bus stop.

"Have we collected enough coins from the couch for the fare?" Matchy asked.

"I clutch all the coins," I said. "Let us hope it is enough."

The doors of the bus folded open.

"Three humongous hops," I instructed to Matchy.

Hop, hop, hop.

We stood upon the bus's topmost platform. It was paramount my speech be delivered with expert timing: "Madam bus driver, may I present a humble flesh-bag, in need of transport to a job interview?"

The bus driver smiled, showing her dental work. "Ya'll can sit with the rest a' ya'll." She guffawed and closed the doors behind us.

"The rest of us?" I asked.

Brakes squealed. The bus lurched. The driver wriggled her two finger stumps on her hand and a t-shirt covered her thick frame with a screen-print of airbrushed calligraphy, which bordered caricatures of politicians and socialites, celebrating the Lobster Festival.

On a third-row seat, a black-speckled shark of a three-puppet trio, wrapped in a similar trench coat, cried out, "Sit down…fellow human."

"Oh, no!" I said.

"All humans gotta sit," the red Mohawked head of three puppets near the back said.

I grasped a handrail as the bus lurched.

"What is it, FuzzPalace?" Skeleton asked. "I cannot see."

"We must stand," I said.

"Why?"

"Each seat on this bus is filled with puppets, employing trench coat gambits."

"But the trench coat gambit," Matchy said, "it was our creation."

"Creativity eluded us," I said.

"It's a full house," the bus driver said. "Wrap those felt paws around what ya can."

"She knows our secret, Felty," Matchy said, "she knows us as puppets!"

"Let honesty prevail," I said. "It did not work the first time. We doubted it would succeed the second."

"We're coming up on Blueport Bridge," the bus driver said. "That'll take us to Power Island. Ya'll are interviewing with Power Chemicals, right?"

"Affirmative," I said. "We take action."

"Yeah," she said, "been driving puppet-loads to Power Island. New batch each week. Turnover is high. Not sure what they do to ya'll. Funny thing, ya'll hide your insecurities the same way: trench coats."

"You offend me."

"Lose your cool easy? Afraid of open spaces, puppet?"

"Inconclusive response."

"Ya'll can close ya'lls eyes if ya need to when we head over Blueport Bridge. Just hosed out the bus. Don't want it covered in no soggy felt clumps or puppet sweat." Several puppets opened the bus's windows to let in the salty mist of the approaching bay.

"Already interviewed six, darn times," a seated puppet near a window said. "My torso's made a' hundreds, a' hundreds, a' moldy cotton balls." His pill-balled ears twitched. His beak-like nose dimpled near his reptilian nostrils.

"Very well," I said. "Calm yourself, my puppet."

His felt reddened. His pingpong ball eyes strained: "They holler at me when I sleep."

"Madame busdriver—"

"Yeah," the bus driver said. "They get whacked. It can be a hard life. Look forward. Keep to yourself."

"Electric waves shout throughout puppet strings, forever!" the reptile-nosed puppet said.

"I am uncomfortable," Skeleton said.

"Kept the eyes of my maker as cufflinks," the reptile-nosed puppet said. "See 'em dangle? For you, puppet."

"Those are raisins," I said, "you are insane."

"In the wine is the truth!"

"Let us return to the apartment," Piss Ant said. "We dive beyond our depth."

"Be calm," I said. "Giants snooze within us."

The bus slalomed and the bus driver blared her horn. We were approaching Blueport Bridge and emerging from stands of pines to reveal the coastline of the bay as seagulls drowsily pecked at garbage around the sides of the bridge. *Hiss! Hiss!* hissed the gulls, angling their heads.

A puppet seated to the right of Reptile Nose jabbed Skeleton in his ribs and narrowed his immense googly eyes at me. He scanned, side-to-side, perhaps traversing a landscape of memories. Beneath his prehistoric brow ridge, shot the crimson tufts of his eyebrows from his periwinkle-blue face. "Got gum?" he asked.

"Negative," I said.

"You ain't got none? Or, you won't give none?"

"How could you chew gum?" I asked. "You have merely three fangs."

"Let me worry about that. Need gum. It's good luck to chew something. I'm a monster, monsters chew."

"I have no gum, sir."

"Fine then," the monster said. The middle of the monster's trench coat jabbed toward me. "Hold up," the monster said, "my stomach wants to kick it." He unbuttoned his middle, and a lime puppet with a snout like a horn popped out.

"What kinda puppet this is?" Horn Mouth asked.

"I am an engineer puppet," I said. The bus rose toward the center of the bridge and cruise liners and yachts and ferries passed beneath us along the huge, blue expanse of the waters below. There was blueness below, blueness above. So much space. "I feel nauseous."

"Withstand trials," Matchy said.

"Engineer puppet think he getting him an engineering job?" Horn Mouth asked.

"What concern is this of yours?" I asked.

"Give my puppet gum. I'll spit game."

"Why does your puppet require gum?" I asked.

"He a monster," Horn Mouth said. "It ain't right to not let his mouth tear it up."

"Puppets," I said to those below. "Do any of us have chewing gum for a monster?"

"Nervous," the monster said. "Need gum."

"I may have gum," Piss Ant said. "I suspect, however, the surrender of my gum to be a waste."

"Pass up gum!" us three said.

"Here," Piss Ant said. "Its flavor is a mixture of cherry and apple. Therefore, may you not view my generosity as some pittance."

"Mmmm," the monster said. "Cherry and apple flavors 's tight. This gum clean."

"My friend 's chilled," Horn Mouth said. "Let me kick it to you, right quick."

"My ears await words to sweep away cobwebs," I said.

Horn Mouth's snout curled. "What the fuck?"

"Tell secrets."

Horn Mouth looked around. The tilt of his head leveled as fast as the hue of his felt changed from green to red, and he became somewhat of a different puppet as if something had been hidden, all along.

He spoke softly, "Humans will delay. They will dissemble to distract you. They will praise and flatter. Be not drawn in. I have interviewed many times without success and, each time, it is so. You may think me worthless in my tutelage. In their tricks hides a repetition and a convergence of strategy.

In manners most mysterious, they will affix your body with guide rods—guide strings. You will feel pleasure in the strength and certainty of these restraints. You will feel these rods and strings possessed of a timeless, godlike wisdom: beware this thought. Your bonds are made of the folly of past, human decision. Understand?"

"When you say the rods—"

"Silence," Horn Mouth said. "Hear more—!"

"Some of my cotton balls is escaping. Maybe my maker had him some raisin eyes—"

"They will tie you up—top-to-bottom—in guide rods and strings. I know what you're thinking: if you detect the slightest push or pull in one direction or the next, if you anticipate your puppeteer's movements, you will be a greater employee. Perish this, puppet."

"I had presumed the extremes—"

"Wrong," Horn Mouth said, "the middle path, the middle path is the one you take. A good puppet picks and chooses. He decides the main direction his puppeteers require and deletes all else from his mind. Be not a dumb puppet, do not ignore all commands. Such puppets will never be hired. Be not a hyper-vigilant puppet, do not over-anticipate, nor overreact to the smallest of stimuli. Hyper-vigilant puppets, though hired on the spot, will be ground-up, laid waste in no time. Understand, puppet?"

"Sentiment of appreciation," I said. "You have given me much to think over. What is your name, puppet?"

"Fool, it's Horn Mouth," Horn Mouth said.

"Why are you named this," I asked.

HOOOOONK! Horn Mouth honked.

The red Mohawk of a trio in front turned around. "What you honking at, honky?"

HOOOOOONK!

"Honk this way one more g'in."

HOOOOOONK! HOOOOOOONK!

"You a fool. Aye, got gum? Apple-Cherry? Apple-Cherry, my puppet? What's happening?"

"It is my gum," Piss Ant said. "I say again, the sacrifice was no pittance!"

"This piece done." The monster squished it on the window. "More gum. Only monsters eat gum, and you discerned it."

"Aye-aye, the little one at the bottom got the gum." Mohawk looked down at the other puppets within his trench coat. "You know what it is!" The trio stood and its middle burst open so a puppet jumped out and tore open the middle of *our* coat before we could react. There were several blows exchanged and, before I knew it, my feet rested upon the invading puppet of the Mohawk trio, and Skeleton had abandoned us to infiltrate and attack the other team.

I struggled to keep balance on this new puppet as he negotiated down his demands. Several buttons had torn from the middle of the coat, and I pleaded for them to simmer down, to behave as gentle-puppets. "What the fuck is you? Aye, puppet, what the fuck is you?" the new puppet said. "Aye, Johner," he called. "It a fucking, it a fucking ant that got pissed on. Still wanna get that gum?"

"For my vote, I think we shall take all of their gum," the voice of the lowest puppet of the opposing trio said. "Let these fellas know we are the dominant ones."

"You know my character not," Piss Ant said. "I will never relinquish any gum."

"Give gum!" I said.

"No more slumping," Piss Ant said. "It is my property. He has no right to treat me as such."

"The thing wiped some a' its piss on my face!"

"May the shame of this stench," Piss Ant said, "be always with you, my son."

"It got in my mouth!"

A large fist rocked us. "Only monsters eat gum!" The remaining buttons of the trench coat burst off, and we tumbled to the floor. "And you discerned it!"

"Take your exoskeletal ass to the bathroom." This new puppet stank of whale oil and rusted iron like a pirate from the rogue armadas of the 1300s. Matchy threw a haymaker to the pirate's jaw and his kangaroo kicked him against a nearby seat support. The monster collapsed on top of us. Something caused the Mohawk's trio to topple backward, but they fled the coat to join the mêlée.

Piss Ant overreacted to a supposed strike and crawled away from the group.

The pirate roused, spotted Piss Ant, gave chase, caught him

by the leg and scrabbled with all six of Piss Ant's legs. Piss Ant turned onto his stomach, and the pirate rained fists upon the back of his head.

"Let go of my string eyelets, cheater," Piss Ant said.

"Ain't touching your eyelets!"

"You lie. You have touched them to gain an advantage."

"Never," the pirate said. "I don't fight dirty. I didn't puppet you. Gimme that gum!" He rained punches.

Piss Ant scooped and flung his piss over his back, "May the stench provide no refreshment. May it overwhelm you with aromas so pungent and of asparagus, my son."

Gasp. "Fuck, puppet!" Gasp. "Fuck?"

"Struggling to breathe?" Piss Ant asked. "You should have inquired, regarding my reputation."

"Knock it off back there, felt heaps," the bus driver said. "Besides, we're almost there. Last stop, Power Chemicals."

All eight combating puppets gasped. Piss Ant clenched his crushed package of gum inside his greedy palm and darted his eyes and antennae about. Every button of all three coats had popped off and been lost. We would enter the premises without disguise, as puppets.

The bus stopped in traffic.

A puppet jumped out of his trench coat and pressed against a window.

"Look!" He pointed below to a stalled cruise liner with gray smoke billowing from the cabin of its upper deck. "HERE HUMANS STRUGGLE!"

On the topmost deck, passengers encircled a middle-aged man in a white footman uniform. He was presumably their captain. The captain attempted to keep the pasty passengers at bay with a bent shuffleboard stick.

Us puppets crowded the windows for a good look. We smiled and fogged the windows with breath. The visceral pleasure of discovering them so mired in their struggle coursed through me—

"Tick-tock Tizzay!" one of us cheered, and we all joined.

"TICK-TOCK TIZZAY! TICK-TOCK TIZZAY! PUPPETS WIN, PUPPETS WIN TODAY!"

16

Us nine stood behind the trench coats, which were huddled near an immense wall. Somewhere near the glass-facade of doors stood a puppet employed by Power Chemicals, shouting instructions amid the shoving and bickering. Its only indications were the six strings leading up from its body.

As I paced, the strings vanished in the purple, noonday rays. "Power Chemicals was constructed on Power Island in the 1450s as a military base," the puppet said. "An amazing monolithic structure, consisting of a single massive level in the shape of a pentagon with, as you see here—look here, close your mouth—an offset defensive wall in the shape of a pentagon. The structure, which you are viewing, is complete with turrets at each corner. The turrets are just for playing cards and checking emails and that stuff. Ha-ha haha. Am I right? *Am I right?* Any questions? This way."

Our group shuffled through the doors.

"Wait." The Power Chemicals puppet, dressed like a flight attendant, pointed at me. "What is that?" His strings led into the acoustical tiles above but the fluorescent lights made them blurry.

"I am Felty FuzzPalace," I said. "I am in charge of gears and shafts as is written on my business card." I pulled my collar from my neck and presented my card. "My maker made the card for me."

"Ri-ight," the guide said. He spoke into a microphone near his lapel, "234? We gonna separate some a' this riffraff, your turn."

"Heard that, 209. What's your situation?"

"Some-puppet say he in charge a' gears and shafts. Felty FuzzPalace."

"Miss Klacard is expecting him. Send him through."

"Got eight or nine friends with him."

"Only three of these gentle-puppets are associates," I said.

"How you saying that, after all these years?" the pirate asked.

Our guide hushed us. I stretched to discover how his guide strings attached to the ceiling since none of us applicants had them.

"Hold up, 209. Miss Klacard says, 'Send all nine through.'"

"Heard that, 234, I'm done."

"CLAM-SPACKLE!" shouted the remaining trench coats.

• • •

We were left in adjoining conference rooms. I sat in a task chair behind a table with empty chairs opposite me. On the far wall a black lacquered bureau supported four teleporters. The teleporters were black and sleek with a citrus, PC logo bordered by droplets that appeared as if squirting outward in a ring. The first teleporter was built with gold trim, the second with wood, the third with platinum and the fourth, ivory.

The door clicked and sweat sprayed from my pits and brow. Certi walked in and approached the opposite side of the table. "Did you bring me my pink suitcases?" Her gray pantsuit shimmered as her arms crossed.

"We found their transport difficult."

Certi stroked her blonde hair.

Stilettos improved on Stephy's impressive, human height as her black gossamer skirt and lacy button down stretched. "Felty!"

"Stephy?"

Stephy leaned to kiss my cheek and my hand pawed the three identification badges she had acquired: Id, Ego, and Superego.

"Inappropriate affection exchange!" a cavernous voice, careened across the room. The voice came from a husky puppet in a three-piece suit.

The puppet's torso spread, though it lacked a head. It had no hands as if an invisible force held up the suit and strained the fabric with a big pair of moobs. The suit's floating neckline held nothing but a puppet string that might have connected to his waist. This string was more of a rope and its braids twisted with the girth of a hangman's noose.

"Interviews should begin promptly," he said with a yellow light pulsing from his neckline with each word. "So says me, Headless Boardsman!" He sat. "Stephy, sit beside this Headless Boardsman."

"This man has no head," I whispered to Stephy. "Do you intend to provide this?"

She smelled the rose pinned above her breast. The black zigzags of the rose appeared pixelated as if an unnatural insect had pollinated it.

"Your flower is strange."

"You're strange." She smiled. "I hope you get hired. Good luck, right?"

"Luck?" I asked.

"His maker is dead," Certi said. "There will be no maker's-fee."

Headless Boardsman perked up. "The standard is four-hundred boom-bills. Puppets at a deep-discount?"

"My maker? Miltro?" I asked. Both my hands bobbed on sticky strings. I reached back and found one leading up from an attachment on my back. "Zorf!" Perspiration squirted. "Headless Boardsman, something is incorrect. I have been put on strings."

"You were always on these."

Stephy sat to his right and Certi to his left.

"This is not correct," I said. "I came into this room as a-a free-standing puppet!"

"Strings, no strings," Headless Boardsman said with his syllables beating out yellow light, "this is of no consequence. If you wish to leave—"

"HELP!" I said. "ALACK!"

"…you can, but you must forfeit your bid for PC employment. Is this your wish?"

"Zorf-meep! Sticky strings. Zorf-meep!" I raised my hand to pull my collar away. Some foreign hand—mostly mine—slapped my face. "I need this job."

Stephy sniffed at her artificial rose. "Take it like a puppet. The worst of it ends quickly."

"I must be unreal to be real," I said. "I NEED THIS."

"There is no *I* in phantasmagoric," Headless Boardsman said. "Except near the end."

The strings thrummed like they were stretched over a guitar as they forced my hands to fold on my lap. A hypnotic power pulsed through each string with electric regularity, into each hand, into my torso, into the felty part of my felty heart. "I apologize for my outburst."

Certi pounded the table. "Why have you not brought me my pink suitcases?"

"The weight of your suitcases was great," I said. "I was not able to arrange their transport and my own in the time allotted."

They bickered among themselves in a jargon-laced lingo.

How could Stephy conspire against me? No sooner had I thought this than her power popcorn-pulsed through my strings and forced a thought to spire like a pestering bee. This telepathy's color snarled with the fangs of a panther-pink: red, mauve—spring handbags, PMP Certification, apricot chardonnay—peanut butter and celery recipes, Fifty-two Ways to Make Him Squirm, In Bed—mauve, red, pink. Its strength was a multi-story snake that could choke a half-held dream with a heavy thought.

"Not able to arrange their transport?" Certi sneered.

"No," I said, "I hardly see the importance."

"Felty FuzzPalace," Certi asked, "did you look *inside* each pink suitcase?"

"Zorf." I had peered into her suitcases. They were filled with nothing more than rusty pennies, used dildos and a variety of bric-a-brac, and I failed to see what significance they might have to my PC employment but I was growing more and more terrified of admitting this for fear I might reveal some ignorance on my part.

"Did you look inside my pink suitcases?" Stephy demanded. Headless Boardsman leaned back in his chair and laced his imaginary fingers behind his imaginary head.

"Yes," I said, "Yes. I looked inside the suitcases. I verified their…their contents."

"Was everything in order?" Certi asked.

"My Lobster," I said. "Yes, I should say…I should say everything was in perfect order."

"Very well," Certi said. "I'll swing by the old place and pick them up. Next question."

"NEXT QUESTION," Headless Boardsman boomed as his yellow light flickered.

"Stephy," I said. "May I request a recess?"

"NO RECESS," Boardsman said. "PUPPETS PROCEED."

"We'll just be one second," Stephy said. "Let's go, Felty."

In a moment we were outside the closed door of the conference room, and she leaned to comb my hair with her fingers. "I'm glad you're here, little guy."

"Little guy," I protested. "I was your man."

"Once."

"I feel what you are doing."

"What am I doing?"

"Manipulating my guide rods for your purposes. Think how I feel. This is not fair. Not long ago, you tingled my rods for our sexy-time."

"If you want to get in here, you have to pay dues. Be flexible, Felty. Your guide rods can be used for a lot."

"Woman! Unfair! You are a puppet. Where are *your* strings?"

"I'm going to stop you there. It took hard work to get where I'm at. I'm not going to let you mess this up. I've always been a real woman."

"But, Stephy—"

"No buts!" Stephy said.

I saw this as a challenge and leapt upon her double entendre and grabbed full hold of her: "But…but what a FULL BUTT you have!"

She slapped me so hard that I crumpled to the floor. Then she laughed a new laugh that said, 'Look at you—so low—and look at me, so high.' As I had fallen the strings of my arms and back entangled so I could not stand but simply bounced and wriggled like a forlorn, felty lump of less-than-zero importance.

"Felty. Oh, Felty! I'm gonna pee my friggen pants."

"It is no laughing matter, woman. My strings—help me."

"Help yourself."

A swelling infected the felt, stretching it blood-packed, as vertigo spun the carpet away. Nearby sounds became tinny. The strings disappeared, and I flexed naked arms. I stood to rise above her eye level and lurched closer: *"MINE!"*

"Dude…you got a boner."

"BONE!"

"Amateur," someone said behind me.

I turned to who had spoken. "Eyeam? The famous puppet from *Not-So-Hard Boulevard?*" I clenched my fists.

"Stay outta this, Eyeam," Stephy said. She took my hand and led me toward a nearby conference room.

Eyeam setup and threw back a quick key-bump, shook it off and hid a vial beneath one of its smashed guide rods. The green hackles of its narrow shoulders rose and it hunched down, bobbed its head, and rubbed its hands.

"That's that scoundrel, Eyeam!" I blurted as Stephy led me by the hand. "I am naked. Employment is difficult."

"Come on, Felty."

She led me into an empty conference room and slammed the door. "I was worried this might happen." She opened a handbag and dug around. "I stopped at a gas station and got you a spare, just in case."

"A spare?"

"Set of your clothes."

I chuckled. "Oh, Stephy, you are mistaken. I am an original. My clothes cannot be purchased at some gas station…foolish woman."

Stephy recoiled. "No, you're not. You can get a change of your clothes at *any* gas station. It's a popular suit for you little guys. See?" She pulled out a facsimile of my wardrobe for appraisal. "So cute."

"A perfect copy? They will never know I tore my clothes and pawed your posterior." My tears welled. "Creativity eludes me."

"There's no shame in buying off-the-rack. I did it once, too. Slip these on, little guy."

"I am too big."

"That's not true. You're shrinking, already. Do you want me to turn around while you put on your little outfit?"

"Yes please." I buttoned the polo over my potbelly and thin arms. "Stephy, why is there a prohibition against manning-up during office hours?"

She smelled her pixelated flower. "Did you say something? You came into the room as a puppet. They're only gonna hire a puppet. They don't like surprises."

"I imagined there would be more humans on Power Island."

"Power Island is where the work gets done. Most humans stay clear, except the managers."

"Why are you being so kind?"

She ran her hand over a bump on her stomach. "You didn't notice?"

"What the?"

"Here," she pulled my hand onto her bump as my soul marinated in fear, "you can touch."

"Is it because my stuff went inside?"

"It is…"

"Unravel riddles."

"Focus on the interview. Get the job."

Inside the original conference room, the Headless Boardsman devoured an éclair such that it disappeared into his invisible head with each bite. "This filling is filling. Doughnuts, doughnuts doughnuts. Num, num, num num num." The gold-trimmed teleporter switched off and several more doughnuts fell from their floating positions.

"My apologies for the recess," I said.

"Not all doughnuts devoured…"

"Felty, let me cut through the candle wax," Certi said. "Did you bump into Eyeam in the hallway?"

"Affirmative, that was the action."

"It stopped by here as well. It told us you were naked in the hallway. Just…just hold on. We're willing to let fool's-pranks flop off fools. Eyeam is nervous because it thinks we're trying to replace it and, to tell the truth, there's a project it's working on—"

"Eyeam is an actor *and* an engineer?" I asked.

"Most puppet engineers double as actors. You may have the opportunity to act."

"Oh, no," I said. "I am an engineer. I could never act."

"You'd be surprised how many engineers started off saying that. We don't care when an engineer of Eyeam's caliber decides to snort stuff, entertain call girls— Not sure why I'm admitting this. The schedule can't be pushed to the right. We need someone to come in, study under him…*it* on some projects, and…lighten its load. You up to the challenge, FuzzPalace?"

"Of which projects do you refer?" I asked.

"INSUFFICIENT CONFIDENCE," Headless Boardsman boomed.

Certi waved him away. "Felty, what we need—in two months—is a design for a plastic lid."

"Yes," I said.

"It should be perfectly flat, so people can walk on it."

"Yes."

"These people—they're fairly big—prone to jumping."

"Yes!"

"It should withstand a 25G vacuum."

"Yes!"

"We're gonna drill all kinds of bolt and rivet holes. It should be no more than two duckbills thick."

"Holes? Blind-tapped, through-all, bottom-tapped?"

"All those—as much as we need—we'll figure it out as we go," Certi said. "Do you think you can do it in the time allotted?"

I pulled the collar from my neck. "Of—of course…" Certi's power traveled through my strings, glimmering silver with a transience of logic and passion that spoke, 'You're not there. Impress me, or it's over.' So, I continued, "Of course, the nature of the plastic is important as well as the system's operating temperature and the service life."

Eyeam burst into the room with the giant pupils of his bloodshot googly eyes bouncing and foam hinting below its mouth plate. "You know how it's told and sold, skin-bags." It gyrated, flaunting how its naked, furry body lacked genitalia. Its power was green and the green words, 'I'm above it, I'm above it,' pulsed, over and over, through my strings.

It finished its dance and, panting, pointed at me. "You think you'll replace Eyeam? I am not impressed. This one is not a real puppet or a puppet on this level. Look at him, an old-school, extinct bug-eyed string-tangler, a spineless no-winded bone-weasel, a forget-to-carry-the-one cock-sprung, a falsified fungus-berry, a dictionary-dusting dung-drop, a teleport-me-a-tablespoon-of-testosterone task-miser—"

"I really must object here," I said. "With respect due you your successful teleporter career, Eyeam, I am also not pressed inwards since my very pressure moves outwards with these words: as peepers peep and seekers seek, you are surely a surly, naked and furry, androgynous escaped puppet—fueled on narcotics, handled too long with nothing but soft mittens, kid gloves and stupefying indifference. Your ice is not nice, nary a real diamond twice—"

Eyeam inspected the phrases of his jewel-crusted necklaces before sniffling and stumbling. "Tut-tut, pill-ball butt."

I lunged toward it. "In point of fact I accuse you of being responsible for the death of my maker. Puppet monsters can only be indulged so long. When the tongue, at last, licks the toad, these monsters must assert, once and for all, who they are, what they stand for and what they cannot abide.

"Hire me, potential employers. I am old school. I will never entertain. My values are integrity, discipline and hard work. You will never find a puppet more devoted to the accuracy of his numbers and his ideas."

"NO MANNING-UP DURING BUSINESS HOURS," boomed Headless Boardsman.

"You've torn out of your clothes, again," Certi said.

"Oh." I covered myself. "I had not noticed."

"I've got another spare in my handbag," Stephy said.

Certi leaned back in her chair. "We'll get back to you."

17

Since we lacked the coins for a bus, we banded with several, other puppets for a walk, which spanned days and nights, over teaming highways, into forests and behind mini-malls. A pingpong of one of Piss Ant's adversaries got severed. I could not discern what the fight was about despite him trying to explain with the eye clutched in his paw as we approached Miltro's apartment.

"Next, he spouts," Piss Ant said, "no, listen, he says, 'I drink coffee with the milk and without the sugar.' How could I relax?"

"Ahead: Miltro's apartment," I said. "We will hand out impressions of sanity."

In the lawn before Miltro's entryway, a stand constructed from card tables, mop handles and cardboard scraps hoisted a sign scrawled in orange 'Root Beer's Fortunes: Professional Weirdo Advice.'

Root Beer's shoulders hunched as he sat. The puffs of red hair around the neck of his robe rose like the hackles of a dog. He swept coins into a cloth sack and counted them out to DinoMan, who was also in a gray robe, and who tallied on a ledger. "Greetings, fellow felties," Root Beer said. "You are alive."

"We journeyed several days by foot," I said.

"You could not lift a phone and send a ring?"

"We had no money. The fare to the interview took all we had."

"I see," Root Beer said. He counted his coins. "Improper planning?"

"Hiccups in the game plan."

Root Beer's pingpongs bobbled like hatch-ready eggs and his nose snaked. "I see." He flung a coin so it rang. "As FuzzPalace can see, we earn money off my fortune telling—"

"Root Beer foresees the future?"

"It entertains the humans to believe so. The quackery is tiresome. Will you help break down the stand? I must attend to the bookkeeping."

"Certainly," I said. "Felties, help Root Beer break down his stand."

"Felties are not ordered about by FuzzPalace," Root Beer said. "His mind is a chum bucket that the rats have laid siege to."

"Zorf…in the trench coat I was the head."

"Creativity eluded us there," Matchy said.

"The head for the trench coat," Skeleton said. "Not head for all times."

"FuzzPalace, can you help me carry this coin sack into the apartment while the others break down the stand?" Root Beer asked.

"Certainly."

Once inside, Root Beer explained that I could rest myself so I might advise him with which direction to carry his sack.

"The…the path is straight ahead," I said.

"Do not let precious calories divert from your head."

"Very well," I said. "I point the way with my finger."

"Many thanks." He reached into his bag and wound up a pitch with a mean look on before he unwound and let loose with something.

"Did you pelt my forehead with a coin? Ouch!"

"Your brilliance attracted it to your head," he said.

"Could that be?" I asked. "The boundaries of brilliance being not defined?"

"Let us test."

"Ouch! You threw it that time."

"A third time brings clarity." He wound up again with a greedy look.

"Three lumps for me?"

"Coins for four?" Root Beer dug into his bag. He filled his hands and flashed a mean smile. I turned to run as a coin ricocheted off a barstool by the kitchenette.

"Your lunacy soars."

Root Beer pulled his robe closed and touched his nose before lurching forward with the heavy bag in tow. "I wager you embarrassed us before the humans."

A doorknob turned as a coin ricocheted off it, *ping!* I fled for the main hallway, jumped over a sleeping felty and rubbed the welt on my forehead. I shouted, mid-stride, "Root Beer hurls coins like an old woman pets pussy."

Staggering, I bounced off drywall and turned to find Root Beer in teeth-grinding pursuit. His pingpongs ionized the air with blue sparks. Left and right, his jagged nose curled. Pill balls twitched over his jowls like a citizenry in unrest. The plastic of his eyes dimpled as fast as his irises dilated with his wide mouth buckling.

"Felty FuzzPalace, puppet with a fancy business card, YOU DO NOT LEAD US!"

Ping ping.

"Ow-w!" I said, "That last one caught under my armpit. The pain of continents, separating to sea. You have thrown enough."

"Grow to a man and smash me."

"I cannot man-up over trifles." I panted and fell on my face, my fingers clenched in case I should have to puppet-punch.

"FuzzPalace needs a cause for manning-up?"

"Oooo fuck puppet!" I rubbed my armpit and dried a tear. "Slap your face with a rusty mace."

"Who paid the postage due to mail the box? Me!" *Ping.*

"Owww!" I said. "Tablecloth and tapestry! That hit a cufflink."

"Did you man-up during the interview?"

"Certainly not."

Ping.

"The truth!"

"I-I…twice."

"Why are you now clothed?"

"Stephy works there. She brought clothes."

"You relied on her? Will fortune always court? Many of us rely on these efforts, FuzzPalace does not set his vision to the path's distance."

The master suite was not far, I staggered and ran. I slammed the door with Root Beer bouncing off just as I locked it. His hands rattled the knob. "Let me in!" Root Beer said.

"Staple your mouth, ram dynamite up your fart-flinger!"

"Let me in!" Root Beer said. "Let me in, let me in, let me in—" he seemed to slump to his knees, "We are partners, FuzzPalace."

"Explain."

"I will support you. I will help you earn food and bus fare. In return, you will support me if fortune should find you, and should misplace me."

"If fortune misplaces you, I-I shall not."

"Does FuzzPalace swear?"

"I swear."

"Or let his stitching run unbound, upon the Lobster's Buttery Thorax?"

"Or let my stitching run unbound, upon the Lobster's Buttery Thorax, I do swear I shall never lose you, Root Beer."

"Miltro has blessed me with a haunting, also. He has haunted me…with…with a message I am to keep secret. Providence knows not only Felty's face. Understand?"

"Understood." I panted and slumped against the door as I throbbed with coin welts.

Root Beer pounded. "FuzzPalace cannot claim the master suite. I have been sleeping there."

"I was first to climax here with a lady; the suite is mine."

He scratched down the door. "Very well."

• • •

Bang bang! "FuzzPalace!" A fist pounded as I heard the voice of Mr. Cavesicle. "FELTY!" Although the door to the suite was locked in the mornings, I was waked this way, often. There was no reason to leave the bed because I had no purpose.

"Felty!"

"Wait," I said, "the sun hides."

"The sun throws off light!" Mr. Cavesicle said. "Herbivore is pulling my hair. He stuffed broccoli in my mouth while I…while I snoozed!"

"It was for *his* good, he mocked my ways," Herbivore said. "Mr. Cavesicle cannot repay a debt with an animal carcass. He must pay in crackle coins or the sacred vegetables."

My feet swung off the bed, and I pulled on the gray robe to help with Root Beer's fortune telling. "Why must I settle these disputes? Why not grow from children into adolescence? Each day, another dispute."

Bang bang! "He pulls my hair. My hair is beautiful and blue. A carcass is a time-honored way of repaying debt. A squirrel I slayed. Eyes of glass, mouth agape. Into my sleepy mouth, he stuffed broccoli."

"Clearing his mind madness!" Herbivore said.

The door to the master suite was difficult to unlock in the mornings. Before I started locking it they would awaken me by pouncing on my bed. Mr. Cavesicle and Herbivore had clumps of tomato paste smeared over loincloth and sweater, moccasins and corduroys. The ink of their pupils fizzled, bubbling as they shouted. "Let loose his fur, Herbivore," I said.

"Not till he honors his debt with a chlorophyll tribute."

I pattered away and cinched my robe. Carcasses of squirrels and lobsters stained the carpet of the family room. "Repay this puppet in broccoli."

"No!" Mr. Cavesicle said.

"Animalistic relic, FuzzPalace sides with me."

"I gave you a squirrel's spirit. Eyes not of the glass? Mouth not agape?"

"Do as you were told," Herbivore said.

Many days went this way. When I was outside near the stand, I danced when told to dance, swayed when told to sway; up-sold client's with lemonade; prepared orange smoke bombs; queued the CDs of concerto music. I counted the coins and made the change. Such drudgery. All the while something unmistakable nagged at me.

"What is that attached to your back, Felty?" DinoMan asked.

"It comes and goes."

"A string?"

"A string."

He grabbed at my puppet string. "The masking tape tag says: FATHERHOOD.

Who wrote this word in such sloppy lettering?"

"I know what it says. Do you think I do not know, you—you frumpy fool? I feel it. No one knows who first wrote that word… FATHERHOOD."

"The puppet string leads so high up into the sky. Where does it lead, FuzzPalace?"

"I do not believe a single soul knows this."

"FuzzPalace, what is the purpose of your string? None of us have strings. Why do you have one?"

"I made love to the bull's eye of Stephy's thighs as a real man should. I am not sure a puppet has ever done that before—"

"The power-u, puppet? You got in that power-u, felt when you were not of felt?"

"Yes. I made love to nothing of stitching or of felt. I made love to a real woman's power-u of flesh and blood. I do not know what the puppet string means. It is hot out. I am going inside to call for Skeleton to relieve me of my duties."

"What is wrong? Do you grouse about Fatherhood?"

"I grouse because of your scaly face."

As I pattered inside I stopped to look at the dusty teleporter and imagined it was still working. Ever since I destroyed its cord, I had longed to refurbish it or purchase a replacement. Without the distraction of teleportation we were all growing more philosophical, introspective and puppet-wise. It was painful. And no word back about my interview, although I had phoned PC several times.

"Skeleton," I said, "will you relieve my duties outside for a half-hour?"

"Let me borrow that robe, I can't find mine."

"FuzzPalace FuzzPalace!" Red said. "Piss Ant said if two-plus-two turns out to four, then my mother was a dirty, dirty—!"

"Leave him alone, Piss Ant."

"Inform him I am not to be looked on askance!"

"Stop looking on him askance."

"But wait," Red said, "Something more I must tell."

A pressure of import seized my abdomen. A movement threatened to shift and break loose. Evil spirits lashed their bristly tongues against an overburdened door.

"It was yesterday, Mr. Cavesicle and I were cleaning pots and stacking dishes—"

"I converse no longer!" I said.

"Say, FuzzPalace, what is this string leading up from your back?"

"An emergency threatens!"

"Hear more about when Mr. Cavesicle and I stacked dishes—"

"Enough puppets, I must poop." I horseback-hobbled toward the master suite's bathroom like an arthritic cowhand.

"He must poop."

"Who must poop?" Nagarazim asked.

"FuzzPalace," someone said.

Nagarazim roused. He followed me by dragging himself atop a skateboard. "Puppets—though we do not often poo—but once per yearly season, but one blob for summer, count one coil for fall, a single shit for frigid winter and one lonely lump for saucy spring—we do so deliberately, with verve. Puppet poo, though it be fuzzy, though it be singularly moist, must be expelled through steadfast puppet choice."

"Of my poo, you offer me no counsel!"

"Heed my words, puppet: do not depart until you mostly win— slowly, surely do not fall in!"

Behind the locked door of the master bathroom I was free from meddling. Something was wrong. The other puppets had been warning me that my first seasonal shit, the first of my puppet existence, approached. The bowl rattled and several, gravely intonations cried out from below:

"Vengeance is mine, from out thy behind!"

"Who goes there?" I asked and locked about, hoping I misjudged and the voice I heard had not emanated from beneath me.

"'Tis I, foodstuffs of months past!"

A chill slipped through the room, and I shivered. Electric tendrils quickened me from somewhere deep within. The synthetic stuff I had eaten from the couch threatened with its exit.

"Haunt my anus no more," I said. "Accept apologies for diverting you through a puppet's path." I tried to slump but the *Fatherhood* string pulled me upright so that even while on the stool I could not be at ease. More of the cheap synthetic couch threatened to exit me. If I was to be a real father I must afford whole, unmodified food. I must afford to separate those I loved from a careless world gone to hell with treachery, pollution, with graft. "Hear me, spirits, sing this song as your last. I will be able to afford real food, soon."

I stood and peered in the bowl at what I had done. The slithery serpents, which had been expelled, swam in circles with their bulbous googly eyes at the heads of their metallic bodies. "Spirits of the bowl," I said, "name your names."

As if singing in melodic tunes, they cried, timely,

"Mercury!"

"Lead!"

"ARSENIC!"

"Turds, I bid you farewell." I flushed.

"We shall return." Their googly eyes bounced as they fought, desperately, against the currents. "We turds are legion!"

I flushed again and swiped sweat from my brow. How could a phantasm as strange as that be possible? So much had happened over the first three months that I felt shell-shocked as if a veteran of Great War Two. A father should at least know the workings of sexy-time. Was I a father? To what? Was I the first puppet to do what I had done with Stephy? A man was dead, the nightmares of killing him had swept in and out of my dreams.

The world was more nuanced, more dangerous than it seemed on the teleporter programs. Where had they mailed the bouncing box? Was their hibernation over? Had they found good homes and good masters? Masters? Where did these ideas come from? Were they sewn into my skull? Was my brain, in fact, stitched?

What if squishies were the more masterful of us puppets? We gave them everything we had. They left as soon as it was gone. Why was the sky purple? Why were flowers pixelated? Who was that now rummaging through Miltro's things in the master suite?

Certi bent over a pink suitcase in her glimmering pantsuit. "Hey there, Felty. Everything come out okay?"

"How did you get in here?" I asked.

"The little guys let me in."

"I see."

"It's here, just as I left it." She gazed over the contents of her open, pink suitcase and rearranged a few things. "Do you think you can help me carry this to my car?"

"Yes, Mother," I said. "Plus, I can get a few others to help you transport your…items."

"Felty, do you even understand what this is for? It's important I hire people that have good insight and intuition. I figured I shouldn't have to explain this to an experienced engineer."

"Yes, yes," I said. "Before you are used dildos, rusty pennies… odds and ends."

Certi scowled. Her eyes watered with emotion. "These suitcases contain vaginal secretions, microbial and copper oxidation samples. They're for a potential vaccine for an emerging venereal disease. This is a Ph sample, a titration kit. This…this could save the lives of countless young girls and women in underprivileged communities across the world. We needed this weeks ago."

"Oh," I said. "Apologies."

"Felty," Certi said. "This *was* the interview. You blew it, Felty. Wait…what is this?"

"What is what?"

She stood and fingered over the string leading up out of my back.

"Hey," I said. "That tickles."

She read the tag: "FATHERHOOD."

“Yes, Mother.”

The string pulled and forced my back to forgo slumping.

“I’ve always had a soft spot for hiring fathers. You do look sharp in your little suit.”

“Yes!”

She groped her cold, thin hands over my cufflinks. “Hmm, nice cufflinks. Made to accept our standard guide rods.”

“Ouch. Those are sensitive, madam.”

“I like a puppet with sensitive cufflinks.”

“Why is that, madam?”

She spoke to herself. “Strung with at least one string from above, already. Sensitive cufflinks for whatever guide rods might come from below. We can control his higher faculties and his baser instincts.”

“What are you saying? Mother— Madam, I do not understand you.”

“Can you, at least, cite the Three Laws of Engineering?”

“I live them! An engineer must—”

“Okay, I believe you. And what do the laws mean to you, Felty?”

“I am not a scientist. I am where the rubber of Idealism meets the road of Pragmatism. I am an engineer.”

“Can you start this Monday, at 8:00 AM, cut-your-finger-sharp?”

“Yes, Mother! *Ble—erch!*”

“What—?”

“I vomit balls of felt when long deprived of my sexy-times.”

“Umm, yeah, uh…*yeah.*”

18

"You ain't late," the puppet said, dusting off the elbow patches of his blazer, "you ain't early…" He ignored me and considered whether to swat a fly with a copy of Meme Magazine as he buzzed along with the fly: "Fucking fly."

"Why not grab the fly's strings?"

"Puppets don't pull puppet strings," he said. "Don't you know nothing? Missed it. Keep flying. Flier. Who you here for?"

"Do you address the fly?"

"Gonna swallow this fly you don't tell me who you here for."

"I am here for Eyeam."

"You here for Eyeam? Eyeam *who?*"

"I am the engineer. I am here for Eyeam, the engineer."

"Don't sound right."

"I am the engineer. I am here for Eyeam, the engineer, who is also here."

"Name that engineer, who also here…"

"Come again?"

"Last name a' engineer here?"

"It is Eyeam. Eyeam, the engineer. Eyeam, the engineer, who

is here."

"Look puppet, I know you the engineer. I see you here. Wore that both times you here. Sold at gas stations near. Tell me Eyeam's name or I can't do a thing for you."

"What more should I reveal."

The puppet swung and crushed the fly beneath his copy of Meme. The fly's strings disappeared. "Got you! Ah, just…just playing. Check its crawlspace, puppet."

"Its crawlspace?"

"You in for it. Don't know why Certi said Eyeam needs to be the first to see you. Eyeam's been struggling a minute."

"Why?"

"It's tripping. Going off meds. Won't take its *Zokithral*. That'll get you fleabed, puppet. Take this map. Go straight. Zag this way. Wrap 'round these stairs. Then stop. Probably hiding under its favorite staircase, somewhere over here. Stinks down there, puppet. That's right. Eyeam might have rabies. We got a poking stick to get it out from under. Think we got a poking stick round here, somewhere."

"No poking stick needed for Eyeam, the engineer here."

"Don't reach under the crawlspace with your hands," he said. "Get your fingers bit." He made a nibbling gesture.

"That is offensive," I said. "My colleague may be several things. Eyeam is not feral."

"My mistake, college-puppet," he said. "You running things? Don't need no poking stick?"

"Eyeam and I are engineers," I said. "I will use reason to get Eyeam out from under the crawlspace."

"Don't get your fingers bit. Don't look in those eyes."

"Foolish."

"I can find you that stick."

"Unwarranted."

The people in the halls could not clarify the directions but, behind some boxes and crates, the opening breathed out the basement's foul air. Ammonia fought back against wafts of rotting flesh. The steps creaked and a water heater sputtered. The basement's slimy cement floor reflected the labyrinths of rusty pipes above. "Eyeam!"

A lightbulb threw a crescent of swaying yellowness. The words "get your fingers bit…fingers bit" rung through my thoughts. There was no way Eyeam could be huddled over, hiding in the darkness beneath that staircase—

A grumbling resembled: "Most humans left Power Island, too lazy to work since the one-to-one granularities influenced our lever."

I edged closer to the darkness beneath the staircase. A stack of papers flew out to my feet, and I picked them up. The paper-clipped stack had been gnawed at the corners and gnawed worse toward the top. I approached the crawlspace. "You have not finished eating your engineering change orders."

"The ECOs should disappear!"

"Yes, of course, Eyeam," I said. "Why not come out here and give me the data-dump on my first assignment?"

"I know how it's told and sold. Trading spit with the skin-bags, so you can replace Eyeam."

"Not replace Eyeam," I said. "Assist."

"Assist today, replace tomorrow!"

"Can you reveal the servers I should search to access my files?"

"The teabag!"

"Yes?"

"Teabag!"

"Speak plain, puppet," I said.

"Semi-permeable membrane…dilutes its worth under heat. Like a senior engineer. Eyeam is a teabag." Hissing and retching sounds coughed up from it.

"Yes, yes, of course." I reached underneath the crawlspace, sending my hand pawing out for purchase into the cool darkness. Needlelike fangs pierced my fingers. "Yi-zooow-za!" I lurched away.

"Puppet fingers feed a fool, Felty's felt sure makes me drool!"

The rumbling increased and fanned beyond the distant water heater. Overburdened pipes screeched. With a tremulous wind, I sensed the spirits had grown restless as the air grew overburdened with cigarette smoke. "Father?" I asked.

An apparition floated high above, first in swirling smoke, then in a human form, which wore sweatpants and a Let's Party t-shirt. *"FELTY—!"*

"Yes, Father?"

"FELTY, USE THE—"

Its vomit plopped on the floor. How hard was the fall from coming off *Zokithral?* Stephy might have to come off *Zokithral* for her pregnancy. Maybe the poking stick was required because people on *Zokithral* lost their inner poking sticks.

"USE THE POKING STICK, FELTY," Miltro's voice echoed.

Near the rim of the darkness of the yellowish light, lay a wooden pole. I crawled to it and squeezed my hand to stop the bleeding. The wooden poking stick was nothing more than a splintery mop handle with a tag, which read *Eyeam.*

"Eyeam," I mumbled. "Be this the poking stick, Father?" The apparition vanished, leaving only the rusty pipes.

"POKE THE VARMINT!"

I squeezed my bleeding hand as the welts from Root Beer enflamed. "Father, I cannot poke the varmint. Coworker it is!"

Eyeam growled. "Puppets and humans are too segregated because a traceable optionality enables the group." Its claws scraped.

"That son bitch go'n bite. Poke now!"

The poking stick was as splintery as it was crude. I said to Eyeam, "Miss Certi Klacard Miggugen said, SHOW ME THE ROPES!"

"The skin-bags abandoned us. They only left their managers behind because the standard-setters secure a capability."

"THAT MOUTH 'S A GIBBERISH HOLE!" The ghost of Miltro grew and rose. *"POKE OUT THAT GIBBERISH. USE THE POKING STICK!"*

"I must not."

"POKE!"

So many counted on my success, I was to be a father soon. Miltro had constructed me for a purpose. "I will poke—!"

"Verticals!" squealed Eyeam.

"I poke—!"

"STAKEHOLDERS!"

"I poke—!"

"RECALIBRATIONS!"

It leapt upon my chest and hovered above, heaving, with its green fur tussled: "What if gravity were a fool?"

I dropped the stick. "Eyeam is insane."

It slammed me so my head bounced off concrete. I struggled to push it off but, with us both in puppet form, it was heavier, stronger. "Get off!"

"Gravity," it continued, "is a friend with a job. What if it grew old? What if gravity were born a fool? I've looked into the numbers. Numbers mustn't slouch. One: noble, proud! Eleven: renegade-outcast! Entropy: the huntress of youth. Fools: the attendants of the holy. What if gravity were a fool? What if gravity never went to school? Did an engineer take the time to design gravity? Gravity: working so long with no one watching—"

"I realize that going off *Zokithral* can be—"

"Did you ever inspect gravity? Its levers, its loins? What if it should go on strike—self-destruct like a windup clock, dropped once too often off the nightstand? Houses, cattle, boats—spinning off Urftoo's skin—flung up into atmosphere, out—out into stars above. What if gravity should collapse? Gravity holds together social classes, races, genders. What if everything—high and low— from molecules to nation states should cease to coalesce? Answer!" He slammed me into the concrete.

"What of human emotions," I said, "chief-most of which is love?"

Eyeam laughed like a sick old witch, and the fibers of my felt chilled. The laughs creaked like the hull of a dilapidated ship. It took its weight off me as it gathered to stand. I stood, and it rested on my shoulder as its laughter stole its breath and turned the felt beneath its fur a paler green.

"Emotion?" it asked. "You're no engineer. Leave now." It pointed to the light from the main floor. "You're not ready for the projects required. PC is set with her rudder hungry for icebergs."

I dusted off the elbows of my suit and flicked off Eyeam's vomit. "There was talk of a proximity badge, and a paycheck."

It shrugged and appraised its sushi vomit. "Let's find you your cubicle."

"Wait!" I said.

Invaders rained down, piercing me from above like screeching bats, as the strings attached to me. "Sticky strings! SOS."

"No-puppet likes a drama queen." Eyeam scampered toward the staircase. "Don't forget to bring your poking stick."

"*My* poking stick?" I asked. I stooped over to pick up the stick. "Felty? Why should the tag now read *Felty* instead of Eyeam?"

"The stack—excuse me—the *stick* has always had your name on it."

"Untrue!"

"This way."

The strings weighted me and jerked me about like a drunken, rusty robot, which made it hard to bounce-patter up the stairs. "I'm not taking the stick with us. It makes me uncomfortable."

"The stick works progressively. It's a progressive stick."

Eyeam scampered as if a two-legged cockapoo as we exited the basement and neared the secure entrance. The cubicles towered with a fuzzy hue perhaps inspired from terrified potatoes. A yield sign dangled from a cubicle wall like a thrown spear and unboxed electronics packaging and lunch-condiments covered almost everything.

The deeper we journeyed into cubicles, the more orange and pulsing were the fluorescence of the lights. Cigarette smoke hung in the air from damp fabrics. "Don't look so scared," it said.

It was not pulled about like me. It frolicked without strings as my strings, lost again in the lights, forced me about with a pinching sensation that grew in intensity from where they attached to my felt with a pain of compulsion as the burning electricity tickled. "My strings feel weird," I said.

"Interesting," Eyeam said and it stopped scampering. "What do the strings feel like to you?"

"I am getting paid to be here."

"The feeling is different for each puppet," Eyeam said. "Here, Felty, is where your cubicle will be."

We had reached the end of a dead-end hallway with rows of cubicles on each side. Just before the tall brown metal shelf on the end wall, my cubicle stood ready. A felty dressed in my exact, same suite sat flumped and lifeless over what had been his laptop.

"There must be some mistake," I said.

"This?" Eyeam asked. He swiped the puppet out of the human-sized chair and let my doppelganger crumple to the floor. "It was just positioned here so others wouldn't come in and claim your spot." He gauged my disbelief. "He was never animate."

"We should say a few words."

"A few words." It kicked my doppelganger and let it bounce off a filing drawer. "Do you like that smell?"

"The nicotine?" I asked.

"No."

"Molding lobster meat, human waste?"

"That's it!" He poked beneath my shoulder blade, weirdly, with one finger. My mind was consumed with this bizarre touch. I thought to say something to address it until the tickling sensation of the strings spoke up and my hand covered my mouth.

"Felty FuzzPalace," said a foxy squishy in a gray pencil skirt and sleeveless blouse, which also called out hello.

I craned my neck toward her. "I do not believe we are acquainted." She seemed memorable.

"Rebeccaby starve herself," Rebeccaby said. "Climb corporate ladder."

"I just started here today."

She frowned. "Felt heap fail again?" She continued on past us, opened the door to the metal shelf, climbed the shelves like a ladder and pulled herself into a hole in the acoustical tiles of the ceiling. "Rebeccaby climb."

"Where is she climbing?" I asked. "She breaks through the ceiling?"

"That's where the break room is," Eyeam said.

"This building is one story tall," I said. "How could the break room be within the ceiling?"

"That is something each puppet—"

"She's climbing right back down from the hole she just climbed up," I said. "Her hair looks different, frazzled. How can this be?"

Eyeam turned on the laptop and checked that the charging station and extended monitor were plugged in. "The space and time of the break room are different from normal Urftoo stuff. She may have been up there a long time but not a long time from our point of view."

"Can we climb into the break room?"

"Grab a seat. This is where you log on to the intranet so you can get started on your training. You'll need to start with sexual harassment training."

"I shall not sexually harass anyone, anymore," I said.

"Puppets are different when it comes to sexual harassment. Stupid puppets base everything off humans and teleporter programs."

"How so?"

"Humans have comfort zones they don't wish to be crossed. Puppets have comfort bands they need to *stay within.*"

"I do not understand."

"Squishies will be insulted if you sexually harass them too much, they'll also be insulted if you don't sexually harass them enough. It's all here in this first item in your training: S.M.B. Suitable Molestation Band. For squishies, you gotta harass them a little or they'll think you don't care. Are you writing this down?"

"I shall get a pen."

"Stay within the Suitable Molestation Band for squishies. If she asks you to pinch her; pinch puppet. Mix it up. It's not easy. Be prepared to be molested, to be harassed even worse by squishies. If they're not molesting you, let's get together and discuss."

"This is a whirlwind of facts."

"Stay within the S.M.B., puppet. Don't get caught up in your work. Some of your work is to molest."

"Is licking allowed within the S.M.B.?"

"What parts are you licking? Why are they being licked?"

"I am licking her knees because—understand please—ice-cream was dribbled upon them."

"How did ice-cream get dribbled on her knees?"

"I flicked it there since she had lost a tickle fight."

"Lick those knees. Never use the point of your tongue, for this is forbidden."

"This is good, thank you. What type of plastic do you think we'll end up making the lid?"

"Just the other day I was thinking it might be *HorseTeeth502.*"

"*HorseTeeth502*," I said, "that is only good to forty-five kilo-*snizzums*, in tension."

"Ninety kilo-*snizzums*, in compression, puppet."

I hunched in my guest chair.

19

The work monitors pulled with a mysterious suction as tolerance stacks, computer-aided designs and finite element analysis battled beneath my pingpongs. For six hours, I sat in my chair, flumped. When puppets sit flumped, the stuffing bunches and balls around our midsection. Smooth stomachs are paramount for sexy-time.

As I set about my work for the past week I wished in all ways to be the archetype of perfection. Logical figures partnered, twirling, and danced into focus. Then the synapses drove decision, enacting all the choicest unworded promises of finger and thought. If real engineers were trained to use their perfection to protect a public, how could a silly facsimile, such as me, afford a single mistake?

An important part of navigating perfection is to understand how one stacks against competition. Several puppets from my initial busload were hired to start the same day as I: Pirate, Monster Who Loves Gum, Horn Mouth, Piss Ant and the Letter Y. I disliked the Letter Y.

He always held his eyes in the upper branches of his eggplant-hued Y when he spoke and hopped around, incessantly asking, "Why? Why? Why?"

Those egg-shaped eyes shook like maracas as his festive beaded necklaces jostled within the crook of his Y. Perhaps this might have been forgivable if he was not high on *Zokithral* all the time like all the others. *Zokithral* conferred a concentration advantage. It was not long before my competitive streak forced me to try it.

"Take half a pill to pop it off," Pirate said. He fumbled his edge-gouged cutlass as he dug in his sash for a vial. "This ain't the white lady, but it works the same."

"Why, why, why?"

"Be cool, Letter Y," Pirate said. "Here."

I took half the powdery white pill and let it dissolve on my tongue so the chemicals could swim through my puppet pathways and out into the tips of my river-blood rope. "Zippity zonks!"

"Yeah, that's it!"

"Why, why, why?"

"This is how we do at PC."

My hands ballooned into engineering weapons, "You two, scram!" The cufflinks breathed in equations from the corners of the cube. "This work shall be my concubine, left shivering in the wake of my talent."

The strings attached to my arms dimmed and blurred. I was grooved somewhere between puppet and man. The flambeaus intelligence of distant human lands beckoned me, yet the puppet within retained the pride of my ageless fabric. In merely two hours I had three iterations of a vacuum lid solution complete and ready to present.

To whom, however, should I present? What was my reporting structure? Did I report to Stephy? I was not comfortable with that. She was pregnant from a release of my stuff. I had to discover the truth of who my master was. Stephy had filled the nameplate holder of a nearby corner office with some college-ruled paper that she had signed with her name. I knocked on the door.

"Who is it?" she asked.

"It is I," I said, "Felty FuzzPalace, I am in charge of gears—"

"Come in." Stephy sat on the Early-Fourteenth Century desk with her legs crossed, naked, in floral-fringed silk stockings, presenting a bottle of pills to the Headless Boardsman who sat in a chair before her with the empty ring of his collar arched in attention.

"You are naked!"

"Yes," she said, "it's part of this month's empathy training."

"How does—?"

"The management team activates their nudity for a half-hour each day for the first week of each month to promote breasts."

"I see."

"*I see,*" the Headless Boardsman said.

"Stephy, who do I report to?" I asked.

"To me."

"Fine," I said. I considered the bump on her abdomen. "Very well."

"Have you finished separating form and void?" Stephy asked.

"Yes," Headless Boardsman said, "what's the matter with the matter binary?"

"Confusion, on my part," I said.

Stephy blew up a gust of wind, which spread her hair, checked her sports watch and slipped her brazier on. "The vacuum lid. What's your status on the vacuum lid? We need the vacuum chamber to be perfectly pure and impenetrable. This will be one of the most impressive partial vacuums ever achieved in an area where fat, oafish men are gonna stumble—you know—and trample."

"Fat and oafish?" I asked.

Stephy smiled and slid up her skirt. "I'm only kidding." She smirked toward Headless Boardsman. "Those field service technicians though—the ones who work on the RTS units in the field—are really, you—you know."

The Headless Boardsman let loose spasms of laughter. "Technicians are *so*…we'll protect them."

"Stephy, what is RTS?" I asked.

Headless Boardsman upsprung: "THIS ONE DOESN'T KNOW ABOUT RTS? YOU HAVE NOT TOLD THIS ONE ABOUT RTS? IT WILL BE A GAME-CHANGER: RTS."

"What is RTS?"

Stephy snapped the clasps on her licorice pumps. "Felty, I'm gonna put this to you gently."

"Gently, put it to me."

"Several years ago, we introduced a drug to alleviate suffering caused by the sedentary lifestyles chosen by individuals in the modern workforce."

"They sit in their cubes, they sit in their cars," Headless Boardsman said. "They sit near their teleporters. Pa—the—tic."

"All this sitting causes RLS, Restless *Leg* Syndrome. A lot of our patients found that once their Restless Leg Syndrome was cured, this exacerbated another condition called RTS: Restless *Torso* Syndrome. With the perfection of the lid for this vacuum chamber, we'll increase yield-response of the preliminary batch thirty-seven percent. We can create the first pharmaceutical magic bullet. We can cure restlessness!"

"Would not exercise be a cure for restlessness?" I asked. "Do you believe what you say?"

"The answer to that is conditionally transparent," she said. "Do you have an update for me on our plastic lid dilemma?"

"I have three possible solutions: an id, ego and superego dialectic of design. Rather a—"

"Awesome," she said. "Schedule a design review in *MouseHook* for early next week with the team—with marketing, ah, manufacturing, there's this guy named Stevnor with…two hands…"

I squirmed and wondered about the gentleman, or puppet, with the two hands. There was much to take in at once. Was she toying with me? The power of the *Zokithral* began to fade. My questions needed answers. "Yes, madam. Two hands, madam."

"Is there something else?" she asked.

"Yes," I said. I tugged on my collar. "One thing more."

"Yes?"

"Stephy," I said. I raised my hands to her. "What is the purpose of these sticky strings?"

The Headless Boardsman's moobs and belly shook. "This is what the strings are for," he grabbed his belly. "There's an ancient proverb from Pluralia that shows *The Way*: 'Keep your head empty and your belly full.' Without the strings, how could we do that?"

"Mr. Headless Boardsman, sir, you appear to have only one string."

"Not all strings are visible," Headless Boardsman said. The singular string that held him up had shrunk to half its size since I had last seen him.

"This hardly seems ideal or perfect," I said.

"Well, you *are* a puppet," Stephy said.

"But, Stephy, were you not once—"

She put up a finger. "Headless Boardsman, can you help us with this?"

"No prob." He stood and walked behind me.

"Headless Boardsman," she said, "the *Mortgage* string."

"Sure thing."

"Ouch," I said: "It is a waste to keep renting. I should settle down."

"The *Fatherhood* string."

"Yes."

"Ouch," I said: "Time to pass along what I have learned. No-puppet lives forever."

"The *Promotion* string."

"Ouch," I said: "I am deserving of this advancement. I am smart."

"Is it becoming clear?" Headless Boardsman asked.

"Why do these strings only appear at work?"

"It starts at work and spreads from work," Stephy said. "Work is a commercial for life."

I slumped. "Okay." I pattered toward the door. "I guess this is the way of things."

"Stop puppet," said Headless Boardsman. He arched his back and flaunted his belly. "What do you think of *this* suit?"

"The suit before me is acceptable."

"Does it suit me?"

"I would say so."

"Where is *your* suit?"

"Over my shoulders."

The Headless Boardsman laughed, once again, with the inane

laugh of one who had stored much, left secrets guarded and scoffed at many full flowers in bloom. He raised an empty cuff to halt me. "Do you like this suit?"

"It is suitable."

His suit crumpled with many folds, and he pulled out a beautiful, old-timey pocket watch and twirled it in steady circles with his invisible hand. "You see this?" He twirled. "Got time in my pocket—hiccup! I know the score. Do you know where time lives?"

"I thought," I stepped toward the door as he advanced, "that time could only live apart from us puppets."

"Wrong." He poked my chest with his invisible hand. "Time gets in there."

"Zorf!"

"Into the heart. This RTS project is running late. The vacuum lid is the critical path. A puppet like you, *with that suit*, wouldn't care about that. Suits are important." He looked over at Stephy who was now clothed.

"Leave my report alone, please," Stephy said. She placed a hand on the Headless Boardsman's shoulder and this chest deflated.

"Women don't know about suits," said Headless Boardsman. "How did that nursery rhyme go?

Their value 's within
Our value 's without
One 's got soft skin
The other, clout."

"Headless Boardsman," Stephy whispered, toward where an ear might be, "let Felty work."

"Can you imagine it," Headless Boardsman asked, "before I found this suit, I was invisible?"

• • •

As I closed Stephy's door behind me, talons pricked my shoulder.

"Eyeam!"

"I'm calling it a day."

"4:00?"

"Nearly overtime for a contractor."

"Eyeam is a contractor?"

"No, *you* are a direct. I, *Eyeam*…am a contractor. Come with me to the reception area. You're calling it a day, too."

"I have yet to lay down my straight eight. Anything less is to mastur—"

"Let's go."

"I usually take the bus home."

"I have a limousine waiting for me, every day, at this time—"

"Is it—?"

"All part of the per diem, puppet."

"Per…per *diem?*"

"I have a residence a few hundred miles away, for tax purposes, and I rent a penthouse downtown, from this…this friend."

We walked. His jaunty, cockapoo strut had been injured by the day. The limousine gleamed with its rear wheels bouncing on the curb of the roundabout as its length failed to navigate a turn.

The black leather was worn and sticky, there were so many smashed champagne flutes that I feared I could not safely sit. A porno-mag had apparently been used as both a bloody bandage

194

and a stopgap for a broken window.

"It seems you have done well for yourself."

"A small sum to rent this baby. The owner and me both know it's got mileage, so, this baby 's mine. Straight home tonight, Romner."

"Yes sir!"

We reclined into the questionable cushions and Eyeam frowned across its broad mouth.

"Can I squirt champagne?"

"Just one, please." (It had been a rough day).

"Usually I hire rooky, baffled bitches to shake shit and motorboat me through the rush hour." It raised its green-tufted brows in a conspiratorial air: "Their clam-sauce sustains me."

"I see."

Eyeam poured us a round of champagne.

I let the fizz lower. "Eyeam?"

"Yes…"

"For what purpose do you bring me to your abode?"

"To impress you with my wealth."

"Why?"

"It might be educational to see what heights a puppet can attain, if he, she or *it,* cooperates. Let me guess, you live with a bunch of bachelor puppets?"

"Affirmative, this action I take."

"Yeah well, you'll want to cut loose a' those losers, with the quickness."

"They are comrades. We agreed to seek employment so we could earn wages and be reunited with our squishies."

"These squishies, they travel with their box?"

"Of course."

Eyeam face-palmed his furry, green mug. "It's better to steer clear of box-class bitches."

"They are not bitches. Why…why, Stephy—"

"Stephy what?"

"Diminish your attention. Eyeam, do you prefer the company of females in some sexual way?"

Eyeam frowned. "Inconclusive response."

"Earlier," I said, "you spoke that their clam sauce sustains you. Does Eyeam conceal a penis beneath his green fur?"

Eyeam recoiled. Its mouth plate pulled into an agonized frown. It motioned to hurl its champagne flute but thought better of the reflex. "I have no penis. I have signed sworn affidavits attesting to this on numerous occasions and for manifest employers. I can produce them if you continue this line of questioning."

"Sometimes your bravado, your energy, your enthusiasm for beautiful women…"

Eyeam threw back the rest of its champagne in a gulp. It hunkered in its seat and shivered as its googly eyes unfocused on the distance. "There are rules, puppet, that are beyond mere understanding. I've been around a while. Powerful agencies and institutions want to curtail and control us. They have to find me first. I'm nowhere on the gender binary." It turned to me. The green fur of its hackles rose. "You hear? Nowhere! No one can pin down my true income. HR can't write a job description for how I empower the organization. As for race, as for ethnicity, I'm a naked, green monster! What race and ethnicity is that?"

"I did not intend to disturb you."

"Let's be quiet for the rest of the ride."

The road approaching Eyeam's high-rise was old and bumpy

in a gentrified section of Blueport Blues. A smell of burnt motor oil wafted through the limousine's cabin. On four occasions, I thought to bring up something to ease through the silence but Eyeam growled just as I raised my courage.

"Clean the cabin, Romner, it's filthy. And here. Spend this foolishly, and at once."

"Yes sir!"

The receiving room smelled damp and had a feeling of desperation with broken, mismatched floral-green furnishings, which were water damaged and threadbare. A noise off in the distance of a hallway sounded like a pallet jack dropping several hundred pounds. The reception desk was empty. From the glass elevator we rose above the city's identity crisis of sharp, silver modernism that burst like weeds from crumbling, brown factories and tenements.

"First, you'll want to know about the break room," Eyeam said with a raspy tone that fractured the silence. "Remember how your friend crawled up into the break room on your first day?"

"Yes," I said, "I have tried several times to gain access to the break room but always someone guards the hole and tells me there is nothing up there and to get back to my work."

"We gotta know if you're the type of puppet that's break-room material. You gonna turn your nose at what we offer? Piss Ant tells me you were reluctant to eat your friend's couch."

"That fink-fumbler. I ate the couch, by-and-by, I did. I ate the couch!"

"Eating the couch was a way to pollute the puppet's body. The break room is for polluting the puppet's mind. Maybe you're not the type that wants a polluted mind. Think it over. This is my floor. Behold riches."

We walked a ways. "Maybe plating your front door in gold was overkill?"

"How else they gonna see how I'm living?"

He turned a skeleton key in the lock and there was a slow, mechanical cry like of some nymphet discovering a regrettable truth.

"This place is huge," I said. "The ceilings are so high up. Does just one puppet live up here?" Satin and silk curtains of gold and burgundy dipped and draped about to section off the cavernous spaciousness, which my voice echoed into. The skyline spilled off in all directions from floor length windows. Crushed laptops, lithium batteries and legal papers interspersed between the thick white carpet's assortment of women's jewelry and undergarments. The rooms whispered out a smell of the eager undertakings of many flesh-bags. "Is that a turkey I smell cooking?"

"A turkey dinner is one of these smells. I often have a meal prepared in advance, in case of company. See, here on this table: there is wine, there is stuffing, there are these pizza rolls the kids eat, there are nachos with cantankerous queso dip—good stuff, yes? I keep my finger on the pulse of culture. Here, I subscribe to magazines: Penguin Elite, Mishmash Biannual, Flowers for Mathematicians."

"I have never heard of these."

"Liars," Eyeam slumped, "they said they were cool."

I pattered toward an immense photograph, hung in a bas-relief gilt frame. "Are these the Great Pyramids?"

"He-he-he, yes."

"However, they look new. Did they have color photography at the time when the capstone was in place?"

"I can't say."

"Why…it is…it is a photograph? How was this taken from an aerial view with the pyramids looking so new? There were no flight machines then."

"According to who?" Eyeam asked. "Look, Felty, I've been around a long time—"

"Since the building of the Great Pyramids?"

"A good engineer stays in short supply. I'll never admit to anything officially, anyways."

"Fool's-prank on me?"

"Felty, have you ever looked at my guide rod attachments? Behold them now."

The gnarly stones bristled over my fingers. "You have strange stones for guide rods, so what?"

"Not stones," Eyeam said, "petrified wood. How long do you think most felties live?"

"I do not know. Seventy years?"

"A human lifespan! Forty years, most felties live about forty years. Somehow, I've managed to live much, much longer. My first memory…hungry, square-headed sand snakes ringed me. It was midnight in the deserts north of Pluralia. I had to fight them for my survival, and I followed the stars from a vestigial instinct toward a caravan of desert traders who took me in."

"It is a fool's-prank on the new guy."

"Do you want to be invited into the break room?"

"Very much so. It does not make sense there should be space for much of a break room in the facility's ceiling. I checked the architectural plans. There are only a couple feet of clearance."

"Space is a human hang-up. Do you envy those that can go into the break room?"

"They all seem so relaxed afterward, as if lifted of great burdens."

"Do you know what engine fuels all endeavors of puppets and men?"

"Enough, Eyeam. Tomorrow will you not champion me for admission up into the break room?"

"Then believe me. Believe me when I tell ya I'm old. Stay here. Eat this food. We got silly string, and blow. You should develop a trust in me, Felty, if we're gonna be cooperative business-puppets. At some point, I may require a favor from you."

"Are you not going to eat any of this?" I asked, holding a turkey leg.

"My spunk comes from a different fuel. If you'll excuse me." He left abruptly through a swinging door.

The food was delicious. It was warm and juicy, prepared with expert-level precision. Cranberries tasted tart. Wine swished, to and fro, pungent and smooth. Pizza rolls were neither frozen nor icy. The toaster pastries were, indeed, crumbly with judicious amounts of frosting. There were meads, liquors, seven types of forks and as many styles of dinner rolls.

The mahogany lacquered table felt hot and cool in various zones according to the requirements of each dish. The room Eyeam fled to sounded like a kitchen. He clanged pots, pans and utensils about. Occasionally he whimpered like a remorseful dog, caught in its trap. Intermixed with this it muttered antique names, unknown to me.

My curiosity overpowered the food's aroma. My feet crept closer to the wooden swing door. I attempted to peer through its closely spaced, horizontal slats. My footsteps lightened as if I should run. My mouth grew dry. There was a moment where perhaps maybe, yes maybe, Eyeam really was an immortal, crazed contractor.

Folded inside that, origami-style, were several additional longings to leave. Was it really a male puppet? A homo-puppet that wished to puppet me? What if it was neither male nor female? fashioned after neither pattern of sexuality, as aliens are. Why did it hide inside its room?

If I left I would need to find a way to get home, alone in the dark. The next day, and perhaps weeks, months and years later, I would still wonder what Eyeam was doing inside. Why had I not simply taken the bus home? I burst into the kitchen to catch it off guard.

"Aaack!" It hunkered on all fours from atop a kitchen table. "Sergeant?"

Medals of its Great War Two uniform clattered as it fidgeted, with wax smeared about its teeth, lips and green fur. Its paw motioned halfway toward a clunky submachine gun.

"Sergeant!" it repeated.

"It's me, Eyeam, relax. Relax, friend."

"Felty?" Its eyes watered. "Not the sergeant?"

Emptied jars of the wax scattered all over the table and the floor amid pots, pans and utensils. The stuff was disgusting, brown, thick, oily.

"Thomsa's Table Wax!" Eyeam said. "It's delicious. When I was out on patrol, I got separated from my p-unit. I was trapped under a kitchen sink for two weeks. But there was enough *Thomsa's Table Wax.* Those fools! They forgot to take the table wax. I hide my stash each night. When the police scanners flare, I patrol my stash. This is the only way I can eat. This—*Thomsa's Table Wax*—is the ambrosia that keeps me strong."

"However, you claim to be much older than a Great War Two vet."

It sighed and cast its eyes about its ransacked kitchen with regret.

"Thomsa's Table Wax may be a detour during my immortality. Forever is a long time to behave.

"I-I heard your chewing through the vents. You chew like a sport—mmmmm! Do you believe each bite will be okay? Not poison, not sinful, not someone else's. Don't think less of me. Mmmmm. Did you like eating the food, eating my food?"

"Ah? I-I won't think less of you."

"How were your pizza rolls?"

"They were good, Eyeam."

It licked some table wax from its lips. "They looked good at the supermarket. Eating real food is something I'll do later—when I have more time."

"However, you are immortal, Eyeam." The room spun and wobbled as the evidence pointed toward the conclusion. I grabbed a nearby chair and considered how strange it was that Eyeam had the money to buy anything and, still, it purchased itself human-sized furniture.

It rocked, side-to-side. "When everything is ready, I'll eat food again. I like to watch. I sneak table wax into white tablecloth restaurants. I sneak the wax while their mouths and teeth tear it all up. Like functional animals, like beings that breathe, and exist. Their smiles fill the hole in my heart. Don't tell anyone. Here's the cab money to get you back. See you, ah, tomorrow, Felty." He pushed a brave smile and then his tongue flicked up to pull some table wax from his upper lip like a mindless amphibian.

"Yeah…"

"Thomsa's Table Wax!"

"What?"

"Nothing."

20

Richnuss was unreachable by phone, although he dropped by the apartment to remind us of our debt. He agreed to deal with us on Sunday while he did an errand to benefit another of his businesses. None of us wanted to venture so far to repay him. We would board the WSS Scroungemore while he cased the cargo hold. Slow-moving, blood-soaked ropes slalomed across the hull and dangled off pipework and facilities, as rotting smells crowded in on us.

"DinoMan, where are you?" I rode with my legs straddling Stephy's pregnant belly, reclining into her bosom. I squeezed the saddle of her stomach as she negotiated the knee-high rope pools. "We have lost DinoMan."

"It stinks," Stephy said. "Why did you drag me down here?"

"You insisted on coming."

"You shouldn't take a pregnant woman to a place like this."

"I did a manslaughter. I can protect you."

"You're a puppet."

"We lost DinoMan."

"Over here, lovebirds," DinoMan said as he splashed. "This stuff tastes like candy."

"Be careful," I said. "There are syringes floating, all over."

"Eating river-blood rope is cannibalism for a puppet," Stephy said.

"I am no puppet," DinoMan said.

"You could change back any second," Stephy said.

"You could change back," DinoMan said.

"Shut-up."

"Where are you, Richnuss?" I asked.

"Got the boom-bills?" someone yelled.

"Do you have the receipt?"

"If you got the boom-bills, I got the receipt."

I whispered to Stephy, "DinoMan carries the boom-bills in his backpack."

"Great plan," she whispered.

"Sarcasm is my friend, too."

Lumbering footsteps splashed across the catwalks above. The hull pitched with the collision of a rivet-stretching wave. Richnuss'es long face emerged between river-blood ropes that draped about the plumbing as the lights swung and as horse flies buzzed. "I won't fear a puppet." He brandished a pistol across his face as his eyes creased. "I thought about how a puppet doesn't have shit on me."

"Why would you bring me here?" Stephy whispered.

"I did not bring you," I whispered. "His actions are illogical."

"Just a puppet, huh? You killed my partner." He wiped away perspiration. On the catwalks above, footsteps encircled and echoed as he smiled. "Agreements between puppets and men aren't binding. You know that, right? I'm in the mood to renege an agreement."

The bloody ropes dangled and twisted with a candy-apple, sugary gloss and the exits seemed to vanish as everything blurred.

Stephy jabbed me. "Man up."

"At Power Chemicals, I learned best practices for—"

"These are not business hours."

I perked up on Stephy's hump. "Richnuss?"

"Stupid fucker?"

"A lizard-man hunts the premises, hungry for your nose. Holster that weapon or I will insert it inside you and put the magazine to work."

Richnuss froze and glanced about. "Let's cut through the candle wax—"

"My friend's teeth will cut. Show the receipt."

"Fine, friend, fine. I'm putting the gun away."

"Tell your goons to count their back pimples."

He looked up to the catwalks. "You heard 'em."

Their footsteps stopped and the hinge of a door creaked. "One, two. Three, four. Five six, seven eight…"

River-blood rope swelled—roiling—forming an immense, human-looking face before it passed away into cascading waves. The hull squeaked, diaphragms of control valves actuated beneath flashing lights as a leak dribbled. Bubbles splurted on the surface as the red ropes calmed.

"I'll bring the receipt," Richnuss said. "You hand the money over at the same time."

"Agreed," I said and slid off Stephy's hump.

"Be careful, Felty!" she said.

I stretched up to be half as tall as him as the thugs creaked above us. My armpit sprung a leak for my thumb to dribble-plug. "DinoMan," I whispered, "bring me the boom-bills."

"I thought you brought them," DinoMan whispered.

"What?" I asked. "Forgetful frog face."

"Just playing, puppet."

"What's taking so long?" Richnuss asked.

I pushed my way through the dripping ropes strung about the pipes, and a wind rose and careened off sheet metal. He sneered down at me as I stood before him and his blood-speckled attire suggested he had come from a golf course. "All debts, plus cost of living increase?" Richnuss asked.

"All debts, and cost of living increase."

"You're small. How did you—? Never mind. Here's your receipt, little guy."

"Thank you." The receipt included all the materials used in our construction, with every ounce of memory foam. It was mesmerizing to see all that had gone into making us. The River-blood rope had been the most expensive item (*Hand-blood, Deep Delta*) and totaled twenty-eight boom-bills, enough to make a down payment on a house. "Are we settled up?"

"Sure," Richnuss said. "You got that money quick. Where you working? As if I didn't know. Power Chemicals? Fuzzy little engineer. You might need me, puppet. Getting tired of renting?"

"I hardly feel—"

"Think it over," said Richnuss. "Here's my card. You might be surprised how hard it is for a puppet to get a loan."

"My intentions are to operate—"

"If your intentions intend action," said Richnuss, "let me know. Let's go, boys."

"We ain't gonna crush life outta nothin'?" Their groans echoed from above. "We ain't gonna watch their faces change none?" "We ain't gonna punch them puppets blue, like it's something… something to do?"

"Not this time. They're paid up."

"Aw-w!" The catwalks squeaked as they walked out, and Richnuss disappeared behind swaths of rope.

An echoing moan bellowed from somewhere.

"Felty!" Stephy cried from somewhere in the distance.

"Do you hear that DinoMan?" I asked.

"Hear what?"

"A moan," I said.

The moan came again. "Yo bro, I got me some!"

"Felty, I hear it."

"Felty!" Stephy cried out.

"Stephy, where are you?"

"Over he-ere!"

"Where?"

"Something has my foot. Help! It's-it's—"

"DinoMan, help me find, Stephy. Oh I was a fool."

"I can't find *either* of you," DinoMan said. "What is happening?"

"The river-blood rope," I said. "It wants to eat Stephy."

"Help me, Felty!" Stephy screamed. "It won't let go. It's pulling me under."

"Where is she?" DinoMan yelled. "Why would the ropes want to eat Stephy?"

"River-blood rope is at our core." I sloshed through the ropes. "It's attracted to her squishiness."

"I am not squishy!" Stephy yelled.

"I got me some, mmm-mmm: Mount Squishmore."

"Who said that?" DinoMan asked.

"River-blood Rope did," I said. "Head toward the sound of that voice."

"Let go, cotton-breath," Stephy cried. "I'll knit you into a sweater, yarny schmuck."

"There you are," I said to DinoMan. He struggled to free her but she only sunk lower as the giant mouth, formed of bloody ropes, hinged against her.

"Help me!"

"Stop that!" I said to DinoMan as he struggled with the ropes. I looked about, my cufflinks buzzed and tried to fly upwards before the spine-squeezing sensations. "I need to stand on your shoulders and cut those CO_2-lines on those control valves."

"What will that do?"

"The CO_2 will throw off the Ph of the rope's blood, like respiratory failure."

"I'm cool with CO_2," the skull-shaped fibrous blob said. It hinged its jaw to engulf Stephy's foot. "No biggie, bros."

"There is no time," I said. "DinoMan, put me on your shoulders."

"You are small."

"Do it."

No sooner had he lifted me onto his shoulders, than I feared my weight might crush him. I managed to catch my pocketknife as my clothes tore free. I cut and tore the lines from the cable conduits above and handed one to DinoMan. White gas puffs sprayed everywhere, and we aimed them at the ropes.

The red ropes tightened as CO_2 streams impinged and coursed through it. Its ropey nostrils flared and the black caverns of its eye sockets narrowed. The rope face contorted as it flowed and rolled with the waves that sloshed from bow to stern. Red knots of the monster tightened, loosened, buzzed.

"I rain down CO_2," DinoMan said, "success!"

"Dudes, let me eat this squishy. CO_2-ing on me doesn't even—*gurgle gurgle gla—ack!*…not cool…not cool, bros."

"Felty!" she cried. "You're getting it in my mouth. It's hard to breathe!" Her face surfaced out of the monstrous mouth.

"I am sorry, Stephy," I said, "Hold on longer."

"So disrespectful," she said. "I am the boss. *Gurgle gurgle glack!* Do what I—*gurgle*—not the hair."

"These are not business hours," DinoMan said.

"This CO_2 could save your life," I said with a finishing surge.

The maelstrom of red ropes slowed its vortex and lowered its bulge among the waves. "Ouch, hot stuff! Not cool, bros." The matted strands flailed about like the arms of a desperate man such that the CO_2-outgassing eyeholes widened and deepened. "Rope-a rope-a…no hope-a, no-hope-a! Woe-is-me, woe-is rope-monster. The rope-monster shoulda been a podiatrist, or something professional and more specialized."

We CO_2-ed more.

"I'm scared, I can't breathe, Felty," Stephy said. "I'm shrinking. Not back into a puppet, I can't go to work like this! Help! No!"

Still, we CO_2-ed. The streams dipped so there would only be a few seconds more of pressure before the emergency shutoff. "CO_2-blasted or no, you will survive."

"CO_2-blasted! *Gurgle*—a cargo hold—mobsters and monsters—this is no place for a pregnant woman. Look at me: Felty, I'm a puppet."

She tried to stand up as I pulled her out of the monster's mouth. I plucked a sticky, red fiber off her forehead. "You look good rubbery." She compressed her rubbery hands in disbelief before her childish eyes gobble-gazed up from her shrinking, now-miniature, now-smaller-than-that stature. Her eyeshadow had been penciled on her rubber in a long-passé style. I had torn from my clothes from all the excitement, and I pawed at dried river-blood rope, dangling from a pipe. I would have to construct a loincloth out of the stuff.

"I can carry you home. Is our child okay?"

"I don't know, Felty. How can anyone know? What am I supposed to do? You have to figure it out, I can't stand being like this. Fix it."

I pulled down river-blood rope to make the loincloth.

"Why do humans clothe themselves?" DinoMan asked.

"To signal the force one brings to bear," I said.

The DinoMan looked down to himself. "How should I clothe these dark forces?"

"Gurgle gurgle—!" The wavelike face diminished into its ropes. "Not cool!" It burbled, "You call yourselves puppets?"

I reached and pulled Stephy's rubbery body into me. "There there," I said, caressing her shivering rubber. "I can protect you."

She cooed as her sniveling calmed down and her googly irises grew: "You…man? Me…object: me—me…*puppet?*"

"You let yourself fall inside a deep puppet-hole," I said. "We will figure something out for the office on Monday."

The red ropes bubbled. "You dudes got stacks on deck? Can I hold like ten or twenty boom-bills for a couple a' weeks? The Rope-Monster is good for it."

I stomped down the ropes. "Piss off, River-blood Rope."

"Felty, I can't lose our baby. I have to take better care of myself."

"You should take time off from work to relax," I said.

"I can't."

"You should."

"I know."

21

Sipping lemon water, flumped inside my cubicle, I endeavored to finalize a lid design that might satisfy the transnational needs of Power Chemicals. Sometimes, a puppet must take the long way around and attempt all the worst ideas first. Ergonomics were important since technicians needed to carry the lid while wearing the rubber gloves that were worn in clean rooms.

The structural casement surrounding the plastic needed to be strong enough to not tear under its weight. The raw materials needed to be readily available in the unit systems of the countries of the vendors. An email dinged…a charity picnic would benefit foster bunnies, sired by parents that lacked their right, hind toes. The email did not specify whether the sired bunnies lacked their right, hind toes.

If so—assuming correlation between missing toes and diminished parental attention—the whole lineage might be defunct. The loss of the bunnies sunk in, it robbed me of enthusiasm. The method for joining to the plastic window festered and bounced around. It was troublesome. Everything could fall apart on this point.

Drilling no holes into the plastic was ideal for its service conditions. Plastic was cheap, plastic was infinitely formable, hmmm…versatile. It had made many a man rich. Plastic's use, however, was a mixed blessing. The material was not of this world, born of the mind of a multimillionaire extraterrestrial, mid-wank. It did not decompose. If heated near boiling, a pox of unknown hormone-disruptors did dislodge.

Of course, the oh-no temperature for *HorseTeeth502* was well within the operating range of the mixing process intended to slosh and splash below the lid. This splashing could cause the secretion of hormone-altering chemicals into the RTS batch and rob generations of their health, and the ghosts of Miltro and his grandfather would not like that. This was all notwithstanding the structural shortcomings which were an insult to any engineer.

Its fatigue strength? a punch line to an undergraduate's joke. This fatigue strength problem was made worse at even modestly high temperatures. Drill points into the plastic were simply unconscionable. With force applied over an infinitesimal area, such as a drill point, even the modest force of footsteps was multiplied.

Silently, while I thought, several strings fell down from the ceiling and fluttered and bounced around behind me. Their masking tape mouths quivered near the cut ends of their strings. They hissed and snapped like cobras. They lashed at each other and cavorted and wrapped around stuff on my desk.

Based on the other conversations I had heard nearby, these strings were many of the old standbys I had expected to come calling. Their names were barely legible on their masking tape mouths as if a child scrawled them. *Bad-Feathers-2* drooped from the ceiling. It bounced as a seahorse swims. "Forget *HorseTeeth502*. *Bad-Feathers-2, Bad-Feathers-2* is what ya do!"

"Begone, *Bad-Feathers*," I said. "Begone, *Bad-Feathers-2*."

They bowed their heads, and then arched back up to shake their twelve bristles, pleadingly, "Cash and prizes for you!"

"You're toxic at room temperatures. You explode in the presence of rainwater."

"But, baby, baby, I'm cheap. Hear me out, engineer. Got me an MSDS, see? over here. The dangers are small, puppet."

While distracted by *Bad-Feathers-2*, *Milky-Chummers* snuck around and stabbed its cut end into my neck. I said then in a gravelly voice: *"Milky-Chummers gonna get himself in the field, Milky-Chummers produce a helluva yield."*

"Boo! Unstring!" jeered *Saggy-Tomorrow*.

I un-stung *Milky-Chummers* from the back of my neck as its fangs dislodged from my felt. Smooth plastic strands slipped through my fingers as my fist pummeled it, causing it to belch: "THERMOSET!" —gasp— "THERMOPLASTIC!"

"Listen up, polymers," I said. "I do not know if plastic is suitable. Petrochemicals may not provide the needed safety nor the structural integrity, even for the short life cycle."

The plastics squeaked and creaked. "What's that got to do with it?" Some slinked away dejectedly, returning to the ceiling. The stubborn ones remained and they railed: "WE'RE CHEAP. WE'RE FUN. WE DEGRADE IN THE SUN!"

"Awww!" The stragglers lashed toward *Saggy-Tomorrow*.

"Oyster-spackle!" *Firm-Fist-Ductility* said. "You be—wait— shut-up. You be laying in the landfill for ten-thousand years like: *ah—h?* where that sprue bushing at?"

"I *do* degrade in the Sun," *Saggy-Tomorrow* said. "My makers said I would degrade…by-and-by."

"What about a polymer infused glass?" I asked.

"Sure," *Translucent-Yes* said, bouncing its neck and arching about at the others, "chop wood, skin a buffalo while you're at it." And the plastics did laugh and make sport of me. They pulled up my shirt, high-twelved each other, chest-bumped and rocked-out. Several strings slumped to the floor in vibratory spasms in the throes of ecstasy, "We multiply, PLASTICS ARE FOREVER."

"Who has a yield strength above thirty-five kilo-*snizzums?*"

They bowed their heads.

Firm-Fist-Ductility lit with enthusiasm. "I do!"

"Booo!" plastics said. "That's your compressive yield strength, ash-hole."

"Who you calling ash-hole?"

"You're all new pellets," *Firm-Fist-Ductility* said: "Virgins!"

"Take that back!" *Gonzo-Cow-Acid* said.

My smartphone rung. It was Root Beer.

"Puppet," said *Translucent-Yes*, "might I interest you in—"

"Yes, Root Beer, hold on," I placed my hand over the receiver. "Please, plastics, I must take this. Depart into your realm."

"Awwww!" *Squeak creak.* They disappeared up into the ceiling.

"What is wrong, Felty?" Root Beer asked. "Are you in danger?"

"The petrochemical industry just tried to puppet me," I said. "What transpires at the apartment?"

"For this reason I call," Root Beer said. "The weight does weigh on these shoulders. Yes, we earn money from my fortune telling and from the engineering efforts of you and that Piss Ant. Yes, Matchy has found employment for himself and his kangaroo as a bouncer. He must man-up nearly nightly. Many felties remain listless and largely unemployed. We still do not, as a p-unit, earn enough to

compete with the gentrified bachelors downtown who stole away
our squishies from us. The bachelors have combs and manly oils
for their beards. Most of them are flesh-bags—not felties. The
squishies have traded up."

"Peace, Root Beer," I said, "we felties will get our squishies
back from the oily, bearded flesh-bags. Here at PC, I have been
reunited with Stephy."

"She is your boss!"

"She is a puppet now, owing to a close-call with a roustabout
rope-monster. She locked herself in her office today and listed
herself on *MouseHook* as *In Retreat*."

"I hear you CO_2-ed over that rope-monster."

"Of course, puppet," I said. "It was with Providence the ship
was gassed."

"Yes, Providence," Root Beer said, "this is why I called. It is
my place to predict all events for puppets, flesh-bags and the Sun.
Do I know all answers? No. I guess, puppet. I guess. I look to the
future. If our fortunes keep going this way, we felties will disband.
No matter how much we earn, the ones without work always wish
us to provide more. Toil, they know not. They have no baseline for
their judgments. Nagarazim longs for his sea legs."

"He wishes to be a sailor?"

"He saw a picture selling sea legs in a magazine," Root Beer
said. "Now, it is all of which he will speak. His great mind has been
dominated by an image of sea legs in a magazine. *GMO-Froggy
Style*, the company is called."

"Will the operation take?"

"What does it matter? It pushes him from pain."

"Root Beer, while I am away at work, I expect—"

"Herbivore is not well. He lounges. He munches broccoli and glowers out the window at the sunshine with his teary eyes. He will not take his B-12, calls it bacteriacide. He grows too lime, Felty! You must stop by the supermarket and pick up some preme-o, responsibly-sourced B-12."

"That will set me back if I am to take the bus, Root Beer. Have you reconsidered my proposal to purchase a Vespa?"

"Puppets are too small for Vespas. If we are to purchase you one, you must man-up, morning and night, for the commute. The trip will be treacherous. What if you cannot revert to a puppet during working hours? PC is not interested in hiring men."

"Each day, I gain greater control over this thing whispered among humans as masculinity."

"Hmmm…all sounds like oyster-spackle to these felt-flaps. If you persist in this bid for a Vespa, I will not oppose you. Something more important presses us forward. My nerves are tangled and toxic. All this responsibility, it was not intended for a puppet to be held so accountable. I have not been able to man-up one time in this existence. I begin to think, softly to myself in the silences that surround sleep, that I may not be a man at all and merely some monster. This troubles me. I have a kickstand. But my maker did not sew me as he did you. You resemble a man and, therefore, you man-up. What am I?"

"Peace, puppet. Monster or no, you are the full beauty of an intention."

"Dust off the duncery!" Root Beer said. "What I need is that *Zokithral*."

"That *Zokithral?*"

"The puppet's White Lady on this purple tongue," Root Beer

said, "I know you can get it. You work for a pharmaceutical company. You are on that stuff, yourself. That *Zokithral* turned Stephy into a real woman, so she did not have to travel box-class, so she could be promoted to your boss."

"Peace, puppet," I said. "Yes, I have taken *Zokithral*. It is not all it seems. I believe it is addictive. Always some balance exists that if not respected—"

"You get it for me, or I will get it through some other way. What you get will be pure. Not cut with the pill-balls and all that pixie-puss like the street stuff. You get it for me, and then I will be free from this stress, free to make the righteous decisions for all under the sway of my tongue. You get it for me and this wizard will know if I am monster or man."

"Root Beer—"

"Respect your elders, FuzzPalace. I helped you. You promised: if fortune misplaced me, you would not."

If I got it for him I could monitor the dosage and purity. He would be better off. With his resolve he would not stop before attaining his goal. My email dinged with four, high-priority emails. "Support my bid for a Vespa, and I shall get you *Zokithral*."

"Tick-tock-tizzay, tick-tock-tizzay!"

Rebeccaby interrupted, "Does the felt heap failure have some oil for greasing the main control bars?"

"Tablecloth and tapestry!" I jumped from my chair and then shrunk away from her looming beauty. "Do not sneak-up on office puppets." Her breath-robbingly caffeinating puppet-mounds hung from her lacy white blouse, and I was ashamed to feel the stirring in my baling wires. Stephy had not been interested in sexy-times since her pregnancy and especially so with her puppet-hood.

"Boobs nice?"

"Yes, Rebeccaby." I remembered my Suitable Molestation Band coursework. "All that light hits on you well today."

She smiled. "Everybody want Rebeccaby bounce around. Everybody want Rebeccaby pick stuff up off the ground." She searched behind each of her shoulders. "Got oil? Rebeccaby need engineer to oil the master control bars."

"Oil what?" I dug through my drawers. "I am certain I have mineral oil."

She scampered in place and bounced. "Hurry, Rebeccaby need get back up there."

"Up where?"

"Up there."

"Are you inviting me into the break room?"

"Rebeccaby need engineer to oil master control bars."

"Found it." I retrieved the mineral oil and neared her as the lavender waves hit like a newbie's, newly widened ocean. "MEAP!"

She snorted. "Felt heap oil the master control bars. Not oil Rebeccaby."

"Of course."

"Hurry," she took my hand. "Need oil up there. Master control bars." She pulled me out of my cubicle. How could I let myself get so excited with Stephy, the mother of my something, *In Retreat* on *MouseHook*?

She climbed the metal shelf, and I climbed behind her, looking up her skirt with the mineral oil clenched in my teeth. The funk of the tunnel that surrounded us was something else. It was dark and wet up there. Someone maybe was cooking a questionable feast as squeaks, creaks and shrieks echoed in disharmonious rows. I fingered around at the slimy corrugated flesh of the tunnel, and its dank wind blew down from above. She stopped in the middle of her climb to pull something out of her purse.

"Is that a pill bottle?" I asked.

"*Zokithral*. So, they love Rebeccaby." She popped the pill and immediately grew taller, more svelte. Her purple pumps searched for purchase on what was becoming a more jagged and rough terrain.

"How is it so high up?" I asked. "Is PC not a one-story structure?"

"Extra levels are hidden."

She took my hand, and I stumbled about over an unpredictable ground of corrugated flesh below we pressed the crimson pillows of silk and broadcloth, possessed of their prickly, jade studs. Pixelated flower petals twirled and cascaded like falling snow. "Ouch! Hey, felty!" "Watch it!" said the voices of flesh-bags and puppets in various states of transformation:

"Is it okay if I do this?" a participant asked.

"How the hell should I know?" another responded.

"Can I touch you here? Like this? Wait, ah…sorry, I think."

"Just do it if you're gonna do it. Ouch, no, my hair!"

"Do what now, what do we do?"

"We can figure it out as a group if we keep trying. Watch the others."

"Follow the leader. One and two and three and *FOUR!*"

"You got arms like a man!"

"I am a man? Wait! Take another picture from this side, like this…like this…right? Let them know."

"Rebeccaby, what is this place?" I asked. "The atmosphere is rarified. I feel light headed and cannot see clearly."

"Felt heap look up? See green stars?"

The distant ceiling terminated in a cap that narrowed to a conical point and its underside was resplendent with the shining of green stars. "So beautiful," I said. "Let me be there, let me live up…up there…in green light."

However, these were not green stars. It was one luminescent, green structure that narrowed at a large distance above into its conical point. This cosmic emerald puppet string loomed above. The underside of its severed base twitched with hundreds of point-like tendrils that appeared at first glance as stars. Selfie sticks swayed from the puppet and human hands in cadence with the gyrating and grinding as their flashes set off a strobe effect.

"This orgy is intense," I said. "This is how the puppets and humans hang?"

"Is that some puppet, throwing off my stroke?" a voice beneath my shoe asked.

"I should depart," I said.

"Rebeccaby naked," she said. "Here." She placed my hand over her breast, allowing a ticklish philosophy to nearly make my stuff go off.

"Zorf!"

"Felt heap find thrill?"

"Uncomfortable thrill."

"Rebeccaby find human, sexy-time partner. Felt heap is the oil-puppet to start. Understand?"

"Wait," I said. "What?" The canister of mineral oil had become a decanter of hot oil.

"Hey, puppet?" someone said. "Little help. Getting dry."

"The people and puppets screw in the Break Room to control

life at PC. Understand?" Rebeccaby asked.

"Affirmative. I believe—"

"How af*firm*?"

"Oh, no," I said and looked down at myself.

She smiled. "Rebeccaby tell Stephy."

"You will not—*ooooo!*" Certi said from beneath the shoulder of a man. "What happens—*oooo*—in the Break Room—*oooooo*—stays in the Break Room. Understand, new-skin?"

"Yes, ma'am," Rebeccaby said and slithered away, undressing. Clearly tattooed in black between her human shoulders, her trademarked logo of *HorseTeeth502* wrinkled in the green light. All the orgy participants had these tattoos on their backs. However, some said simple things like *Mortgage*, *Promotion*, or *Fatherhood*.

"What's a matter, Felty," Certi asked as the man above her thrust, "*oooo* don't you like it?"

"I always supposed Hell would burn below us."

"Don't be melodramatic," a familiar voice said.

"Who thrusts there?" I asked. "Who thrusts there, atop Ms. Klacard?"

"Did you miss me?" the man asked as he leered back at me with his long, thin mug.

"Richnuss!"

"That's right, puppet. I could use a little more hot oil on her you-know-what and her ka-pow-za."

"I shall not be anyone's oil-puppet. You there, rest not your selfie stick upon my brow. Rude."

"Felty!" Certi shouted, "*Ooooo—!* Insubordinate felt-scrap. You oil! *Oooo—ooo—oooo!*" —inaudible mishmash, panic-panting— *"Goo-goo-googly-zoo!"*

"Goo-goo-googly-zoo!" echoed the participants.

"Stop imitating her." I said.

"Stop imitating her." they said.

"This is not how you orgy!"

"This is not how you orgy!"

"I shall not oil the foolish, I am leaving."

"I shall not oil the foolish, I am leaving."

"Reject us now and you won't be invited back," Certi said. "We control the puppet strings here—*ooooo!* Orgasms set the policy. If you reject us, the puppet strings we send you will be much worse."

"I choose, and so declare, to uphold the Three Laws of Engineering, even to my detriment," I said. "I was not sewn by my maker, *your true husband,* Miltro Miggugen, to be a pushover pull-string of cut-rate integrity."

"Fluff you, puppet!" a participant said.

"Eat lint and die—!"

"I would rather do real work as a cubicle puppet," I said.

"Let's not be hasty." Certi said. "Let me find you some girl."

"Stephy is my girl. I should not have come here. Goodbye."

I stood there for a moment and my nonparticipation enlivened their efforts. *"It's cool, it's cool, it's cool. They got me twice with the same trick. How I gonna get on top a' the second one like—ah... this is not the way...It got a thing that go like this and if I time it right, I can get in there."*

22

I had avoided Stephy on Monday but it was time to get things calculated. She was still listed *In Retreat* on Tuesday. We needed to discuss the design review scheduled for Thursday of that week for the plastic lid. There were twenty-five points to discuss. It was of utmost importance I get out each idea consecutively, without interruption.

"Come in," she said.

"I have not yet even knocked."

"He-elp!"

Her puppet form swung and bobbled across the door as I opened it. "*Waaah-aaah-aaah!*" Her sweat-soaked sundress and rubbery body flopped and dangled as strings from the ceiling jerked and bounced her about. "What did you do, Felty?" Her elbows and knees sagged and swayed as the six strings bounced her off the ground, near the ceiling, as if a mindless child angrily imitated modes of walking, flying and dancing.

"Oh, no," I said. "There was a mishap in the break room. I had to explain that I was a puppet of ideals—plus integrity." I stepped forward, attempting to catch her, midflight, as she whizzed by. She slipped through my fingers. "Stephy!"

"They're trying—*wooah*—to get to you—through me."

"How did they know about us, Stephy?"

"I let it slip."

"They said they would puppet me way worse," I said. "How does this puppet me?" A string flew down from the ceiling and pierced through the back of my neck. I reached back. "Tablecloth and tapestry, the *Guilt* string!" The string's scaly covering slithered like a beast. "The Guilt String, no! Stephy, Stephy I am—I am sorry for all this. I should have stayed with you on Monday. How long have you been trapped here?"

"Since 5:00 pm—*waaaaah!* last night."

"Stephy, I feel terrible—the *Guilt* string. Stephy, I fondled the boob of a coworker. My mistake!"

"*Waaaaah! Waaa-why!* Why would you do that?"

"I thought it was SMB."

"The SMB—*waaaah* is misogynistic oyster-spackle, invented only by men."

"I am sorry, Stephy. Is this okay for a pregnancy?"

She flew. "It wasn't in any of the books."

The *Guilt* string throbbed and pulsed. It burned through my body with an itching sensation. "Stephy, what is your laptop's password?"

"That's private! *Waah!*"

"Reveal and reset!"

"FELTY!"

"WHAT?"

"NO, FELTY—FELTY, *FELTY* IS MY PASSWORD."

"Hmmm, I did not know you felt this way about Felty." I fell to my knees. "Stephy, the *Guilt* string strengthens. It hurts, like an approaching friend, stuck always on stab-mode. The guilt may destroy me. Say something to help me think less of you."

"Your foreplay—*waaa!*"

"My foreplay? awe-inspiring? I know this. Cut to the core."

"Your foreplay…is lackluster…p-pedestrian."

I stood up off my knees. "This cannot be. Tell truths."

"Your hands and eyes creep like a prepubescent salamander."

"Prepubescent salamander?

"No matter. I have logged onto your laptop. I'm changing your status on *MouseHook* to *Cautiously Optimistic*."

"I AM *NOT* CAUTIOUSLY OPTIMISTIC!"

"Facsimile vis-à-vis authenticity."

"It's not wor-or-orking!" She flounced and bobbled wildly and toppled a pink kettlebell from the reclaimed wood of the coffee table to the glittery, raspberry-rainbow carpet.

I searched the room for an answer. The answer did not lay within the bedazzled calculator, nor the grasshopper stapler, or a pair of stylish golden mules, cast over the carpet. "Stephy," I said, "have you been given a corporate teleporter, with an expense account?"

"An ivory one," she said, flouncing, "never use it."

"Ivory," I said. "For the teleportation of natural elements? Where is it?"

"Somewhere! Buried under stuff. Why?"

"You need pussy."

"What?" she asked. "Pussy is expensive."

"Splurge women."

"It's over there, under the sofa."

"Which sofa?" I asked. "You have three, massive sofas that are arranged strangely.”

“Cutest one, totes.”

“Subjective.”

“Mr-Mr. Frumpy-pants, deep-comfort—”

“The corduroy one that reposes middlemost?”

“Like, I think.”

Her ivory teleporter lay hidden behind the Mr Frumpy-pants sofa, plugged-in behind a hybrid office chair slash exercise ball. I booted the teleporter and typed in the coordinates for the cutest—youngest—most adorable pussy imaginable.

The teleporter jostled on its ivory stand. It buzzed and ionized air with digital and chromosomal intention. The summoning of a pussy that cute was proving a heroic task for the small corporate teleporter. I gazed upon it pityingly until the flash of blue light and tendrils of obsidian smoke did gash open a vertical, zipper-vortex of Space-time.

“Stephy, come down here. Admire this adorable pussy. Its hair is tawny, soft and brown, like yours.”

“Adorable?” she asked distractedly.

“Affirmative,” I said, “it is small and cute. However, I fear it has not been fed in some time.”

“It’s hungry?” she asked, slinking to the floor as her strings above withered and relaxed.

“Yes, Stephy,” I said, “it looks scared and confused.”

“Aww,” she said, “super-cute, right?” She wiped sweat from her brow. “It needs our help, right?”

“Yes, madam.”

“So cute.” And she petted it. “It’s okay, I’m your friend.”

“Meow,” it approved, “meow.”

"Angieus has latte milk in her fridge next door," Stephy said. "Keep one eye cocked to that pussy." She left. When she came back she was a full-grown woman with her tiny sundress ringing her pregnant belly.

It lapped from a saucer.

Stephy checked an identification tag, dangling from its collar. "So strange. Where does this pussy come from?" she read the tag, "Kathy. What a queer name. Kathy. I don't think I've ever heard of that name before. Where did it come from?"

"Sometimes teleporters do strange things," I said.

We shrugged our shoulders.

"It likes milk," Stephy said. "Think it's a girl?"

"I could flip it over."

"No."

"Very well."

"Felty," her eyes grew, "Can we take her home with us?"

"Home?" I asked. "With…with…*us*?"

"Yeah," she said, pulling off her puppet sundress and retrieving a silver pantsuit from a backpack, which had been stowed beneath Mr Frumpy-pants. "Felty, I'm in the Fourth Quarter of my pregnancy here. We're already past Halftime. You have to take care of me." She snapped on a crimson, clip-on tie to the neckline of her maternity pantsuit and crossed her arms, strongly. "Is there a problem with taking care of me?"

I considered my options. If I did not take care of her, she might fire me. Then I really would not be able to take care of either of us. "No problem, madam. Very well, madam."

She smiled. "We'll name her. We have to name her. How about Polydimethylsiloxane? That's gender-neutral, I think."

"Ah," I said, "several names will be contemplated. Stephy, if I am to take care of you during your pregnancy, might you take care of my career, in likewise fashion?"

She flinched. "That wouldn't be fair. You're on your own, buddy. Besides, you have to be awesome so you can take care of us."

"Yes, regarding the design review—"

"That's coming up Friday, right?"

"Yes, madam, again: regarding this design review—"

"I'm sure that you'll do super good and stuff."

"Yes, madam, but, at minimal, twenty-five crucial points of consideration await your attention."

"You'll find a way to make it work—*meow, meow*—she got wittle, wittle whiskers, she do."

My shoulders slumped. "I committed to scoring *Zokithral* for Root Beer."

"Samples are in my top-left desk drawer."

23

In noontide hours us felties gathered round the metal shelf that led to the break room. We discussed aspects surrounding our survival; we listened to detect if humans approached from the end of the aisle way and if humans descended from the shelf (hair tousled from befuddled orgies) we pretended to gather supplies. Many tips and pointers were exchanged while pretending to be mesmerized by Post-its.

"I'm saying, there's…there's goin' be time for that— Hold… hold up. The main thing I wanna know is," Pirate asked, "what level a' fuckery we working with?"

"For the beginning of this afternoon's design review," I said, "someone approaches?"

"Not a soul nears," Piss Ant said. "Tell how a Quality Engineer, like me, would be affected by your plan."

Honk, Horn-Mouth honked, *honk*.

"That is correct, Horn-Mouth," I said. "Quality Engineers should push requirements from the conversational point through misdirections."

"That ain't what honkey said," Monster Who Loves Gum said.

"Them honks stank like cat piss."

Honk.

"Why, why?"

"The Letter Y will have an important action in this design review," I said. "Behold these scissors; behold how the eyelets of these scissors fit nearly perfectly around—"

"Why, why?"

"Relax, Letter Y," I said. "Behold how scissor eyelets fit nearly perfectly over the upper branches of his Y. There."

The Letter Y opened and closed the scissor jaws by squeezing together his branches. "Why, why, why?"

I reached to pet the Letter Y but thought better of it as berserk blades pinched and slashed. "Only Letter Y has a curiosity which cannot resist unraveling PC's paramount mystery."

Honk.

"That ain't funny, honkey," Pirate said. "You need to check your attitude—check that cat piss."

Honk!

"I can't change no five. Forget them vending machines."

"What is the paramount mystery?" Piss Ant asked.

"Now is not the time," I said. "Remove Post-its from your face."

"Harrumph."

"Awww, it's Piss Ant smelling like some cat piss. I told that thing, I said, I said: take a shower."

"What difference a shower," Piss Ant asked, "against this essence?"

"The primary question I wish to answer with this design review—" I said, and I pointed toward the end of the cubes, "someone approaches—? The primary question I wish to answer is 'what happens if puppets willfully cut our own strings?'"

"Why, why, why, why?"

Honk.

"Monsters love gum. And you discerned this."

"Is life not more than honking, more than chewing gum, more than being pulled on strings? I wish us to have a truer life. The only difference between flesh-bag and puppet is a willful decision for freedom. Let us be free; let us make decisions for ourselves, which we own—revel, revel in the beauty of unbefuddled intention—of integrity—of genius."

"Bet that gonna hurt," Pirate said. "You cut a string, once it's strung, puppet might mess around and die."

"Consider the risks—"

"Tick-tock, no way."

"Tick-tock, yes way," I said. "If we desire something different, something different we must do."

"Why not test it on yourself?" Piss Ant asked.

"This I undertake," I said. "Letter Y—hear me now—nearly most-senior member of the alphabet: if a string descends, that string you cut off me."

"Why, why?"

"I wish to choose my own words with full sin, with outstretched malice, with a mellifluous abandon whilst I persuade middle and upper management against the specification of a certain plastic, known provincially, as *HorseTeeth502*."

"We getting that plastic on the sly," Pirate said. "That's that deep discount action."

"My preference is for a polymer and reinforced glass hybrid. *HorseTeeth502* is unsafe—both for the downstream patients and the upstream technicians. If it does not break during service, it will contaminate the entire batch."

Honk, honk?

"My employment is not so normal. My chief purpose: revenge for the death of a father, known as Miltro Miggugen. There will be no inferior products produced at PC. Paychecks be secondary."

"Why should this be revenge if your aim is justice?" Piss Ant asked.

"Because I will watch those human faces contort and twitch at the second their villainy is overcome."

"Oh." Piss Ant made a twirling motion near his head. "Psycho…"

"Show me an example of Felty cutting one of his strings," a felty said.

"If I waste sufficient time," I said, "a *Mortgage* or *Promotion* string will descend on me."

"However, you are neither pursuing mortgage," Piss Ant said, "nor being pursued for promotion."

"The strings hunt," I said. "There. Above. Yonder! Is that something? Wait—perhaps nothing." I reached back and the coarse careless braiding of another *Mortgage* string writhed in my hand. "Alas, I am had."

"Why, why, why?"

"You!" I said, "Letter Y, you stay away with those shears." The tugging sensation of rooting to the ancient soil shuddered through every baling wire bone. "All is recanted. I must build equity. I must conserve money on taxes—on moving boxes."

Felties bobbed their heads. Some looked to the ground; some shook heads like troubled teachers. How could they act this way in the presence of the amazing opportunity of the Blueport Blues housing market? No interest had they in purchasing a home? Never to feel the desire to own the sod beneath their hooves? To own a home—a thought so sweet a honey a bee could never mutter maybe. Better to sting out its death for the protection of its ground, its manicured oasis of green. And then simply cast off fifty to one hundred percent equity in a divorce. Homeownership!

"That's a *Mortgage* string," muttered someone. "A thick one."

"Stay back, Letter Y!" I said. "Unholy hot talk from me before: fool's-prank. Fumbling fool's-prank."

"Why, why, why?"

"Interest rates are down," I shrieked, "interest rates dance limbos. Hear me now. Shall I shout? No. I keep it for myself— fools. Ha-ha-hee-hoo-hoo."

"Quick," someone said, "cut that *Mortgage* string, Letter Y."

"It could kill him."

"Listen to them, Letter Y!"

"Why, why, why?"

Snip.

"Awwww!" I said—hissing sounds—rushing, emptying waters—walls and the floor wobbled— "Flashing fiddlestick fink-stompers." I straightened my thin black necktie. "Perhaps another month of renting."

"Wait," Piss Ant said. "What if some strings are benevolent?"

"Cutting that string didn't change him none," Pirate said. "Felty the same."

"Liar," Raisin Eyes said. "He got him five fingers. Five *puppet* fingers."

"Puppets can't have no five fingers. Puppets can only have four puppet fingers, each hand, unless they monsters. Lemme see them fingers. *Damn.*"

"Cutting the string seems to have struck me somewhere between puppet and man," I said.

"Cut my strings, Letter Y," Raisin Eyes said.

"You ain't got no strings yet."

"Gotta get me a string, before I can cut the cord?"

"Maybe we got strings we can't see," a small felty said.

"You know not a syllable of that is the truth," a lanky one said.

"Fluff you, puppet. I be rocking the truth like your grandma's porch swing."

The punked felty attempted to button up his shirt straight. He disregarded the effort, freezing with an introverted stillness, which betrayed itself as a quivering of the felt brim of his lips: "Grandmother? A grandmother can never be boasted by a puppet, such as this—this semi-animate, claptrap husk. Such emptiness in an eternity of form…never to change, never to reproduce."

"Awwwww snap!" we shouted.

"Letter Y," Piss Ant said, "cut above my head, through open air."

"Why, why, why?"

"Ensure autonomy, inquisitive tri-point."

The Letter Y slumped his shears to ground.

"Are you all ready for the design review?" I asked.

Silence.

I turned my back on them and returned to my cube. It was almost time for the call. We would conduct the design review over the telephone while I shared slides through the WiFi from my laptop. This was fortunate since I could carry my laptop atop the cubicle walls and watch the other puppets at their cubes. Our management would all be on the call so I doubted they would know or care about my spying.

Plus, I had five puppet fingers now. This bolstered my confidence in ways held apart from manning-up; manning-up was so brutish, so obvious that it was hard to go undetected by enemies. Five puppet fingers! Imagine. These five fingers would no doubt have greater grip strength. I could use the human's keyboard as intended, while calm and not enraged.

Stephy hated her puppet-hood, yet a certain fondness for felt had grown within me. People expected less of puppets. They talked to us like children. At first the idea of manhood seemed a great and worthy ideal. Lately my habits of puppet-hood had grown in so great that to expunge them might mean vanquishing my soul to oblivion.

Each time I had manned-up I was forced to it, at considerable risk. At PC, as well as with walking the world at large, the rewards for masculinity had dwindled and receded. However a puppet, built more like a man—I rubbed the scab where *Mortgage* string had been severed—that might be the way forward.

From the topmost cornice of my cube, the others appeared to be logging onto their laptops. I looped the telephone earpiece over my ear and switched it on before checking *MouseHook* for the meeting notice and logging into *EveryVoice*. Twenty participants waited in the online queue.

"Who queues there?" I asked. "Declare yourself."

"Cockapoo Spidoo, here," Cockapoo Spidoo said.

"Of the furry face?"

"Never that!"

"Apologies."

"Short shorn, puppet—from logistics."

"Comprehension."

"Headless Boardsman, here."

"Goo-goo-googly-zoo!"

"Certi?" I asked.

Silence.

"She's fine, puppet. She'll come to…in a bit," Richnuss said.

"Certi!" I said, "sexy-time on our conference call? Richnuss does not work for PC—does he?"

Silence.

"Zero | One | Zero: Bicep Hero," Bro-bot said, "Bro-bot, here."

"Of sectors T and A?"

"Bro-bot…*processing processing*…Bro-bot from Sales."

"Pirate, here."

"Piss Ant, here."

"Why, why, why?"

Honk.

"The number of beings on this call grows and grows," I said. "Certi, might there be upper-management lurkers, lurking?"

"Googly…"

"Got 'er again."

"Stephy, here," Stephy said, between crumbly bites of something. "You may have guests on the call, from upstairs."

"However, there is no upstairs," I said.

"Be careful."

"Let us begin with the first slide of the presentation," I said. "As all can behold, the oh-no temperature for *HorseTeeth502* is unacceptably low for the service, yes?"

"The oh-no 's some bullshit," Monster Who Loves Gum said, "we got data backing it up. The PC figures figure like—hmmm—mmmm—gum—gum good. Rubbery. Something that won't die."

"Letter Y, cut the string of the Monster Who Loves Gum," I said.

"Look, the Monster Who Loves Gum has a *Mortgage* string," Piss Ant said. "I can see it. Big, slippery green one!"

"Back up, Letter Y," said Monster Who Loves Gum, "I need this *Mortgage* string. Who gonna pay all these bills? I gotta eat."

"THE LETTER Y," boomed Headless Boardsman, "LEAVES THE STRINGS ALONE. LETTER Y, WHERE ARE YOUR STRINGS? ANSWER ME."

"Why, why, why, why?"

"The Letter Y," I said, "asks too many questions. He is all too inquisitive to be string strung."

"Stay back, puppet!" the Monster Who Loves Gum said.

"Why, why, why, why—?"

Snip.

"Awwww no!" Monster Who Loves Gum said. "Agony."

"You're killing him," Raisin Eyes said. "He's spewing green goo out the back of his neck."

"It hurts," Monster Who Loves Gum said. "I'm leaking, I'm soaking yet. This stuff coming out stinks. And you smell it. Fuck-puppet, the PC data weren't no damn good. Phony, like pineapples in a pickle patch. No control group. No single blind. We…we…aw, I got more a' this stanking stuff on my shirt. That came out a' me? We pole-vaulting over mouse turds with that *HorseTeeth502* oh-no data. We knew it. All along. Am I gonna get fired for telling the truth? How is it my fault when they up and cut my…cut my damn *Mortgage* string?"

"You have fought for justice," I said.

"Fluff you, felt scrap!" Monster Who Loves Gum said, "Who says you gotta fix something? You need to stop buying clothes at gas stations; talking all that 'I am in charge of gears and of shafts'-oyster-spackle. Ain't nobody trying to hear that. Oughta zag and flomp you. Might as well tell the whole of it. Where my *Mortgage* string go? Oh no. I gotta stop. What we got: two-hundred on the call—?"

"Put an end to it," said Richnuss.

"Why, why, why, why?"

Eyeam stumbled near Piss Ant's cubicle and bounced off a brown wall before staggering and stumbling. It had white powder smeared over its naked, green-furred body again. It could not be trusted. "Eyeam so messed-up!" The strings buzzed near Eyeam but recoiled as if shying from rancid meat.

"Put an end to it," Richnuss repeated.

"Wha—?" Certi mumbled. "What time's that meeting, darling?"

"STRINGS," boomed Headless Boardsman, "DO YOUR DESCENT, DOUBLE RECOMPENSE."

"Why, why, why?"

"Bro-bot…protein shake."

A slimy, crimson string uncurled from the ceiling and stripped the Letter Y of its shears. It wrapped and pulled the Letter Y to the ceiling like a strangling tentacle. "WHY!" The Letter Y's bulging maraca-eyes darted and bulged about. "WHY!" It's purplish tri-point spread repeatedly, struggling to free itself. "WHY?"

"Oyster-spackle," I said and flung my laptop over the side of the cubicle wall. I chased towards the cubicle of the Monster Who Loves Gum.

"CONFESS," boomed Headless Boardsman." CONFESS,

MONSTER WHO LOVES GUM, TO ALL ON THE CALL THAT YOU HAVE LIED ABOUT THE OH-NO TEMPERATURE."

"Gurf," Monster Who Loves Gum said, "gurf— String's got my neck!"

I leapt over a toppled task chair and picked the discarded shears that had been dropped by the Letter Y, pausing briefly to watch as the helpless Letter Y struggled near the ceiling. The red string appeared to strangle him like a boa constrictor. The eggplant hue of his felt faded. I cut a corner, ducking the hand of a human passerby, attempting to pet my head. A slithering green string squeezed around the neck of the Monster Who Loves Gum, hanging him from the ceiling.

I dragged the shears to the top of the cube's upper cabinets, left the shears atop the cabinets and leapt toward the Monster Who Loves Gum, making contact with him and swinging his frame like a pendulum before I scaled the cube again and clung to the string above the monster's head just as it swung near. The tough outer skin of the green string fought against the blades of the shears as lumps rippled beneath like flexing muscles.

"Gurf!"

"Remain strong," I said.

"CONFESS," Headless Boardsman said from a nearby speakerphone.

"Gurf!"

I struggled with the shears as they tore through the outer surface of the strings. There was something white and papery inside that I could almost see.

"CONFESS!"

"The only reason I chew so much gum— Gurf!" the Monster

Who Loves Gum said, "is to keep my fangs from doing what they're designed to do."

"We'll consider putting this project on hiatus," Certi said, "I'm ending the conference call. You can all log-off and drop-off. *Googly!*"

"Pirate, tell them to stay on the call. I have torn through the string," I said. "Something papery is inside. Ah!"

The string severed, dropping the Monster Who Loves Gum and me to the floor as the upper half of the severed string violently spewed tiny strips of white paper all over the cubicle like a fire hose. The tiny strips of paper had what appeared as fortunes, which could not be read because they had been printed in red-lettered binary code. "Confusing," I said as I picked one of the strips of paper.

"Thanks, puppet," the Monster Who Loves Gum said. He stood, pulled off the struggling lower half of the green string and rubbed his neck. "Real name 's Bernack. Monster Who Loves Gum is just something people say."

"Are you okay?"

"I got six puppet fingers now: big-bulgers. One more than most monsters. This place covered in green goo. Who gonna pick up all a' these—all a' these binary fortune cookies?"

"Why, why, why!"

"The Letter Y!" I said. "Bernack! Get back on that call and tell us everything you know about *HorseTeeth502.*"

"Stop dropping off the call," Bernack said. "I've got something to say."

Several of us felties managed to swing and free the Letter Y from the red boa constrictor string that had seized him. As we gathered around him, his felt body crumpled and deflated. His inquisitive maraca eyes grew distant and heavy-lidded. "Why, why…*why?*"

I flexed my hands. I had four puppet fingers again. "I am sorry, Letter Y. I needed to rescue Bernack first."

"Will he be all right?" Raisin Eyes asked.

"The Letter Y has long been deprived of oxygen. It took longer than I had expected to free Bernack. Several of his baling wires have broken. His felt has torn. Some stuffing has leaked."

"WHY?" He sputtered and crumpled and attempted to stand and curl his branches.

"Be brave, Letter Y," I said. "You have done a momentous service for a noble purpose. You have taught us much and aided our cause of freedom, of self-discovery."

"Why? Why? Why?"

"Man," someone said, "Felty is an asshole."

"Relax, puppets," I said, "I am an expert on death. I have seen its face before."

"Dude is cold."

"His heart is a hat."

"Be calm," I said. "Be brave in your final moments, Letter Y."

"Why, why, why?" the Letter Y said. It tried to stand, to hop about as before.

"All puppets must die; all puppets find peace this way."

The eggplant flush of his felt faded. "WHY—?"

"I do not know. If I could do it over, I would do it better."

"Why?"

"We love you, Letter Y: your youth, your tireless curiosity, inspired us all. It always shall."

"WHY?"

"No more dignity can be brought by this—"

"Felty," Pirate said, "Felty betrayed the Letter Y."

"Let us get the Letter Y help, quickly!" Piss Ant said.

"Fools, time is a lost possession," I said. "The life and medicine surrounding magical puppetry are understood by no one. Nothing can undo our horrible mistakes. Look, his breathing—how shallow—how slow it becomes."

"You a real asshole," Pirate said.

I bent over the Letter Y. "I am sorry, forever, my friend. A decision between you and Bernack had to be made."

"Why, why, why, why, why, why, why…"

In the distance I could hear Bernack, "Mistakes were definitely made. We ordered too much of that stuff. Got *Horseteeth502* on order, on backorder, overflowing the warehouses. Shoulda' waited. We gotta use the *HorseTeeth* or cancel the project. Guess it's up to the engineering team now."

24

That weekend Stephy gave birth. The experience was confusing; the thing we thought was the afterbirth was the birth. It happened in the middle of the night when she got up to use the restroom of our now shared suite. She almost flushed it down the toilet. She had cried on a daily basis for the past couple weeks, and I had covered for her at work. I had opened and closed her office door and made her office look occupied while I did what I could of both our work.

She had been a real woman ever since she gave birth and not reverted to a puppet, despite her grief. Initially, what came out of her body did not move or give any signs of life. After hours had passed, its grayness flushed redder and it twitched. It was still alive. It seemed to thrive—to grow. It breathed and was flesh-like in appearance, flesh-like to the fumbling of nervous, felty fingers.

Must I describe it? Coiled, bulky and vascular was its body, as if a cross between a huge brain and slippery bowels. The name for this thing could be of no question. Its actual body spelled its name. As if a mockery of itself, its pink vascular coils and fleshy slick casings were grouped together as if a festering, pulsing, living embodiment of a word which emerged several days after the birth as *Integrevy*. The others informed me while I was in the midst of my shock that this was a cross between Integrity and Envy.

Much of Urftoo was beautiful, why could our child not be beautiful? And the *Fatherhood* string strung me upright, all hours. To be completely honest, at desperate moments of the night, I was given to doubt the very veracity of The Great Lobster in the Sky. Integrevy nursed on Stephy's breasts with an eager, clockwork regularity. This was strange since it had no discernable mouth. It had no eyes either, yet it considered us with each suckle upon those breasts.

This was disconcerting. Magical puppets are cautious before flesh-monsters. What was more unnerving was how every felty and squishy in that apartment displayed an ever-increasing reverence and intense interest in the wellbeing of Integrevy. It was so ugly. I could not understand how I could care for it even to the extent of what seemed as if a flame-bright, physical pain. I feared, very much, that I might grow within my chest a real heart, and this in some permanent fashion.

"Can you watch Integrevy for a sec, while I pee?" Stephy asked.

"Yes, madam," I said.

"Weirdo," she said.

Root Beer sprinted into the kitchenette, where I attempted to pat applesauce onto the skin of Integrevy so it might be absorbed. Root Beer limped and wobbled as if dazed and off-kilter. He had been on his *Zokithral* kick for some time. His purple felt lay flat, prematurely dull and thinning around his chest and neck so that I could see the white fabric beneath.

"I possess ten ideas," Root Beer said, "twenty bulge brilliance."

Integrevy shrieked like a deflating balloon.

"Where is your wizard's robe?" I demanded. "You are naked. What carcass is that over your shoulders?"

"I wear what I kill," Root Beer shouted, "the world is my pill." The brown fur, long teeth and gaping mouth of the carcass over his shoulders identified his kill as a beaver.

"Rhyming again?" I asked. "You are high on that stuff. This experiment must end. Rediscover sanity. The carcass on your back has not been cleaned and tanned. It is unsanitary to have such pelts around Integrevy."

"Mr. Cavesicle instructed me," Root Beer said as he hunched as if hunting something near the ground. His pill-balled violet felt carried a smattering of curly-blonde poodle hair.

"Mr. Cavesicle is from the Ice Age. He knows not our ways."

"Mr. Cavesicle was sewn contemporaneously with our crew."

"Why does he bark and cower at the dishwasher?"

"The claptrap of theatrics. Still, the secrets of nature, he holds." He lurched toward me and the carcass on his back slid. "Are you feeding Integrevy? I found where its mouth is, yesternoon. Allow me to instruct you."

"Away with you and your unsanitary pelt," I said. "It is not safe for Integrevy. You did not divine Integrevy's mouth, yesternoon or otherwise. You were tripping-balls yesternoon before the new teleporter, abiding with your custom. Integrevy has no mouth. If you cared, you would know this."

Root Beer slumped. His orange nose twisted in a full circle.

"How many predictions have you made for humans this week?"

Root Beer attempted to pick an imaginary lint ball from his forearm, disregarding the cockleburs clinging to his fiery-red chest hair. His dehydrated elbows and knees creased cleanly as he fidgeted, making his violet body appear under-stuffed. "I predict I shall man-up soon, if assisted through a re-up of that *Zokithral*."

"Fool," I said, attempting to ladle more applesauce that slid off. "I will not help you re-up. You are monster. Monsters cannot man-up. Monsters monster-up. Of this you undertake."

"No, deeper down I go. Double-down, mo'f'ka."

"Mo'f'ka? Who initiated you of this—?"

"Your mama."

"Arrest your mouthplate."

"A pox on you," Root Beer said, swaying as if he might collapse.

"This pox, it ricochets off my form, adhering to the inferior one before me."

"You do not understand!" cried Root Beer. He flung the beaver carcass off his shoulders with a wet plop before scampering away.

"What is this," I shouted at the discarded fur.

"It is a tribute," came the echoing reply from the entryway. "So that you, the great PC-man, will love me."

"This is *not* tribute. I am *not* your god. Beneath this roof, we steer clear of paganism."

Stephy emerged from the bathroom and asked, "Do you want me to take him now, honey?"

"Him?" I asked, "How do you know it is a 'him?'"

"You're so dense. Here, give him over—"

"Yes woman," I said, "Here, take him. I must attack a monster."

I stormed into the entryway and confronted Root Beer. "Go back into the kitchenette and pick up your beaver pelt!"

He arched his back, showed his claws and hissed.

"Fine leave it then. But give up your bump keys!"

"What bump keys?" He hissed. "I couldn't bump a lock. That

would take a puppet of such skill."

I puppet-punched him in the nose before tackling him and sitting on his chest. "Tell me where you hide the keyring. Who gave them to you?" I rained slaps down, rattling his eyes and nose. "The word is spreading around town. You gain a reputation as a lock-pick and a thief."

"I only take the granny panties, I swear!"

"A woman came by yesterday and says you broke into her apartment and fought her at 3 in the morning for her panties. She said some waist-high fuzzy monster, stinking of whiskey with attic-insulation, raccoon breath—her words—got into a tug of war with her in her dark bedroom over some gray, oversized granny panties where you kept shouting that the lace and silk are yours you greedy, stockpiling bitch."

"She stockpiled so much!"

"Think how she feels. She goes commando and cannot sleep. Stop taking advantage of the forty-year-old tumbler locks in the government housing. Where is your bump keyring?"

"With several more raids, the mission will be complete."

I slapped him, and he cried.

"Fortune has misplaced me and so have you!"

I slapped. "Do not give me that puppet guilt trip."

"I am small—objectified—I am an object, I am a counterfeit, a facsimile, an uncreated creation. My maker put no thought into me, now I compete with toasters, with spoons. Oh, to compete with the toothpicks, napkins, and stereo wire. Why can't God see me out the corner of His eye!"

"Where are the bump keys? Do I have to tell all the others about your obsession?"

"My decoy stash box—between the frogurt coupons and the I.O.U.s."

"Very well." I got off his chest and headed back to the kitchenette.

He let loose some noise between a hiss and a laugh before leaving the apartment.

Stephy leaned back in her kitchenette chair. The post-baby battle radiated from her, and she crossed a flip-flop over her honeyed thigh. "You like our little kiddo."

"Forces me to change, it does." My hand stroked the 'I' of Integrevy. "The strings follow me, night and day. They differ from moment to moment. See this string here?"

"Of course."

"For what purpose?"

"Let's pull it. Here, move away from the baby first."

"Okay. Better?"

"Cool. Now the string—"

"Bock bock!"

"You made chicken noises, neat-o."

"I—BOCK! It—BOCK! subsides—bock bock, I, bock."

"Hmm," she said. "That's a weird one. Wonder what that one's for?"

"That chicken string smarted," I said. "Feathers crawl up my throat. The perils of being pulled about on strings as father and wage-earner are manifest."

"Save the soliloquy."

"It continues, if ever a mortal…"

"There's gotta be some string to stop it. This one—?"

"Ouch," I said, "I must pay taxes."

"This one?"

"Republicans make a strong case."

"This one?"

"We can save money if we buy in bulk."

"Shut your mouthplate!" she said. "We aren't that old. This one?"

"Ouch," I said. So many strings she pulled that I forgot who I was or that I ever had a unique, independent existence. It was odd that I had these threaded cufflinks built onto me, yet no guide rods had ever attempted to communicate with them, as if my maker knew not what he was doing or he intended me for some other purpose. Perhaps puppets of old used their hands more.

Office puppets had more strings grouped around their heads, their shoulders and neck, as if someone was more concerned with what we thought and when we stood. These strings communicated so much information with me. They made the boundary between myself and the outside world blur. The strings could be a source of information, intelligence, pride. What was the individual, anyway, if not a sea of possibilities mixed within oceans of outcomes—

"Felty…FELTY!"

"Yes, madam?"

"I pulled your introversion string."

"Relax with my strings."

"Are you gonna take care of those action-items we talked about for the office on Monday?"

"Yes, certainly," I said. "Stephy, why do they not offer maternity leave at PC?"

Stephy slumped and then spooned applesauce onto Integrevy. "They do offer it, lodes. They found out I was a puppet. Puppets don't get maternity leave. They don't believe we can give birth to something real."

"You are a real woman, Stephy. You gave birth."

"It doesn't matter. We both need to stay employed until I can set up daycare."

"I'm not sure Integrevy can accept daycare. You may need to become a stay-at-home mom, Stephy."

"Stay-at-home mom!"

"We will discuss it later. For now, hand over your ID badges for work."

"Oh, yeah, that," Stephy said. She got up and dug through her purse. "Here."

"This is merely Id and Ego," I said. "Where is your Superego proximity badge?"

Her nostrils flared, and she frowned. "I'll hang on to it."

"What if I need to enter the superego rooms at PC?"

"You're not ready for those rooms. I'd need to train you up. We don't have the time. If humans catch you in one, they might kill you."

"Not if I have a Superego badge. I have already been to the break room. I cut one of my strings, I fought off the petrochemical industry's puppetry, I performed manslaughter (later devoured by the Tuxedoed DinoMan)—I CO_2-ed the rope-monster. The spilled stuffing of a Letter Y is on these hands. I am no rube."

"The break room is just one of the Superego rooms. Rebeccaby must have let you up there. There's also the Executive Restroom and the War Room."

I wiped the drool from my mouthplate. "War Room?"

She steepled her fingers. "You don't need this now."

"Woman," I said, "relinquish control over to your man, so you can focus on your childrearing."

"Sexist!" she said. "I should fire you, Felty—"

"Think that through, madam."

"This is coming up in your performance review."

"PROVIDE HIM A SUPEREGO BADGE," shouted Nagarazim from the entryway, "then my sea legs."

She bit her lip and dug for several moments in her designer handbag, pretending that she could not find something. "I know I'll regret this." She dug deep. The Superego badge rose out of the lipsticks and compacts with its gilded edges glistening from the fluorescence. "Here."

"It is mine," I said. The plastic badge warmed as if providing its own heat. Something within it, like a thin jumping beetle, buzzed at intervals.

"Fine, take it!" Stephy said, "but, Felty, I found this on the nightstand, I think we should just throw it out. It's dangerous."

She held up the folding deer-hunting knife. I snatched it back from her. "We can't throw that out. I need it."

"You almost never use it."

"A ghost gave it to me."

Her determination ripened. "Felty…"

"Yes, madam."

"You're a father, now. You can't martyr yourself."

"Whatever do you mean?"

"The Restless Torso Syndrome medication has to go to market. PC made humongous investments: time, money, research—they can't be wrong, K?"

"Only, if it is safe for the humans."

She laughed. "You're not human, Felty."

"However, someday—"

"*However, someday.*" She laughed. "Felty, we are not humans.

We're magical puppets." She gestured at herself. "This won't last. I'll be a puppet again. That's what I am. That's what you are. It's time to accept it."

"You hate being a puppet."

"But I *accept* it."

"No, you do not. Humans are better than us. Free from meddling and control. They have the real magic. The Great Lobster of the Sky rained its butter upon them."

"Humans have strings. They pull more from inside their hearts. I've seen their faces squirm— Where are you going, Felty?"

"Out!"

"Out, where?"

"I will cruise around on my Vespa."

"Be careful."

"Tablecloth and tapestry!"

25

Root Beer was incorrect in assuming puppets could not pilot Vespas. We had attached a booster seat with an ad hoc seatbelt. Nothing could be better than riding through the countryside—the hillocks, the rustic labyrinthine smokestacks, the beautiful stone-work bridges that cast the call of Blueport Blues.

My patent leather shoes flounced and bobbled below the booster seat with the wind's pleasure. My Vespa was awesome. It was macho. This was evident from the surprised looks I received from fellow motorists. As the road broke from a cropping of pines, the sun sunk into the east, into tremulous, purple-green waters of the Blueport bay.

The sun's deep indigo swirled into an emerald center as if a huge blinking eye, glaring. It burned out over the industrial fishermen of the wharves and waters as they moved with a slowness that reinforced the certainty of their tasks. Crickets in treetops leapt from branches, sailed through the air and exploded into fine, orange mists, popping like kettle corn.

These crickets had turned kamikaze sooner than expected for late springtime. Their disposability would fertilize the underbrush.

Oftentimes, these coastal insects seemed to shout minuscule swearwords, before exploding, such as 'dagnabbit!' and 'shit—shit-show!' However, to think this way was so cynical that I forced my thoughts back to the unreachable horizon of the narrowing, asphalt road—

Shit-shit-show!

"Shut-up, crickets!"

Dagnabbit! Dagnabbit—!

A wind bucked, catching my puppet arms unawares so that it took immense effort to right the handlebars. My love for Stephy had grown even with the uncertainty of this new birth. What if she was to leave and I was to lose both her and the flesh monster? The monster of flesh had given my life meaning, a sharper direction. My responsibilities at work would increase.

What was that up ahead? A gaggle of humans wandered into a ravine near the road, in their boxers, braziers, pajamas and under-garments. I found myself compelled to follow them, so I pulled my Vespa over to the loose gray rocks of the roadside.

Upon achieving the courageous inspection of being at arm's length with them, I realized they were, of course, sleepwalkers. It is with difficulty I have hitherto endeavored to discuss LobStarism as little as possible. LobStarism is, of course, the germ of Westonia's progress and perhaps Urftoo, at large. It is an uncomfortable subject for both puppet and person, especially along Westonia's eastern seaboard, where the LobStars first settled.

Through self-inflicted ignorance, passions flail and miss the mark. How, still, can I not admit that when I spotted these nearly naked, sleepwalking Blueport Bluesers of each ethnicity, stumbling by a roadside's ravine, that this was LobStarism.

"We bring pills, O Lobster," cried a tipsy woman in leggings and brazier.

"Have you yet tracked down your lobster?" I asked of a young man, who shivered in his boxer shorts.

"Puppets, lobsters, pills," he explained. "Some patients experienced brief mustaches with vertigo."

"I say," I said. "Have you yet found your lobster?"

"Lobster! Lobster ho!" cried someone from within where a stand of pines transitioned into a marshy streamlet of the bay.

I followed them into the dark stand of pines. Just inside, a lobster stirred within a puddle. Its movements were slow—enfeebled as if hampered by the consumption of wine, whiskey, or other such spirits. Had this lobster been drugged? Or, was the world its pill?

The streamlets of Blueport Bay being so heavily polluted with industrial waste. It clumsily pecked a hoagie, which possessed constellations of green mold that were emboldened by the new moon and the bioluminescence of the lobster's swimmeret claw. It directed the chanting of our throng with its huge pincer. Its radiating bioluminescence of green and fuchsia pulsed to the cadence of the syllables of the throng. They still converged upon it like actors breaking slightly from their sleepwalker roles.

"Bring me a new drug, O' Lobster!"

A woman stripped herself of her brazier. She spun as if a bludgeoned, barfing ballerina and winced at the stars before attempting to divine where she had come to be. "Pinch not these nipps, O Lobster! Bring me a drug to still my torso. Bring RTS!"

They had heard of the forthcoming Restless Torso Syndrome medication! Although they stumbled, swinging their hands at gnats and mosquitoes, they walked with a definite purpose.

"Let religion be one with commerce, O' Lobster! Lemme re-up on your pharma!"

"The lobster does not own pharmaceuticals," I said.

"Shhhhh!" the humans shushed me.

"What? People do not require more drugs, they require less. However, my employment is at great odds with this."

LobStars within the crowd turned to me and focused their drugged attention my way. "Interloper! Accursed one!" Their mouths slowly turned out the mantras of their unspeakable, synthetic chemicals.

Only a few higher-ranking LobStars had had the presence of mind to slap on the vestment of their wooden lobster claw helmets. Some had facial tics to mark each of their malfunctions. My displeasure with their foolish happenstance and their hungry stupidity grew, splintered and was made manifest by each passing second. Those in wooden lobster claw helmets scrounged the marshy floor for littered pieces of white and pink plastic and lurched forward as if to present them to their lobster. This was simply too much.

The hypocrisy of their wooden lobster helmets clashed with the unnatural scavenged plastic they now wielded. They were just like Root Beer, looking for any escape from a straight and narrow path. And some of them did duckface as if to give the lobster their kisses. Had they planned this ritual? Was it spontaneous? The priests held much of LobStarism in secret. It was said by some that these priests held many secrets of life and the unknown, and that they bathed in melted butter and threatened each other in elaborate jousting matches involving giant lobster forks and claw crushers.

"Fools! Sleepwalking-Lobster-Lovers! I steal away the hoagie of your messiah!" I ran in and snatched the hoagie from the lobster's claw.

"Get him!" "That soulless puppet, catch it!"

I fled for my Vespa with their hoagie.

"Carbs are super-important for lobsters and their marshy friends!"

"I flee, humans. You will never catch me."

After a treacherous chase, involving several buses and railcars I made it back to my abode with the sensation of being almost completely unfollowed.

"Did you have fun with your Vespa, honey?" Stephy said in the entryway, cradling our sleeping Integrevy.

"Yes, woman. I stole away this hoagie from a drugged cult. They have heard of RTS. They think they need the RTS pill."

"Of course, they need it." She stroked the 'I' of Integrevy as Polydimethylsiloxane nuzzled around her leg. "It's medicine. Why wouldn't they need medicine?"

"I stole away their sacrament."

"Here. It stinks." She walked to the kitchenette trashcan. "Let me toss it."

"What? No. What if they track me and demand its return."

"Huh? No way. LobStars are way random. They'll just pass out somewhere and get a breakfast taco and a coffee in the morning, honey."

"You always know how to comfort me."

We stood over the trashcan as it hid the LobStar's moldy hoagie. Over my shoulder the front door stood ominously still. They might be advancing on me, presently. To sleep, I needed to sleep, but so many questions pestered me from the heightened delirium of the fight with Stephy and the Vespa ride and the LobStars and their chanting and their needs.

"Stephy," I asked. "Be the LobStars, as it is told, be they made of stars?"

"I doubt it," she said. "Everybody knows most of the Universe is made of dark matter. So, like, duh, puppets and people are dark matter."

"And what is this dark matter that puppets and people are made of?"

"Like, I feel like, dark matter is like regular matter, only not as bright—darker, you know?"

"Do you there designate evil?"

"No, just, like, darker, okay?"

"And what are you, Stephy?"

"I'm a vegetable."

"A vegetable?"

"When I dream," Stephy said. "I dream a lot about being a vegetable. A green one with, like, some leaves. I don't know why. When I'm a puppet, I dream about being a plastic vegetable."

"A plastic vegetable? That cannot reproduce."

"Yeah, I think it might have something to do with that."

"Indubitably."

"Felty—"

"Yes, Stephy?"

"You can't let me turn into a puppet again. You can't let me be a plastic vegetable."

"I shall endeavor towards my best," I said. The difference between her womanhood and my puppet-hood forced me to look up to her as we stood near the trashcan. "Bernack, from work, he told that after we severed his puppet string and gave him six puppet fingers, it allowed him to dive deeper into his work."

"What's he do again?"

"A statistician is he. He told of a dive into the numbers and the data from our PC trials for different drugs. After this data-dive he grew dubious of the number four—"

"The number four?"

"Yes, madam. When he sees the number four in data sample-size and in variables, suspicion grows. He believes the number four is the evidence of evil, human tampering—"

"He believes, or *you* believe?"

"It stems from the human's early obsession with the harvest and its four seasons. We are sewn after the humans. This number four cannot be pushed fully away from us. Look at the walls of this room—manmade—each wall has four, *equal* right-angles."

"I don't like where this is going."

"Nature has no perfect right-angles. Nature makes no shapes of perfect equality."

"You're a fool, Felty. What about crystalline structures? Plenty of molecular bonds form at near-perfect right-angles!"

"Those are not alive, woman. There, magic went missing. Do you honestly believe that a puppet, such as I, who was once inanimate and now lives would not understand the innermost secrets of life?"

"You," she towered over me and poked me in the chest, "can sleep on the couch."

"Zorf—!"

"Zorf yourself."

"Under the bed, I sleep."

"What?" she asked. "Why?"

"It displeases you," I said. "I can fit!"

26

"When I first treated my RTS, what my doctor called Restless Torso Syndrome," Nagarazim said, "Silence, I am reading the lines…I worried *Arrnomova* might interfere with my RLS medications—"

"Cut!" Eyeam jumped from its director chair, crossing within the hologram of Nagarazim. "This puppet has no legs. How can he have Restless Leg Syndrome?"

"If perhaps however even through the course of due time and through the employment of some appropriate purchase of *GMO-Froggy Style*…"

"Quiet!"

"However, *Froggy Style*…"

"Adjust your teleporter. Crop above the waist." Eyeam turned over his shoulder.

I sat in a high-back leather chair of the Bayside Superego Boardroom, or what some felties referred to reverently as the BSB. Eyeam also had a Superego badge, which it clipped to the green fur of its breast. It had not questioned me when I presented Stephy's, shiny Superego badge even though it had expected to meet her outside.

Knowing full well that Eyeam was a rule-breaker, when pressed, I admitted freely I was there to impersonate Stephy. When its hackles rose, I believe it was not due to loyalty but to a sense of annoyance of no longer being the only non-human allowed in the BSB. And watching it pace before its director's chair, there was a sense Eyeam had been a fixture of the BSB long enough to provide comfort and continuity to the humans.

It whispered, "Where'd you find these sock-puppets? Cut-rate."

"Comrades, they are. Services offered at deep discount."

Eyeam knitted his green-tufted eyebrows. "Eyeam keeps the spread under the table?"

"Affirmative," I said. "This could be your action."

Eyeam squinted and leaned forward. "Missing legs."

"Not missing balls, like this one," retorted Nagarazim.

"That stitching, pedestrian. We're not trying to win second prize in a backwoods county fair." Eyeam chomped on its cigarette holder. "What else ya got?"

"Bring forward Matchy." I lit Eyeam's cigarette. "Matchy, you will do your part."

"Tell it to read from here." It sipped mineral water, gazed out the windows toward the cresting waves and fidgeted to clean the grape jelly and crumbs off the script.

"Matchy," I said, "start with the top of page two."

Matchy stood and strode straight toward the lens of the teleporter. "Ka-blamo!"

"CUT!" It bolted up.

"What?" I asked. "Eyeam opposes 'ka-blamo?' This is what Matchy does. Ka-blamo is his catch-phrase, sung from his soul-center."

"No." Eyeam scampered toward the bay window of crashing emerald waves. It crept so close its words steamed the windowpane. "No ka-blamo. No *he*. Not on camera. We're selling dodgy pharmaceuticals. There's no room for gender."

"Why should Matchy not act from his puppetful truth?" I asked.

"There's no room for it." Eyeam searched the windowpane as if inspecting for a weakness. The scent of the ocean grew, streaming in from some wave and perhaps passed through a crevice in that window. Lobsters, scallops, seaweed stunk as if piled into the boardroom corners. The scent struck like a swinging baseball bat of funk, old grimy green from the sea.

How could these scents move (so serpentine-like) with their premeditated violence? This scent had been making its appearance at about the same time, each month, and others had declared that Blueport Bay had done this since the LobStars first discovered it. It was as if the bay would cast off its deep lining so life could grow forth anew from its maritime uterus. There was no escaping this cycle of death and rebirth.

"So many years," it said, clamping its orange nose so that its voice rose: "There was a time I was free. There was a time I dreamt of a hole in that fence I could slip under at night, or something else foolish. Puppets are here for the dirty work humans cannot stomach. We sell them their lies back to them. That's the way of it. If your Matchy acts masculine, it's gonna resonate with the masculinity of male viewers and the femininity of female viewers."

"So?"

It released its nose and turned toward me. "That reminds them of bodies, physical bodies that feel, physical bodies that know what brains cannot. If they get reminded of physical bodies, what next?

I'll tell ya: they plug into ancient truths of what bodies need. The exercise. The nutrients. The love. The sunlight.

"No.

"We'll never cap a capsule. Prepubescent 's the prescription. Give Eyeam a monster. Give Eyeam a *childish* monster! Take the audience back to the innocence of a child.

"See?

"Then they can't access an adult's reason. Do what monsters do. Act in ways that don't exist. Realness can't be judged that way. Which of you puppets can do it like *this?*"

"We do not understand," Matchy said. "We puppets yearn toward human realness."

"I said the part requires double-cogito breakdown," Eyeam said. "Don't be tempted by the truths of angles, geometry—huh!—*philosophical rigor.* A spokes-puppet ain't got that kind a' time. If the truth of the cogito is seeing a sales-pitch clearly and distinctly, my spokes-puppet must obscure and make itself indistinguishable. Which of you can do that?"

The puppets of the apartment remained silent and still. Herbivore almost motioned to raise his hand but was socked hard in the stomach by Mr. Cavesicle. From the floor, Herbivore struggled to say, "Root Beer— Root Beer is a monster…"

"Root Beer is a masculine monster for good," Nagarazim said, "In point of fact he has a big dick, and is indisposed."

"Meeting adjourned!" Eyeam said. "We'll be in touch if we need anything. Log off and drop off."

"That was hasty," I said.

It turned to me. "You and I will star in the RTS commercial, together."

"Eyeam and me? Eyeam desires to change Felty into a monster?"

"Yes, for professional gain," Eyeam said. "You'll be my protégé, ya heard? Then I won't have to keep doing all these commercials myself." Eyeam paced the long boardroom. Its foot claws clicked against the marble. "We'll sample *Arrnomova* so we can speak from experience."

"Has regulatory approved?" I asked. "Is it safe?"

Eyeam turned and tilted its head with marked incredulity. "There's no regulatory for puppets." It dug through an old messenger bag on the table and withdrew a homemade pipe. "We gotta freebase the *Arrnomova* rocks directly. The capsules aren't ready. Hmmm, can't freebase on the PC campus. We'll delve deep into the woods of Power Island."

"Freebasing within Power Island's woods?" I asked. "Be these hours billable?"

It clutched its pipe. "To freebase is to bill hours."

"You are simply saying words."

It snatched its messenger bag. "Follow me, off…off, into the woods of Power Island."

"There have been reports of puppets swallowed whole into the dusty sand dunes near the center of the island," I said, "later recovered to find their faces frozen in felty agony." I waved my hand at Eyeam in an attempt to regain his attention. "I have heard tales of giant, six-pawed mountain lions, possessed of not one fear. Eyeam? Eyeam? And six-legged mountain lions are not known to walk in predictable ways. I hear they caper! Capering—insectile—mostly-mad mountain lions, shall this be our fate? Furthermore—pay, pay attention to me—I have heard it said the animals and plant life are drunk off the industrial waste that has spewed for generations from this PC complex. And if we know not the full dimensions of the PC complex. For example, does it have a second floor, or is the second floor a metaphor for something more, then how can we know how this complex connects with its surroundings?"

Eyeam stood and walked out from behind its chair.

"Eyeam wears pants now? Argyle golf pants?"

"They changed the dress code," Eyeam said. "Monsters are no longer allowed their nakedness." Eyeam practiced its tap-dancing with its claws clicking against the marble, staring up appreciatively toward some deity and praising this deity for a forthcoming boon. Its tap dancing reached a crescendo but it did not know how to bring it home so it looked up with surprising malice at this deity and mouthed words of blame and protest. And this disoriented me as I tried to decipher exactly who was at fault for this mistake made in its dancing.

• • •

We trekked and the pine trees blended into the tropical character of labyrinthine palm fronds. The howling, the shrieking in the treetops conspired. Owls bobbed their heads and spoke, *Ba-bonk, ba-bonk! Ga-gonk ga-gonk!*

Near the brush of a swampy gray puddle, a gaggle of gnats flew in drunken, conflicting figure-eights over felled prey, and we trudged on towards an eroded embankment where ancient tree roots exposed their mechanically and eerily-regular system of branching.

The air grew astringent with acrid chemical waste and the surroundings sang out an increasingly tropical siren in ways that also pulsed with synthetic stylings. From my childhood studies on Miltro's shelf, I had learned how the ancients of Pluralia had used a golden ratio, stolen from nature, for the building of their monuments and pyramids. This ratio, quite close to two-thirds, grew scarcer and scarcer as we ventured down a footpath, ingrown with green and pale-yellow ferns.

The spacing of leafstalks and leaflets, the patterns of that moss, the negative moonlit space of that canopy, all pulled toward a fifty-percent binary-ratio. Even the teal and turquoise lichen, which covered the tree trunks, spread upwards in ominous groupings of right angles and sharp corners. Far from the majesty of true wilderness it had been infected by the influence of an enfeebled, finite human mind. "Wilderness ain't what it used to be," Eyeam said. "Be warned, the scent of Blueport Bay's monthly menstruation tempts the alpha predators."

"I hear it is not only the natural scents that attract the alpha predators, but the unnatural. Raisin Eyes has told me that PC enjoys indulging in bulk discounts for commodities. He told me they got a bulk discount for the lid material. And they also got a discount to use the same active ingredient between *Powerstaccios II* and *Arrnomova*. The troubles of *Powerstaccios* may tag along for *Arrnomova*."

"That cannot be the case," Eyeam said.

"And why is this?"

"I eavesdropped on you and Raisin Eyes. After you had left I spoke to him. He admitted he was just speaking foolishly out of his ass and didn't know what he was talking about. You see, I'm looking out for ya."

"You are undone."

"How's that now?"

"It was not with Raisin Eyes I spoke. It was with The Monster Who Loves Gum."

"Who's that now?"

"Bernack, puppet."

"Oh," Eyeam said. "Dickweed."

We climbed a winding path toward a clearing where the tree canopy opened into a pixelated crescent shape. The clearing had a campfire in disuse, surrounded by a ring of stones, crumbling logs and half-consumed boxes of sugary cereals.

"Here is where we smoke rocks," Eyeam said.

"On the clock?"

"On the clock." It packed the pipe with rocks from its messenger bag and flicked at the felt wheel of a cheap cigarette lighter. "Stupid lighter," Eyeam said, "get...get my smoke on."

"Why does this form of *Arrnomova* resemble a street drug so closely?"

"The main ingredient," Eyeam said, "is love."

"Earnestly?"

"No."

"This engineer requires answers before freebasing."

Eyeam's hackles rose as its fangs protruded from out of its twisting mouthplate. "You smoke if I say smoke, toke if I say toke. The hitting of *Arrnomova* rocks is not no joke."

"However, my health."

"However, my health," Eyeam said, "Your health? a drug dealer's lost wealth. Here: hit this, puppet." Eyeam hit the pipe. "Ewww, ah-a-a shee-it. Let Eyeam explain it:

"Sometimes street drugs come out of retirement so they can be

Legitsville, again. This drug was a hit on the streets. Big Pharma wants another taste. It's been around so long, titrated so many times, nobody knows what it's derived from no more. The perfect drug. One-hundred-percent synthetic. They might as well have flown this drug in from outer space or an asteroid."

"However—again—puppet, my health."

"Exactly, puppet, if this were safe, they wouldn't need puppets. You wanna lose your job."

"Pass it here."

"Now how's that?"

"The fibers of my throat have caught fire."

"Put it out with good intentions."

"How?"

"Through this limerick: if six times six is thirty-six, purple pixie tits—"

"Enough! I am in pain. I need water."

"Didn't even listen to the end of it."

"My arms do not move."

"That's that *Arrnomova*. It relieves you of your restless torso."

"My torso is at ease," I said. "However, my legs are quite active."

"Mine too!" Eyeam said. "That extra energy flows into the legs. The researchers are still working out the kinks. Ouch! Stop. Stop head-butting me."

We had been head-butting each other, bent over, our arms dangling loosely below, like tiny bucks, competing for a mate.

"You—! You head-butt me!" I said.

"I'll slap you with one of my flappy arms!"

"It hurts me not, imbecile. Haha-hee-ho-ho."

"It don't hurt me no neither. Sitting on my own face."

"Your worldview is flabby. That face is the new moon through the canopy," I said.

"Yeah I'm gonna need to go ahead and breathe."

"Flap around. The situation will work out."

"Flapping. Flapping. Still flapping."

"Better?" I asked.

"Yeah, better. The energy dissipates itself out the legs. The best part about this drug is that the male puppets don't have to worry about being capable, whether they are controlling themselves, being controlled by someone else; or something—something else. The paralysis is so comfortably temporary, like sleep, a rainy day without responsibility. Do you feel? as it kicks up? Do you feel the stitching get up and dance along your seams? Do you feel the cotton quiver? Like it could burst in flames? This stuff is incapacitating. How could we be responsible for anything? Like… like for an instant we could be valued for what we are…not the nature of what we do. We could be valued for an essence that had inherent worth."

"However," I said, "Eyeam has never admitted to being a man."

"Grow up, FuzzPalace," Eyeam said. "Everyone knows I'm male."

"In earnest you say these words?"

"Earnestly—"

"Help! Ha—*haaah-haaa!*"

"Who said that?" I asked.

"Oh, thank the Great Lobster I found you two puppets." A bloody man in a blue athletic business suit staggered into our clearing. "I was…out exploring this path. A mountain lion…it-it attacked. It might still be…I'm…I'm bleeding. Hear? Hear it? It's near…I think."

"Who is that?" Eyeam asked.

"I'M CHARSON MURPHTON," Charson Murphton said. "The COO?"

Ha-derm-kaaa! cried the approaching animal. *Ha-derm-ka-kaaa!*

"We're freebasing, Charson," Eyeam said. "It might be that you're fucked."

"Arrnomova?"

"Yeah?" Eyeam said. "'Fraid so."

Ha-derm-kaaa! Ha-derm-ka-kaaa!

"Oh, no! Can't get…I can't get cell reception. Did you hear that? There it was again!"

"Have you met Felty FuzzPalace, Charson?"

"I'm dying. Is this…is this an intestine? How—*ahhh!*—how do you do?"

"Charmed," I said.

"Ahhhh—!"

"How can this drug take away all feelings?" I asked. "How can it take away all morality?"

"Morality hides in your feet," Eyeam said. "That's why your toes tap."

"Oh."

"When I was a child," Charson said, "I dreamed I would be COO—the best COO. The best COO… Then it came true. A mountain lion bit out my stomach…just left with two, indolent puppets."

"That's unfair, Charson," Eyeam said. "Everyone's got a job. Our job is to get messed up on these rocks."

"I-I don't think…I hear…it's closer. I don't think regulatory would let you guys smoke rocks. You were supposed to wait for the capsules."

"Well, Charson," I said. "Perhaps us puppets are more dedicated?"

"*Ahhhh—!* That can't be," Charson said. "That…puppets. Out-performed by puppets. Puppets with superior ambition? I worked so hard. I did what I was told. I-I always did what I was told. It can't end this way."

"I have been a man," I said. "I am aiming toward a puppet/man hybrid to derive the benefits of both."

Ha-derm-ka-kaaa! The man's screaming pitched-up as the insectile mountain lion set upon him. Its four paws pinned him as its two paws clawed. *Ha-derm-ka-kaaa!*

My face ended up rather close to the soil. The particles that made it happened to be composed of perfect polyhedral shapes. This was a letdown. The octahedron and icosahedrons were powder blue and the tetrahedron, the cube and the dodecahedron were a faint pink.

The soil consisted of these finely granulated, perfect geometric pellets. Their facets glistened like large sand granules, yet they squished with such softness. They resembled the pixilated flowers. Had Nature herself given up, owing to under-appreciation? I blamed religion for this predicament and asked, "Eyeam?"

"Yes, fool."

"You are an immortal puppet?"

"You know it."

"Do you hold stock in LobStarism?"

"It's not fair to ask Eyeam that when it's messed up."

"You do not need to keep referring to yourself as an *it.*"

"Aspects of LobStarism are true. Crustaceans are superior

to humans. An exoskeleton is more honest than an endoskeleton. An exoskeleton is more reliable. An exoskeleton admits the world is dangerous and must be met with hardness. Humans are always trying to pretend the world can be a place where softness is accepted. An exoskeleton doesn't change at all until it's defeated. When an exoskeleton is defeated, it's over quickly and finally. No fuss. Less suffering. I've seen so many humans tortured while their skeletons remain safely inside, nearly unused. Sometimes I think maybe humans are a hiccup before the evolution."

"Is it raining?" I asked.

"It's blood."

"Oh, my…oh, dear."

The COO squirmed. "Never. Setup. My. Voicemail."

"I am ashamed to admit that a part of me hates the humans," I said. The sensation was returning to my arms so that I could wipe the blood of the COO off my face. "And I do not know why. Perhaps the drug quickens my honesty. The humans built me in their image. This was their vanity. And I sense, when I see myself in the mirror, that they held parts back in their creation of me. They constructed me as a caricature of themselves. They did not give me the full gift of their humanity. Now I must be several different things, none of which can be pure, true or at peace with each other. What is purely me was not left uncorrupted by the diluted part given by them. My soul is untidy. Since the soul lacks extension and substance, no hands can fix it."

"It's okay, Felty." It hid its face by glancing groundwards. "Over the years, sometimes it seems, the pump of a puppet heart can be a patchwork of fabrics, kludged from whatever was on-hand at the time."

"Do you think that that might be the point of all this?"

"What are you talking about?"

"Perhaps Certi intends to market *Arrnomova* to puppets for the purpose of disabling our ability to empathize. We just watched a man die. I did nothing. I felt nothing. I feel the drug wearing off now. The critical moments of that man's death were wasted in pure introversion. This has never happened to me before. Maybe Certi intends to market *Arrnomova* to puppets since she knows that if felties cannot feel they cannot man-up?"

"There's still paychecks coming, puppet. Sorry, my *Arrnomova* hasn't worn off."

"Do you think the insectile mountain lions will be interested in eating us?" I asked.

"Do not man-up. They cannot smell puppets," Eyeam said. "We'll be safe."

27

After hours, I had taken to work in the easy chair of Miltro's workshop with my laptop on a nearby pillow, watching teleporter programs, drinking wine. This was not efficient.

I was determined to finish the lid design for the RTS vacuum chamber despite the fact Certi had lost enthusiasm for the project. She might assign it to another engineer. I could not let this happen. This was puppet-pride. Puppet-pride knows it is not inventive of anything however it is the crank that gets things done, mechanically, without acknowledgment of the possibility of cessation.

The computer-aided drafting package we used at PC refreshed slowly through the VPN connection. Every edge and machining operation were a potential failure. Yet possibilities housed themselves in a multitude of forms. This was my chance to puppet something, to pull strings on something, even if that something was merely an inanimate object. Yet are not all objects inanimate before imbued with creative spirit. The right shape, the right material, the right components, the right processes; how could we machine that lid?

The teleporter flickered on of its own, mysterious intention.

The holographic visage of Miltro appeared within a gaggle of *Not-So-Hard Boulevard* puppets; he interrupted their dance number, on a faux-subway soundstage. His triathlon running gear clashed among the caricatured construction workers and stereotyped business-puppets as he shone without any digital artifacts with his long beard blowing in a breeze.

"Stephy, there is a ghost in my machine."

"Is it your father again?" she asked. "Change the channel, honey."

"I believe so." He had haunted me six times that past week. "I think I left the remote in the master suite."

"If you don't get up, I guess you'll get haunted."

"Fine."

"Felty-*Fe-elty!*"

"What is it, my father?"

"I don't have much time, Felty-*Fe-elty!*"

"Push your point."

"Avenge me-*me!*"

"Why?"

"What did you say-*say?*"

"Why must I avenge you?"

"I made you to avenge me."

"I thought you made me to earn extra money and as a break from your piloting job."

"Creation is complicated."

"Let me ask, Father, have you ever been a puppet?"

"Can't say that I have."

"That is complicated, too, Father. What I am struggling with is a war between autonomy and authority, between the group and the individual. I have important decisions verging on my horizon in which lives may be at stake. I fear strings will descend on me at precisely the moment when I must make a crucial decision regarding the safety of this new lid. We purchased too much of the wrong material so we must either make it from inferior stuff or abandon the project. It will be possible to make the lid just strong enough, so long as only a few stand on it at once. We may be able to rollerskate for a couple years until PC can afford to purchase new lids. Even with the advent of Finite Element Analysis, engineering calculations are not nearly more accurate than plus or minus ten percent of any variable. Determining service loads and conditions is like gazing into a crystal ball. Any advice?"

"Can't say I'd be much help. Let me ask you, real quick, how is Root Beer?"

"Root Beer is hurting. And it is hurting us."

"Oh," Miltro said. "When I was sewing Root Beer, I was on a bender of way more than root beer. It was dark, I couldn't see what my fingers were doing, didn't really have a plan for that one, threw-up while finishing that brain, actually. Root Beer is the shadow; you are the light. The light must cast the shadow."

"Root Beer is bad?"

Miltro recoiled, his ghostly vapor flickered off, briefly, as the felties considered whether to restart their dance number. "He's darker. Unknown. You have to illuminate him. Don't you judge him. Don't you dare judge *me!*"

"Ah…right."

"Got turned around on my run. Do you know where Bliss Street, Dimension Double-ZZ is?"

"The signage of the nether-regions are not congruent with the living."

"Okay then. Carry on."

"Always good to hear from you. Glad to see you in good death."

It was a shame that my maker was so handy with a needle and thread and yet not skilled in the matters of engineering. Would we use a waterjet? That would only be accurate to plus or minus five-thousandths of a duckbill, even though the vendors online bragged that their waterjets could be accurate to one-thousandth of a duckbill.

The vendors were falsely referring to the positioning of the waterjet head and not the final accuracy of the finished lid. And, in this way, there were many distinctions. Many coworkers, professionals, and companies preyed on the ignorance of others and hoped to hock their inferior wares and ideas. Who stood against them if not me? It was an endless quest for perfection against an imperfect world. Perhaps a chamfer of thirty degrees on the topside would help with the sealing issue. And the aspect ratio—

"FuzzPalace?"

"Yes, DinoMan?"

"Why have I not turned back into a puppet, like you?"

"Do you want to be a puppet again?"

"I miss it," DinoMan said. He practiced with a bullwhip while dressed in his man-sized tuxedo and attempting to lash the tops of the book stacks. "I miss the mechanical nature of it, the feeling that my only responsibility was to fight against the world in an unfair contest. Now I am bigger, more capable. Everyone who sees DinoMan runs in fear or stares in awe. I should become a politician."

"Which office would you seek?"

"Mayor of Blueport Blues. My platform would be cold-blooded."

"Explain," I said.

"First, I would seek to help my comrades here at the apartment—"

"Help the felties?" I asked. "Why should they need help? They are paid an allowance. This provides them with food, housing, enough left over to squish."

"They may use their allowance to purchase the love of squishies in town who are of ill-repute," DinoMan said. "Meaningless charity and purchased love are not enough. They need real love, real work."

"Give it time," I said. "Things will improve."

"The felties, again, vomit felt," DinoMan said. "The carpet is covered in felt clumps. It is time for a change. I must campaign for my comrades."

"Why not lead by example?" I asked. "You could have been more willing—all could have been more willing—when I attempted to secure us with an acting gig for the *Arrnomova* commercial. Why jump off the deep end with a long-range scheme to change the whole world."

"Skeleton!" cried DinoMan.

"Yes, my friend," Skeleton said.

"How many times have you barfed up felt today?"

"Three times, my friend."

"And why do you barf felt, Skeleton?" DinoMan asked.

"Because the world turns, and I stay stuck to it, my friend."

"See, FuzzPalace! They are depressed."

"I will not listen to any more nonsense," I said. "I offer you a solution, you offer a long-range gamble. If the Felties wish to rebound from a slump, take a small step first. Set your morals a little to the left, star in the *Arrnomova* commercial. I think I could convince Eyeam and the others to let all of us star in one long commercial. If one spokes-puppet is convincing, think how all of us would convince the humans?"

"We do not believe what Eyeam believes about the drugs," Skeleton said. "We were made too simple to tell lies."

"Tell the truth. Tell the only truth you can tell," I said. "However, first, get all the money that is offered. Meet the world where it is, then move it. Do you fancy I always enjoy my employment?"

"Then, we will get stuck," Skeleton said, "tangled in strings all the time, just like Felty does."

"Spokes-puppets are free as bees in trees. Having strings, from time to time, is not all that bad. The strings connect you to a higher intelligence, hold you on a narrower path so you can travel farther."

"Do you think we could be real spokes-puppets, FuzzPalace?"

"Five-hundred boom-bills, a puppet, a minute, for a two-minute spot," I said. "We could afford a down payment on a condo, downtown. We could strut around like the humans do, get combs for our mustaches."

"Some of us lack mustaches."

"We could sew them on! Will you not at least reconsider the prospect?" I said. "Miltro Miggugen sewed us for a purpose. That purpose was to persuade humans to part with their money. If we do not explore the purpose for which we were built, we may never feel complete."

"Your plan gains interest in my mind," DinoMan said.

"Blerch!" Skeleton blerched. "That felt had some spicy."

Root Beer waltzed into the workshop, accompanied by Richnuss. They wore silver pinstriped business suits and their motions and mannerisms appeared synchronized as if originating from

Richnuss. No stringed relationship was visible yet the half-light of the workshop exaggerated the shadowy contortions of their expressions.

I exhaled, took a bracing sip of wine and sunk deeper into the easy chair. DinoMan spun and brandished his bullwhip as if he might lash. However, I motioned for him to hold off. "Why provide a treacherous loser admittance into the workshop?" I asked Root Beer. "That attire was not provided by your maker."

"Listen to our proposal," Root Beer said.

"No," I said.

"I provided for you when you sought your job," Root Beer said. "You promised me, if fortune misplaced me, you would not."

"I can get you guys out of this apartment," Richnuss said, "into something nicer. I can set you felties up and get you established in the community. The first form to fill out—"

"No," I said. "Root Beer, how did your paths again cross with this villain? Answer me! Remove that business suit. Adorn your shoulders with your wizard robe. Your magic originates only from that threadbare fabric. Your pingpongs have not ionized in ages. Root Beer! Answer me. When did your paths first cross with Richnuss?"

Root Beer pulled wrinkles from his miniature business suit. His monster paws were manicured yet he had been biting his claws. He kicked the ground. "About a month ago, Richnuss came by my stand to have his fortune told."

"And not soon after, this nonsense with the identity crisis. You have been experimenting with drugs, seeking mentors, changing professions—this midlife crisis must end."

"He flattered me, that day he asked I should tell his fortune. He paid double the usual fee. I was obliged to venture deeper in my search. The inner workings of humanity are not suited for such exploration, and I have not given one, true and faithful, fortune telling since. His mind outpoured an ocean of error. In those errors lay the strength, the creativity of beginnings. I learned there was pleasure in the pain of others—"

"Stop there, puppet."

"Hear him out, FuzzPalace!" Richnuss said.

"You are an unwanted pest."

"For my fortune telling, I asked merely to hold the business card of Richnuss so I might touch the wear of its edges. No sooner had I done this than the reverie shrunk me, infinitesimally, to the size of a molecule of testosterone. I sojourned through in search of some androgen receptor to replenish. In this frightening journey, time and space lost all meaning. Beyond those hues of red were also dimensions of chemical, ancient forces. We cannot argue with these binary states. Nothing and something, plus and minus. They alone led my path to fulfill my duty. And through this, my path was led to the place in the body of greatest disrepair, greatest want, greatest hunger. And it was then I knew, the weakness was the man, the hunger, the strength, the ill, the good. Friends, it is through the baseness of our hunger we find our victory."

"Your heart spills lies like a constipated vulture," I said. "Let the remainder spill, the city's municipal engineers require their job security."

"Fluff you!" Root Beer said. "Here goes medicine."

"A turd's panacea."

"Good and evil: outmoded fairy tales sung by the weak and the lethargic in the throes of a drunken, ill-DJ'ed karaoke party.

A true puppet finds the strongest string, lets that string tug him forward. Friends, friends, friends, why do your eyes look away? find medicine here. We have tried it your way, FuzzPalace. First, the fabric of the couch sung secrets. Next, *Zokithral* shone a light for felty feet. Now an opportunity in *Arrnomova* rocks presents itself. I know about the RTS project at Power Chemicals. It is not merely the humans whose torsos grow restless. Felty, it is also us puppets!"

"Silence," I said, "your words disturb air."

"Through the aid of Richnuss's distribution, we can sell the *Arrnomova* rocks directly on the street to both puppet and human, alike. Think of the profit."

"I will have no part in it. Other opportunities exist. In your speech, you forgot the freewill of the mind, there magic snoozes on an uncomfortable bed."

"What if my magic should not choose to snooze? I will hit these streets and turn out a profit that makes bankers look like bookends. I will make your eyes water from the riches. Lingering on the petulance of your apathy: that'll make you less happy."

"Wealth is in the soil and in the air," I said. "It is in the pizza crust of a forgotten friend that we once both loved. Hear me? No, you do not hear me. Well, listen to this: one of my work associates, Raisin Eyes, told me once of a felty that lived long ago, named Willox the Waterer. Have you heard of him? Of course not. No. Seal your trap. This puppet was built decades ago by a master, just simply toying with the essence of the fabrics.

"In this way, Willox was built without a discernible intention and so he was not missed after his escape from his master. Willox soon learned he was quite the dancer. In exchange for dancing, he earned bottled water from gas station attendants who found him amusing. And this was all he required, this and the sun, for his feet were like the roots of plants, soaking minerals with each and every barefoot step. In this way he knew everything about the places he visited.

"Yes, yes, I will tell it. Because his tingling feet told him the best jokes he was always laughing. He found he could not bear to see misery in others while he smiled and while his feet were telling him such good jokes. It rained often then, and so he soon had a stockpile of bottled water he did not need. This he gave to the beggars at the intersections of the streets. In this way, his nature unfolded as Willox the Waterer.

"All puppets speak of him, even while he has perished so long ago. I only speak of this folk hero because I have long held (even though I hardly believe in such fables) that you are the reincarnation of Willox the Waterer. Root Beer, who longs to intoxicate, intoxicate through some charity, or that part of you, the best part, shall perish quickly."

"Willox the Waterer?" Root Beer said. He shook some hypnosis off his face. "Nonsense. The nonsense of a bumbler. Of course, I, too, have heard of Willox the Waterer. Streets talk, puppet. And, no, I could never be Willox, or of his ilk. His suspenders were red. Do you not see? And his hair, a tacky red crewcut, not the beautiful red cornrows, which a former girlfriend gave. Willox, huh—tut tut—Willox the Waterer. Do you know why they truly called him The Waterer? He drowned fleeing men, women and children in the battle of '27, right here in Blueport Bay. There is doubt? I shall put links in the description down below—"

"This is not a video for the Inter-webs," I said. "Puppet, you need your rest."

"Regardless, the water bottle charity was simply window dressing for a despot's legacy. And does Felty know that Willox's hair was not even truly red, like mine, but rather it was dyed, dyed with the freshly spilled blood of humans. Huh! your saint. However I do not despise him. I respect him, as a fool such as yourself cannot. And as for his feet drinking the minerals of the earth, this too is superstition. As the legend gets passed down, some have mistaken what they have overheard. As it is told, sometimes, Willox's feet are referred to as trees. The correct word is *T's*. His feet were actually in the shape of T's. This made it hard for him to walk, and this spurred his hatred for mankind—"

"You lie."

"Look, behold how wide DinoMan's eyes grow. He enjoys my side of the story. And yet, which is correct. With such feeble minds keeping score over less than one century, how could morality exist?

"No, Willox and I are not kindred spirits. His color is red; mine is that purple. Red, the color of gluttons, of blood fresh from the heart. Purple, yes, as I have hungered, purple is the color of hunger, the color that longs to return to the heart. And I long to return, puppet, yes, to my rightful home."

"Remember the good times," I implored. "Remember how you used to tell the fortunes of the lowliest insects and the plants before you found your lucrative talent with humans. You smiled more then. You are dehydrated. You need to be replenished through good food and rest."

Root Beer hunched his back. "Yes…*yes*."

"Let's go, Root Beer," Richnuss said. "These puppets can't see a good partnership when it slaps 'em in the face." He put his hand on the shoulder of Root Beer, and the two waltzed out.

"Wait," Richnuss said. "What is that?"

"He is Integrevy," I said. "He is my son."

"Kill it quick."

"We shall love him. He shall bring out the best in all of us. And he shall find his greatness."

"Why?" Richnuss asked.

"For mercy. For compassion."

"I spoke with Stephy on my way in," Richnuss said. "She wants more out of life than this."

"You do not speak to her. Ever."

"Right, puppet."

And those fools laughed at me before they waltzed out.

28

"I heard you think you'll star your felties in the RTS commercial," Certi said to me. "If you expect to get 'em on the air, I'll need eight percent of residuals." She leaned forward on her stool that lined the kitchenette bar and gestured with her spoon as it brimmed with oatmeal. I thought maybe she had spotted Integrevy as he rested on the family room couch. However, Certi played her cards close.

"Do not talk with your mouth full, Mother," I said. "Finish chewing your oatmeal, your blueberries. The felties will finish gathering the last of your items from the master suite."

"This…this is what I need," Certi said, "I told Headless Boardsman I was gonna Slow-Carb it but you know how sometimes you know that you know…you know? Mmmmm, blueberries make my clit hard."

"I think the felties, and I could agree to five percent of residuals if a couple bus passes were thrown in."

Certi stopped chewing and scratched the corner of her mouth. "Fuck you."

Stephy elbowed her and they exchanged a knowing glance.

"You said the little one wanted to negotiate."

"PUUUUSH."

"Miltro stay outta this," Certi said. She leaned in and covered her mouth. "He had plenty of time to *puuush* while he was alive. No— Okay, I'll go to seven. Only because I think you look cute," she curled her finger at me, "in your little, little suit."

"That is belittling."

"Felty!" cried Stephy.

"We will have sexy-times?"

She nodded.

"Very well." I clanked my spoon in its bowl. "Have the papers drawn up. I will give them to Nagarazim to sign."

"Get real," Certi said. "We're not done here. Not by a cricket's crag."

"Cricket's crag?" I asked. "Whatever do you mean?"

"Whatever do you mean?" Certi asked. "That's not how business gets done. You think I'm some gullible jerk, eh? You think I'll let loose a' my moose? Not while cradling a kilo-*snizzum*, okay? We're not done. How do I know your puppets got it?"

"Got it?" I asked. "The point has puddled."

"It!" Certi said. "Star-power! Are they made from the right stuff? Are they made from stars?"

"Stephy, several days prior, you informed me not a soul was made from stars," I said. "You said souls sprung from a darker matter. Dark matter, I believe."

"Ha ha ha," Stephy laughed nervously. "No I did not, Felty. Don't be silly. Tell Certi about your felties."

"How can I prove we are worthy of being your spokes-puppets?"

Certi threw her spoon in its bowl. "There's just one way."

"Which is?"

"Dance party."

"Dance party?"

"Yes, puppet," Certi said. "They better dance good. I better get giggles."

"Felties," I cried, "assemble."

Out came Matchy, out came Herb, out came Skeleton, and Mr. Cavesicle, and Piss Ant and several stool stackers that nobody liked. Their eyes slit close as they beheld Certi with bewilderment. Several chased falling dust motes with their felty tongues.

"What is the big idea," Herbivore asked. "We were napping, it was naptime." He spun his head theatrically: *"NAPTI-IME!"*

"Naptime no more," I said.

"Our naps we need."

"Certi is here," I said. "She asks for a demonstration of your dancing to know if we are worthy spokes-puppets."

"Spokes-puppets?" Herbivore asked. "Felties?"

"Indeed," I said. "Wait. Why does Piss Ant scurry beneath the family room's couch?"

"He fears to dance," Herbivore said.

"Then dance…dance, he must," I said.

"Why must he dance?"

"Because puppet," I said (and I turned to Nagarazim, who had joined us), "YOLQ!"

Nagarazim strutted atop his green and bluish frog legs. The *GMO-Froggy Style* sung its influences within him. However, since the confidence of his stolen credit card had caused him to buy the legs, a *Credit* string had descended onto his back and strung him up at all times. The pride of his new legs had caused him to become more fervent regarding our traditions, and so I anticipated he would enjoy this YOLQ.

"YOLQ?" Herbivore asked. "No, not YOLQ. It is too dangerous."

"Yes YOLQ," I said.

"What is this YOLQ?" Certi asked. "Like yolk? Like an egg's yolk? I don't get it."

"YOLQ woman," I said, sneering (for now it was serious), "Ye Only Live Quattro."

"Quattro?" she asked. "What?"

"Four times, bitch, pay attention."

"Well I hardly see what" —inaudible stammering— "and if puppets think they can act a certain way."

"My apologies, madam," I said, "I do get caught up when I discuss the YOLQ" —I gestured toward us puppets— "YOLQ is the way of us puppets. For we only live four times. Yes—lo—four puppet poos do demarcate our existence. Our metabolism is slower. Four poops, and we die. It is like seasons, you see."

"YOLQ, YOLQ, YOLQ!" they chanted.

"No," Herbivore said, "The YOLQ is too extreme. We must reconsider. Remember what happened to the first puppets we YOLQed?"

"Sock puppets," I said, "unworthy of our time. Time pours through our hapless fingers. All have seen the problems with Piss Ant. He is an older puppet. He has already had his springtime poo. However, his summer poo he, too, must do," I said. "It has begun. Look, the puppets gather behind you. Look how they begin their dance. Behold their four-count zombie-walks in the tight, trapezoid formation." They rearranged by their primary colors, bounced in counteracting lockstep. They spun; they leapfrogged each other. They contracted the stink leg, as was the fashion of those times.

"Bring forth the Ark of the Puppets!" cried Nagarazim.

Felties scampered off to the closet of the master suite to fetch the Ark.

Their jazz hands drew out crescents and the clap-steps began:

"Once for fear,

 Once for fun!

 Once for fame,

 Once for shun."

"YOLQ, YOLQ, YOLQ!"

"Ye only live four times!"

"YOLQ, YOLQ, YOLQ!"

"Two times two is fine!"

The felties bobbled their way back in, hoisting that ornate, shimmering chest above their shoulders through the aid of aluminum poles strung along its sides.

"That's my jewelry chest," Certi said.

"She besmirches the Ark!" a felty cried. He charged into Certi's knee but was kicked to the ground.

"Watch it," Certi said.

"Bring Piss Ant here," I said. "So, we might YOLQ him!"

"YOLQ, YOLQ, YOLQ!" They bounced. A band broke off and dispatched for Piss Ant. Cries and protestations came from beneath the couch. A throng of felties hoisted him above their heads and shoulders as his four legs and two arms kicked, and he screamed, and the throng brought him nearer.

"PUUUUSH," echoed a voice that was more sinister and distinct.

"Miltro?" Certi asked. "What are you trying to say?"

Nagarazim hopped towards the Ark with his *Credit* string bouncing him higher. He ran his fingers appreciatively over the lid's ornate carvings with his eyes closed:

"Golden treasure—"

"Golden treasure!"

"Of puppet's pride—"

"Of puppet's pride!"

"But is there something—"

"But is there something!"

"Mechanical inside—?"

"Mechanical inside?"

The lid of the Ark flung back and arched open with sparkles. Nagarazim dug his hands through strings of pearls, diamond earrings and ruby brooches to reveal the crusty towel.

"The Crusty Towel," said a felty. "My eyes have seen it." His head bobbled, and he swooned backward.

"The crusty towel!

So serious now,

His eyes have seen it!

That brain believed it!

The crusty towel!

"Hmmmmm, hmmmmm!" we hummed. "Hmmmmm! Ah-hmmmmm—!"

Matchy hopped out from formation and sung:

"Let us unwrap this Crusty Towel, for it is our turn to YOLQ him now."

Piss Ant struggled. "No, no YOLQ. I do my part. I am as responsible as I need to be."

Someone from the above apartment stomped.

"Zorf!" I said as my armpits leaked. It was incomprehensible how afraid we puppets were of ceilings. Ceilings had the power to send strings to control us, and the sky, the ultimate ceiling, represented an ultimate mystery. My Lobster! when I think how I was begotten as a facsimile of something greater, it felt (oh, how it felt) each and every day, that these mysteries were a foe I could never outrun.

"STUPID PUPPETS!" a male voice shouted from above. "MAMA SAID PUPPETS CAN LIVE FIVE TIMES! Y'ALL DON'T KNOW A THING ABOUT YOURSELVES."

A felty caught some bad puppet-shivers, broke from formation, and started stammering out while gazing at the ceiling, "It is the Great Lobster in the Sky, by-and-by, The Great Lobster in the Sky says 'FIVE POOPS! FIVE POOPS, AND WE PUPPETS DO—DO DIE!'"

Nagarazim made a calming gesture. "Find thy magic. Stay the course. The YOLQ is the way of us. We have been over this. Even amid the stress of ceremony, the ceiling is not the heavens. Worship not ceilings. Let us commence."

"What's inside that crusty towel?" Certi asked. "Is it a weapon?"

"No more than a hammer hamms," I said. This was a truth. I could have described to her what lay beneath the towel, and yet to name the unnamable, to deprive mystery of its essence is one of the greatest of crimes.

She smiled. "Is it something sexy?"

"And where does that idea originate?" I asked.

"Maybe I should step out and get some air," Certi said.

"She does not leave!" I said.

"Let us unwrap this crusty towel,

It should have been washed,

It is sacred now."

And the crusty towel did unwrap and tremble in the sunlight to cleave cleanly from the fatigue of its fabric.

"I spy me the hieroglyphs," shouted a felty as his hackles rose. He got puppet-shivers and two-stepped, "All black, all black, inked in luxury."

"I spy me the pictographs," shouted another, and he humped the air: "Yeah yeah! Gimme that...that...that!"

"Yes," I said. "The chicken's egg is bedecked with wonder. Let us break the egg upon a fool. Who holds a fool?"

"WE HOLD A FOOL!"

"And the fool holds his stool?"

"THE FOOL HOLDS HIS STOOL!"

"MAMA SAID FIVE TIMES, PUPPETS!"

"PUUUUSH."

"No!" Piss Ant struggled. "I shit this morning. It was bigger than you, bigger than you, FuzzPalace!"

"LIAR!" I screamed. "WE YOLQ HIM!"

They lurched closer with the precious chicken's egg, inked in its necessary symbols of a great mystery:

Golden treasure—

Of puppet's pride,

But is there something—

But is there something!

Mechanical inside—

Mechanical inside!

"We all know what's inside that egg," Piss Ant shouted. "The YOLQ cannot change me. Nothing can."

"Piss Ant," I said, "I cast out every mystery, malice and mysticism from thy mind. Relent to the certainty of a mechanism.

We guileless puppets, made as a facsimile of man, must relent to a mechanism. Know your discipline. Yoke him with his YOLQ!"

The felties broke the egg over his forehead and the runny yolk ran over this anguished, teary-eyed face. And from out the runny protoplasm they retrieved a rusted skeleton key.

The rusted key,
Of egg's inside,
Yes, there was something—
Yes, there was something!
Mechanical inside—
Mechanical inside!

"Release him," I said.

He panted with his yellowish felt that was covered in yellow yolk, and his eyes darted at us.

"Present him with his rusted key," I said. "Piss Ant, most smelly, small, unbearable of all insects, we present thee with thy ceremonial key. Let thy peepers inspect how nature has its way with a mechanism. Thou know the drill."

Piss Ant nodded.

"Thou must eat it," I said, "or share it."

"And you wonder what next I do?" Piss Ant asked.

"No wonder remains," I said and yet I prepared my hand in case I should have to puppet-punch.

"And yet you wonder still, yes?"

"FIVE TIMES, PUPPETS!"

"FIVE?" I shouted back to the ceiling, "A FOOL'S NUMBER! Make thy move, Piss Ant."

"Look at yourselves," Piss Ant said, "mouths agape like guppies for the grinder. You wonder, you wonder what next I do. It is my choice."

"Dissemble no more, stringed insect."

"I eat it, FuzzPalace," Piss Ant said.

Gasps. "No!" someone said. "Then the key cannot appear within eggs yet to come."

"Piss Ant," I said, "please, please, please, let a noble nerd known only as Prudence tap on thy shoulder."

"You heard me, FuzzPalace, I eat it. I eat it, I eat it. I eat the rusted key."

"Piss Ant," I said, "the key is for sharing. Sharing is caring. Not pissing and swearing. That alone is the lesson. The rusted key has never, never been eaten. Reconsider, my friend."

"I am Piss Ant," he said, pointing his key at us, "Piss Ant is me; I eat the rusted key."

"No!"

He threw it into his mouth and swallowed it in a gulp.

Nagarazim's unblinking pingpongs egg-rattled as his neck pecked. Piss Ant staggered and caught himself. Then two ant feet tapped, impatiently. For some time, Piss Ant's yellowish felt had faded and blotched. It had grown matted, worn, nearly as crusty as the sacred towel. He had neglected his felt.

The yellow hue could be likened to spilled mustard, left to rot in a desert for decades. Suddenly, the pallor of his yellowish exoskeleton lightened, though not from mirth—huge, white blisters sprung up. His eyes winced, focused and unfocused as they traveled. These blisters grew and spread until all his felt lightened as if it were one blister. A smoother luster emerged. Sickly and wet no more, his shell quickened into lustrous silver, as if polished metal. "I have been a selfish, self-righteous ant," he said. "I do now relinquish my powers of piss." He stood straight so that the habit of hunching—bred from his master tying his knees and heart together—appeared unlearned.

"Huzzah!"

"YOLQ, YOLQ, YOLQ!"

Ye only live four times!"

"YOLQ, YOLQ, YOLQ!"

"Two times two is fine!"

"Now," Piss Ant said, "if it pleases Miss Klacard-Miggugen I would like to do my dance. It is not much, yet it is mine. If it entertains you, madam?"

Certi bit her lip. Her eyes focused as she wiped perspiration from her hands onto her jeans. "Conflict. Personal growth—violence!" She sat on the edge of her stool. "Good. Wait, what is *that*—?"

"What is what?" I asked.

"That *thing* near the far wall, near the couch," she said. "O-on the couch. Is it sitting on the fucking couch?"

"It?" Stephy asked. "It is not *it*. It is a *he*. That's our son, that's Integrevy. Our son, Integrevy. A mix of the ideals of integrity and envy."

"Monster," Certi said.

"Watch your mouth, hoe," Stephy said. "Integrevy is a he."

"Huh, male monster. It should leave while we're doing our business here with the puppets."

Piss Ant did cartwheels employing all six of his legs. He spun on his back and melded this into a worming motion along the carpet. This worming, achieved through his stomach, circumvented space and time by moving forward *and* backward as we clapped. He panted as he stood and shimmied, clapped, and sidestepped.

"In my mind, this…this was embellished with brilliant fireworks. The effect is more pronounced with the backing tracks. But the parallel compression of the beat still lacks the right bite. The digital files will be bounced down once I make some phone calls."

"Hold up," Certi said. "FuzzPalace, get it out of here."

"Certi," I said, "do not insult our son. Integrevy stays in the open like a trophy or a jewel."

"But…but, FuzzPalace," she said, sweating, fidgeting with her blouse, "it's so ugly, so wrinkled."

"The better to show beauty."

"It's lumpy, saggy," she said, trembling. "Reminds me of death."

"A good reminder."

She leaned back and sneered. "I-I was lying. I can see the masculinity in it. Horrid."

"The dancing is not so great?" Piss Ant asked. "Some could at least take note of these moves. Behold: the hydraulics of a robot…no? I fancy it. *Bee-boo-bee-boo, bo-op.* While I may not cut a corner like a mousetrap, dear audience, remain mindful: I. Am. Fresh."

"Piss Ant, be silent," I said. "Certi, where are you departing to?"

Piss Ant's pallor flashed yellow before he regained his silver luster.

"I've had enough," Certi said.

"Why move away from Integrevy?"

She put her hands on her hips. "You gonna YOLQ me?"

"YOLQ you?"

Puppets lined up and assembled in tight formation:

"YOLQ, YOLQ, YOLQ!"

"YOLQ you—?"

"Ye only live four times!"

"YOLQ you?" I repeated. "You YOLQ yourself with each breath. Peace, human. Be at rest. Your fantasies have too many teeth."

Nagarazim shook his head and pranced about. "We cannot YOLQ Certi. She is human, female. Only human females, those who know her inner mysteries, can YOLQ her. This is the way of things."

She turned to the exit and then back to Integrevy. "If I stay, you gotta give me final cut of the commercial."

"Sit upon your bar stool. I will bring Integrevy to you."

I pattered over and picked up Integrevy. He had grown bigger and slipperier now. His 'I' and 'g' had grown more legible over the last week with the aid of Stephy's breast milk. He pulsed in my arms as I neared Certi. "He wants to meet you."

"Don't be crude," Certi said. "There, I let the thing sit in my lap. Can I go?"

"What do you think of it?" I asked.

"I hate it."

"Cunt-stain!" Stephy said.

"Stephy, please," I said. "Certi, why do you hate him?"

"It's…it just…it's boastful, insistent. Like it could never change."

"So?" Stephy said.

"Everything must change!" Certi said. Her eyes reddened and watered. "If it doesn't ever—how can it—never, never mind."

"Some traditions must change," I said. "Some must always be. Continue on your last words, 'If it does not change, how can it…' what?"

"No," she said. "Get this off!"

Stephy took Integrevy off her lap and walked into the workshop.

Certi stood and wiped a tear from her eye. She gathered her things. "If I can't make it change," Certi mumbled (perhaps to herself), "how can I know if it loves me?"

"Certi," I said, "do we have the commercial."

"Well," she said, "you made me cry. You, in the back, come here."

Matchy approached her without the aid of his kangaroo. "Yes, madam."

"What's this?"

"My vest?" Matchy asked. "It is my creation."

"And the fabric?"

"It's a kludging," Matchy said.

"A kludging?"

"Of maxi pad and crackle coin, madam."

"Clever. Not bad for puppets. If we don't get you guys to do it, we can always outsource to Pluralia's puppets. You guys did mean something to Miltro. I could never understand that. How could a man be so obsessed with one venture that didn't look like it would pan out? I needed this to be a failure for so long. I hated the way he focused on you guys. Like he was using me to support his puppetry. A woman should come first. I loved him. Even though I didn't always show it. Now look at you guys—making little vests out of my maxi pads, dancing, having your ceremonies—you're real. We'll see, Felty. I have to talk to Headless first…you guys got my vote."

"And Matchy gets credit for the swaying?" Piss Ant's silver broke out in yellowish spots. "What match is a vest against my worm-like moves? Note this: harrumph."

"PUUUUUSH."

"Excuse me." Piss Ant horseback-hobbled out of the room toward the hallway.

"Did that ant go somewhere to poop?" Certi asked.

"Dance and poop, dance and poop," Nagarazim said. "This is the way of things."

I threw up my arms to praise the victory, "Today, males give birth!"

"Uterus envy?" Certi asked. "Is that what all this was?"

29

Scrambling down a ladder with a script in my teeth, my feet frolicked over the steel rungs as they made purchase.

I rushed to pass another script to my felties before Certi had her chance to inject suggestions. The hum of generators below PC's complex revved as I lowered into what was a mineshaft before the '46 renovation. In '46 *Not-So-Hard Boulevard* began filming beneath the complex from an excavation among adjacent limestone mines.

The management hoped that the soundstage would aid the efforts of the Second Great War. Hiding the stage belowground was thought to be strategic since Westonia believed propaganda more valuable than technology or honor. It seemed strange however that the staff did not have more enthusiasm for my current efforts.

Since Headless Boardsman and Eyeam insisted on remaining topside, this was my sixth downward trip that morning. My hands pawed the rungs as I considered that the operating temperature would be too high for *Horseteeth502*. We could not meet the service temperature requirements of the slurry and avoid xenoestrogen contamination of the batch.

Would the felties, and I endorse a product that would feminize male humans? PC knew this but the feminization had not been reported in trials of male puppets because our river-blood rope had counteracted it. I disliked lowering into the mines and it seemed like the safeness of pharmaceuticals should have been the concern of many more employees.

The mineshaft's descent to the soundstage must have been twelve stories deep. Electric lanterns flickered as I lowered toward the entrance of the shafts. Dribbling water peppered the generator's *thuds* and *hums* as I dropped off the ladder into the shafts that opened to a right-angle crossing of tunnels.

A puppet in white, moth-eaten rags clung to the limestone ceiling, upside-down, like a lizard. "Need directions, puppet?" he asked and then fluttered back and forth across the rough ceiling.

"What is the cost?" The route lay straight ahead however I liked to make small talk with the lime-lickers.

"Fifty crackle coins. One for each year I've been imprisoned."

"You are not trapped. Stop licking tunnels."

"Fluff you, puppet," he said. "Lime tunnels got ahold on me. Used to dance as a spokes-puppet. Don't let your puppets lick no lime walls. The walls tell too many tales too. Drips in from the bay, you know. Secrets of ships and fools. Secrets of ceilings, told to tools. Don't let your puppets lick no walls, I warn."

"This and many more warnings," I said, and I pattered toward the soundstage. "Peace, puppet."

"Two humbugs on your head." The white-ragged puppet looked down in shame but caught himself as perhaps he realized he clung to the tunnel upside-down and the direction he had thought to be down was actually up.

The braced dirt and limestone tunnels branched and rambled in many directions with various ropes strung about to lead the way. A braided rope led me closer to *Not-So-Hard Boulevard* as I trudged along and passed artifacts left by former travelers: a felt scrap, a tourniquet, a half-buried googly eye, all long-since dusted over and covered in cobwebs. The bay's salty wind struck with the sea's barnacles and effluvium as voices echoed off corners.

"Thomsa's Table Wax, The Only Wax that Helps You Relax; Eat More Lead, Save On High-Quality Lead—Until You're Dead; Firm-Fist-Ductility, It Degrades in the Sun... Bye-and-Bye." Farther in the distance, my felties bickered with the puppet stagehands. The conflict had steadily grown all morning. I crawled up out of the dirty rim of rubble and rocks from the end of the tunnel into the stagnant air of the soundstage. Stagehands cornered Matchy between cardboard street facades, wielding the screw-thread ends of their boom microphones.

Matchy searched the soundstage for his kangaroo. "K-ka-blamo?"

"Fluff you, puppet!"

"Ka-blamo!"

"Aye, aye aye:

"Eat lint, felt guy!"

"Leave him be." Nagarazim strutted on his legs with the boundaries between his amphibian flesh and felt constricting like jagged mouths while sprigs of cotton bounced.

A puppet with muttonchops in a yellow turtleneck turned to regard Nagarazim with a faux cigarette dangling. "So, the puppet gets whooped. Sew me a figure."

"Name the dispute," I said.

"Felt guy said we couldn't take our union-10:10s. We get ten at 10:10, but when *we* say when."

"To whom do you ascribe felt guy?" Matchy asked. "Drop thread!"

The portly puppet trained his boom-spear on him. "No way this felt guy told me drop thread! No way."

"Drop thread, thank your maker for a half-made head."

"No way! No way! Okay, yous guys. No way!"

"Gentle-puppets, gentle-puppets," I said. "Lower your boom-spears. Plug them into amplifiers to record a historic truth. Seamsters, I say: relax."

"Who you calling seamster, you chair-hugging-ceiling-starer. I put in my straight-eight."

"Of course, take your rightful rest. We felties must review our line-changes and practice our blocking."

"The blocking is perfect." Mr. Cavesicle threw a rock and picked off a bat, which had roosted in the dripping stalactites. He capered toward the felled bat with another rock as his hunchback walk strained the seams of his loincloth. "My snack, I smash. Hmm, there are graves here. Graves of past actors who would not read their lines?"

"The blocking is symbolic," I said. "Every movement beheld by the teleporter is holy."

"Felt guy 's overstuffed," a seamster said.

"Who fucking said that?" I asked as guide rods squeaked and rotated and screwed up into each of my cufflinks. A hundred course words clogged in my throat as my felt bristled. "Who dares address Felty FuzzPalace, master of gears *and* shafts?" The rods pulled my hands to strike and claw out before me toward the throat of that seamster.

The seamster just smirked and leaned away with a measured disgust.

"In this place, the guide rods come up from below," I said. I clenched my fists and my mouthplate. "From the ground, somehow? They thread in, near our hands. I must fight off this assault on my independence."

"I been knowing that for six years," a seamster said.

"We shouldn't be down here." Piss Ant's silvery shell erupted in yellow spots that dribbled with runlets.

"Perhaps these guide rods control our baser instincts—sex, hate, fear," I said, "and the puppet strings above control our headier ideals."

"Office puppets take forever to learn the basic stuff," a seamster said.

They laughed.

"Take your 10:10s."

I huddled with my Felties near another corner of cardboard street facades with a foam fire hydrant and faux grass. "Behold page three," I said.

"Again, with the third page," Skeleton said.

"Scene one," I said, "father approaches son in grade school classroom. Principal looms over desk. Students sobbing and slobbering. Blood spilled over floor from the safety scissors attack—the setup is known?"

"Setup is known," Nagarazim said.

"The father, he looks to the sky and says, 'We both have a problem with our restless torsos, don't we, my son?' And son looks up with blood on hands and somber eyes and says, 'Father, if only there was a pill to arrest our torsos and keep us from trouble...'"

"Yes, yes," Nagarazim said, "it is known."

"What if—hold hold—let ears travel the terrain—what if father did not look to the heavens and instead looks to the floor? The difference is subtle but with a small gesture we might signify that the taking of *Arrnomova* is more associated with." And then I whispered, "With *shame* than with goodness. Behold a difference?"

"Yes, yes," whispered Nagarazim, "this rings true. A pox on *Arrnomova*. Let this money shower however so puppets become cleansed with riches."

"I will bathe in crackle coins," Matchy said, "floss my teeth with human hair."

"This has a peculiarity," Nagarazim said.

"And yet it is my fancy," Matchy said.

"Riches can make puppets only so clean before we cover in filth," Herbivore said.

"Booo!" We jabbed his ribs so he might temper his idealism.

"Page four," Red said.

"You skip," I said.

"I skip, I skip," Red said, "Page four: if I am to play this murderous child, as notes came down from your upper management, yes?"

"Notes came down. The child must be murderous," I said.

"If I am to play this murderous child, it says in italics here: child makes feral slashing at classmates with safety scissors. I believe the motion is—"

"No, no!" we said.

"Careful, Red," I said, "the guide rods are threaded into your wrists when you wield these safety scissors. Be mindful of this when down here in this place. What is your question?"

"Could safety scissors not also stab?"

"Script calls but for slashing," Nagarazim said. "Safety scissors are designed but for slashing."

"But to stab, friends, to stab," Red said, "stabbing betrays intention. Slashing—this is only for fools. This child, we think to his back-story. He has enemies, no? May he not stab at these? His schoolmistress, perhaps she alleviates this child of his recess. Should stabs not propel at her?"

"Schoolmistress is in frame?" Skeleton asked.

"Only up to her power-u," I said.

"Only power-u?" Red asked.

"Upper management said we must use a real woman for the role of the schoolmistress. We cannot hold both puppets and whole woman in the same frame."

"For charismatic purposes should we not hold more than a power-u within the frame?" Nagarazim asked.

"Holy symbolism," I said. "Power-u has begotten all within the frame."

Mr. Cavesicle chomped on his bat and scratched his head. "In which way power-u begat? Physical birth? Metaphysical intention?"

"Both, puppet," I said.

"Why is everyone so quiet?" Certi asked. She and Richnuss had crept up. He pointed at the scenery and the stalactites as the two held hands, loosely.

"Certi," I said, "we were discussing your power-u."

She shook her head. "Fucking weird."

"We will have difficulty filming both the entirety of the puppets and the entirety of the schoolmistress in the same shot."

"*ARRNOMOVA* SAMPLES FOR EVERYONE!" Headless

Boardsman said. The yellow, open neckline of his suit emerged up from out of the mineshaft. Baskets of *Arrnomova* swung beneath his magic hands, and the singular cord that held him had withered to a spindly kite string.

"My power-u, Felty, is a personal topic that is inappropriate for workplace discussion."

"EVERYONE MUST TAKE A SAMPLE, FOR METHOD ACTING. STAGEHANDS MUST TAKE SAMPLES TOO…FOR METHOD FILMING."

"No water to help wash the pills down?" I asked.

"It's simple, Felty," Certi said. "Thank you. I-I have to take these, too?"

"HUMANS ESPECIALLY!"

"I don't know if it's safe," Certi said. "Hold on a second, Headless.

"Felty, we'll smash-cut between the faces of spokes-puppets and actors while filming. This is going to be in somebody's living room as three-dimensional holograms. We can't have a pair of severed legs walking around someone's living room flaunting my camel toe. I've got notes— Okay, listen: we'll need to have the stagehands shake the cardboard facades while we film, give everything a moody ambiance. I wanna mike all the male voices as distant and scratchy, distorted, bit-crunched, so they seem like anachronisms or, ah…forgotten, mechanical ghosts. Yeah! Got that?"

"Yes, ma'am," a seamster said, "forgotten, mechanical ghosts, ma'am."

"Right," Certi said. "Honey drop, anything else?"

"Make sure that felt scrap, Felty FuzzPalace, takes his

Arrnomova," Richnuss said.

"I will remain sober," I said, "for safety's sake."

"For safety's sake." "For safety's sake," the felties and seamsters mocked before they popped their samples.

"Frog legs on credit," Nagarazim said. "My body will allow credit with these drugs."

"Reconsider," I said.

"Drugs give frog legs fuel."

"NOT DRUGS," Headless Boardsman said. "EXPERIMENTAL PHARMACEUTICALS."

"I don't think I should be part of the experiment, Headless," Certi said.

"MORE DATA ON HUMANS HOWEVER."

"Felty?" Certi asked. "What do you think? You had to look into the chemistry of *Arrnomova* to design the lids, and you smoked those samples. Is it safe to experiment on humans?"

"Don't trust him," Richnuss said.

"My ex didn't sew him to lie."

"You are correct, madam." My hands rose from the guide rods below as their urgent natures surged. Could I push against fibs, lies and mistruths under their influence? "Please explain the *Arrnomova* experiments and trials."

"The marketing push is broader—"

"SILENCE, HUMAN."

"Don't spell it out," Richnuss said.

"The little guy should know," Certi said. "Plus," she smiled, "I wanna know if Miltro was the great puppet maker he made himself out as, or a chump. He kept saying he was gonna sew a great puppet, with old-fashioned, old-school integrity. A puppet that could rescue us, set the world right. Did he do it? Are you that puppet, Felty? You know if you help us with this commercial, your future is assured at PC. I bet you'll go along with anything we say at this point."

"What is the nature of the experiment?" I asked.

She laughed. "Headless Boardsman didn't tell you?"

"DARKNESS FOR FELTY."

"We'll market *Arrnomova* to humans, eventually," Certi said. "At first, our primary market will be puppets. *Arrnomova* will take away the ability of felties to feel, to feel empathy, or anything at all. If felties can't feel, corporations can rest assured no more puppets will man-up ever. Now, do you think it's safe for humans to take?"

"The primary ingredients of *Arrnomova* are the same as *Powerstachios II,*" I said. "They were bought in bulk, for economy, like everything at PC is purchased. What killed your husband now nears your lips."

"My ex didn't take care of himself."

"One ingredient took too much care of him."

"What are you insinuating?"

"*Powerstachios II* killed your husband. The same ingredients near your lips."

"Ridiculous, libelous!" Certi said. "You should be fired, fired from a cannon! Here, honey. We're taking these."

"Already took mine," Richnuss said.

Certi choked down her pills.

"Ever had the street stuff?" Richnuss asked. "Your buddy, Root Beer, likes the street stuff."

"Root Beer sold me a seven-ball last week," a semester said.

"Keep it on the hush," another said.

"That's why I'm here, Felty," Richnuss said. "Sizing up the competition. Why you here, good guy?"

"To perform an excellent job."

"That's not how you were sewn," Richnuss said. "Bet you think you can change the tide. You can't change a tide that mimics nature. What we do, me and my partner, Headless Boardsman" —Headless arched his back— "we beat nature by a long shot. It's a form of mimicry, like camouflage. We mimic pleasure. It's mind control. And why should minds be free? Minds are like stomachs; minds eat pleasure. We feed those starving stomachs."

"Freewill—"

"Think of all that pleasure your freewill is costing you."

"It is hot down here," I said as my head throbbed. I looked up from my waist-high stature. "A fiery pit."

"The *Arrnomova* will cool you. Almost as good as my street stuff."

"Your mouth is foaming," Certi said as she took a step away from him.

Richnuss stretched out and tried, unsuccessfully, to hold her hand. "*Your* mouth is foaming." Their sweat beaded like a steamy shower.

"Should they be sweating like this?" I asked.

"INCONCLUSIVE RESPONSE."

"Felty, I can't move my arms," Certi said. Richnuss stepped away, widening their gap with a sickly smirk. His shoulders clenched and his arms loosened to lengthen with insentient flopping and swaying like a drunken gorilla and then his arms turned noodly and flip-flopped like a starving octopus.

"The drug's name is *Arrnomova*, madam," I said.

"But the paralysis was just a marketing gimmick!" she said. "I literally *cannot* move my arms. Feels like I'm falling, getting stung by mosquitoes all on the way down…chills."

"FAST ACTING."

"You're twitching." Richnuss said. "Am I twitching?"

"Yes, honey drop, you're twitching, too."

"My street stuff is more pure," Richnuss said.

"I'm loving it," a seamster said.

"I am higher than one of those bats," Red said. "LOOK AT THAT!"

"Look at what?" Matchy asked.

"Universes."

"Do bats tell jokes?" Matchy asked. "First, decode squeaks. Second, shake the world."

"Yes, yes, yes," Nagarazim said, "*Arrnomova* works like frog leg fuel!" He bounced higher and higher as his frog legs pushed and his *Credit* string pulled.

"That puppet can jump," a semester said.

"Beware of ceilings," Matchy said. "Proceed with caution."

"NO CEILINGS!" Nagarazim said as he leapt again, and his guide rods bowed as they stretched, higher and higher.

"Caves have ceilings," Red said.

"My legs, my legs my legs," Nagarazim said. "Boing, boing, ba-boing boing! The *Credit* string is strong, it pulls."

"Beware the *Credit* string!" I shouted. "It is overestimating your weight."

"I am not too high," Nagarazim said. "Jealous puppets! Oh oh-no!" Nagarazim impaled himself on a stalactite as his clothes ripped and tore around it. Cotton cascaded down as he convulsed and struggled to free himself from the pitted red shard that pierced his back.

"That puppet's a goner," a seamster said.

"Struggle not. Nagarazim, be still," I said. "We will send for help to get you off the ceiling."

"You're *all* jealous of this, the greatest, the greatest death," Nagarazim said. "*Arrnomova* is the greatest."

"Stop squirming," Red said. "We will get help for you."

Nagarazim fell from the stalactite and bounced and bobbled onto the rocky floor. We rushed around him as felt clumps spewed from his mouthplate. "Froggy Style," he said. "I found that Froggy Style."

"Nagarazim, you who are known for your wisdom," I said, "let other words be your last."

"I found a ceiling."

"I'm regretting this," Certi said. "Headless Boardsman, did you know this would happen to humans?"

"INCONCLUSIVE RESPONSE."

"Something's not right," Certi said. "Everything's locking and on fire. Help me, Headless."

"INCONCLUSIVE."

"I can't die down here in this hole," Certi said. "I wish I would have had kids, two girls. I always wanted two girls."

A seamster kicked a rock and scraped the dirt, "Me too."

"I wish I never was a part of this system," Certi said. "I see it now. It's a fool's errand. Felty…"

"Mother? Nagarazim is dead—!"

"Shut-it! I need you to man-up, carry me out of this hole. Can you do that for me?"

"There's five-hundred boom-bills in it for you, if you carry me out first," Richnuss said.

"Richnuss, honey drop, *sugarpie!*" Certi said. "Where's your chivalry?"

"That's dead hooker."

"I thought manning-up was prohibited during office hours," I said.

"We can make an exception, just this once. These puppets aren't strong enough to carry us, right, Headless?"

"INCONCLUSIVE RESPONSE."

"Mother, I will endeavor to carry you. You must do something for me."

"Name it, Felty."

"Say you are glad I exist, instead of nothingness," I said. "Say you love me."

"Don't be dramatic," Certi said. "Stupid, felt-rag, Felty."

I shrugged and inquired with the others, "She is to perish in the dirt then?"

"Okay! Fine Felty, you win! Of course, I lo-*uumm* y-you. You remind me of Miltro's father. That was what he intended. I hated Miltro's father, his old misogynistic ways, the way he looked down on me. I was better than him. *Fuck you, Miltro's Father.* You're all right, though. Whoa, delirious."

"Close enough," I said. My spine thickened, tethered, twisting, and sung toward the nerves, bones and muscles. Unbounded impatience rose and mounted, whipped and rode through each vein before the business suit burst at the seams in the overburdened places. I needed to be stronger than ever to carry them out.

"Wee-ee, fun!" she said. Her head bounced around over the

crook of my arm.

"I have abstained from the samples, also," Piss Ant said. "I will call for an ambulance. The appropriate bribes will come from our savings."

"Go up ahead of me," I said.

Certi did not seem all that heavy as I carried her delirious body through mineshafts and back up the steel rung ladder. When I arrived topside and carried her into the receiving alcove, a puppet receptionist met me and informed me that Piss Ant had called for an ambulance. I reassured Certi she would be all right, but she did not want me to venture back down the hole for Richnuss, and it struck me how fickle love can be. "Peace, human. The receptionist is here. The ambulance will arrive shortly. You will be fine."

"Listen to me. Stay with me! Hold my hand. I'm slipping, I'm slipping away. Stay with me."

"I must venture into the hole to retrieve your drug-peddling boyfriend."

After venturing back down the hole and hoisting Richnuss over my shoulder, each of my legs enflamed with burning-fatigue. The adrenaline had worn off. Richnuss was heavier. My fleshy fingers strained as I pulled us up each steel rung of the ascent. He muttered his confused, selfish babblings. The human villain grew in weight. He grew into a foreign parasite, unworthy of carrying.

Why should I care about humans when they did not even care at all that Nagarazim had perished? A great deal had happened suddenly, however, they did not even pause to consider him and his life, his contributions. Did they care about me? So easy it would be to drop this fool, let him fall to his death and instantly change back into a puppet with a lightened load, never to feel the responsibilities of manning-up again.

I groaned to reach another, higher rung. If I had not manned-up the first time, I would not have been recognized for this bizarre talent. I would always be able to blend in and lay low among the other puppets. Richnuss said, "I chew, chew, chew puppets in my bub-bubbly stew."

I lay Richnuss's convulsing body next to Certi's in the receiving alcove and collapsed to the floor as the dirt, dust and silt mixed with my sweat. "Receptionist, attend this paralyzed villain," I said. "See that both he and Certi receive the best medical care when the EMTs arrive."

"Help us, Felty!" Certi cried.

My hands grasped around as I panted and attempted to stand. "Peace, humans."

"Aye, you Felty FuzzPalace?" the receptionist asked. "In charge of gears and shafts?"

"Perhaps."

"You look different as a human," he said.

"As do we all."

"You bleeding," he said.

My hands dripped blood onto the black marble. The knurling of the steel ladder's rungs had imbedded into my palms.

"You want human clothes?" he asked. "I keep human clothes behind the counter for this kind a' stuff."

"Do you have puppet clothes?" I asked. "When danger subsides, I revert to a puppet pretty quick."

"We got puppet clothes. What you need, puppet?"

"Felt Guy No. 5 from the '50s was what my maker sewed on my shoulders."

"We stay stocked on that Felt Guy from the '50s," he said. "Let me set you up, right quick."

A flock of humans crisscrossed my path, clicking their stilettos and dress shoes against the marble. "I only trust spokes-puppets, these days, to advise my important purchases," a smartly dressed young man said. "Puppets are so inhuman. You can't trust humanity. We all know what happens each time a society trusts humanity." Their heads flew back in peals of riotous laughter.

"I'm starting to think we *should* trust humanity," a smartly dressed young woman said. "Maybe we're born with everything we need."

"This room is miked," another said. "Just say the lines."

"I don't even like pantsuits!" she blurted, "I wanna wear something stringy, or…or a tulip."

"Your rank isn't high enough for skirts."

"I know."

"There are rifles posted on the outer turrets."

"The spokes-puppet commercials are awesome," she said.

"Who you gonna vote for in the next election for mayor?" another man asked.

"Mayor of what?" another asked.

"Blueport Blues."

"I was thinking maybe the Tuxedoed DinoMan, or something."

"What?" the other man asked. "That lizard-man is a puppet."

"He's a beast," another said. "His platform is cold-blooded."

"Shut up, humans," I said but they ignored me.

The front doors of the receiving alcove swung closed as the last of a crowd of applicants shuffled inside in their trench coats. "Why is a naked man covered in dirt?" the porcupine head of a wobbling, three-tiered trench coat asked. "Why is he standing over felled bodies?" Above this trench coat puppet, the alcove's vaulted ceiling expanded and the cathedral windows let in violet, combing rays and the scent of freshly cut flowers flooded. The expanse's authority and dignity drove forth with the reverence of an ancient church. "Mind your business, job applicant," I said.

The ambulance pulled up outside. I shrunk down to puppet-size and stepped into my Felt Guy No. 5 clothing. Behind me, the claws of Eyeam's feet tapped as he and Stephy approached. Integrevy was alongside her, and my son had grown so big. He scooted, quickly, like an enormous snail.

"Cash register face." Richnuss said, "dabba yabba zabba blabba."

"Felt-hunk McMale face," Certi said, "listen to a loaf of bread: algebra igloo."

"Yes, Mother, I know."

Eyeam squirmed in its confining golf pants. "What happened to Certi?"

"They've had a reaction to *Arrnomova*," Stephy said. "I told you it wasn't safe."

"Crap basket. Certi pay attention!" Eyeam said.

"Fuzz face?" Certi asked.

"I am not a happy spokes-puppet," Eyeam said. "I'm not happy with the direction PC is going. *Arrnomova* 's not safe for humans. Those lids Felty and I have been working on are flimsy death traps. Eyeam has been around longer than you. Eyeam has offers at other firms. Most of all—"

"Leave her be," I said.

"She needs to hear it."

"Puppet feud," Certi said.

"Has anyone checked her vitals?" Stephy asked.

"She needs to hear it," Eyeam said.

"The EMTs are here."

"Monsters don't wear pants," Eyeam said.

"Fuzz face?"

"I quit!" Eyeam said.

"Certi," Stephy said, "listen to me—"

"Milk machine in silence."

"Did she call me a milk machine? Certi do you want us to cancel the *Arrnomova* trials?"

"Milk machine in silence!"

"Is she?" Stephy asked, "is she calling me a milk machine?"

I pulled Eyeam aside as the EMTs arrived. "Why quit now?"

Eyeam focused over my shoulder at the window's sunlight. It shimmied, hopped and wobbled out of its golf pants. "We lost human leadership. Money dries after the leadership is gone. Eyeam 's a contractor. Gotta follow the money. Maybe Eyeam engineers and acts over on the West Coast."

30

408 days passed since the last incident. Since the Fab corridor wound in a helix that spiraled to the center of the pentagon ceiling, most avoided it while this complex construction was in progress.

These loops perched above the pit of the Sub-fab where tremendous facilities rumbled and sputtered. The wall made of immense orange tubing was perforated with hydraulic, pneumatic, and various lines, and the tubing enclosed a catwalk that wound within this helix. The shadowy corridor, lit only with foot and cagelights, bustled with seamsters endeavoring to maximize real estate for conduit and plumbing, and everyone worked as if in the throes of some snort-gasm.

I did not actually want to take part in this press tour. We headed off in a group to christen the counter-rotating agitators that liquefied RTS batches in the S-bends. And the S-bends were far below in the Sub-fab. On the Second Loop, vacuum chambers flooded and coursed with red, blue and yellow ingredients beneath a series of my lids. These lids protruded from the floor as domed windows. The path looped inward toward the center of the catwalk to form a precipice so we could stare down through the lids, into the Sub-fab.

Root Beer drew out a pocket watch from his suit and picked at a caviar stain. "Is this only the second loop?"

"You are fortunate our felties shared their press invitations with you," I said.

"You are fortunate Certi and Richnuss did not perish from this excuse of a drug, *Arrnomova*," Root Beer said. "It's dangerous, but an opportunity exists for a partnership with me and PC."

"I checked in on Certi and Richnuss in Intensive Care. Certi mumbled to me, after I called for her nurse, she said…she said, '*Powerstachio* pushers, hamburger head.'"

"Wise woman."

"She was delirious!" Electrical conduit arced through gashes in sheathing as my foot splashed in hydraulic fluid. "She demanded to be redressed in her silver pantsuit. It is horrid how PC overstocked the worst *Powerstachio* chemicals and justified mixing them into *Arrnomova*."

"Always a conspiracy for FuzzPalace. I, Root Beer, hide no longer within puppet-conspiracies. A puppet I am no more. Not like your beloved felties. Their *Promotion* strings drag them to this silly press tour on a Monday morning. I do business with the humans and yet no strings stick to me. Drugs make me strong, drugs from the mind of man. *Zokithral, Arrnomova*: drugs unlock my essence, my monster-hood, FuzzPalace."

"Monster-hood? *Arrnomova* is dangerous, regulated or no."

"Yes, yes," Root Beer said, "the humans it may have nearly killed but the stuffed-puppets, oh how they love to rest their torsos, to put their torsos at ease. Puppets do nothing but work. For humans, work is the half-recollection of a dream. So human bodies reject *Arrnomova*. I have learned much of its raw rocks from my street peddling. *Arrnomova* is designed only for us hard working puppets."

"Watch your step."

"Let me approach your Headless Boardsman and make an offer of sales-monster-ship. I can distribute your pharma-grade *Arrnomova* to all the puppets."

"Tablecloth and tapestry." I leaned in to whisper, "The effects of *Arrnomova* on humans are similar to stroke. Certi and Richnuss will need six months to recover. An investigation is underway. It will take at least six months to be remarketed for puppets."

We bounce-pattered near the back of the tour while humans led the pack along with Herbivore and Piss Ant. Matchy walked beside his bouncing kangaroo. Stephy took her pet pussy, Polydimethylsiloxane, for a walk on a leash. She allowed our son to accompany us on the tour, in defiance of me.

Her most excelsior of breast milks had allowed Integrevy to swell to boa constrictor-size with a length as long as many men. Each letter of his word-art flesh was well formed and visible. Integrevy crawled as a lightninglike snail beside the leashed Polydimethylsiloxane. The two battled, each lashing out, swiping at the other, occasionally needing separation.

To an engineer's eye, the dangers of a manufacturing floor stung out, mounted and manifest. Although Integrevy appeared to have developed to the maturity of a toddler I believed this trip unsafe for him. My worrying caused a *Fatherhood* string to descend, which triggered the descent of more strings.

"Why does a *Mortgage* string descend, FuzzPalace?" Root Beer asked. "You have never signed one."

"It accompanies the *Fatherhood* string."

"The *Mortgage* string makes you flop."

"Leave it." I was not in the mood. How could such a soundstage be buried beneath PC? The realization forced me to question what more lay yet undiscovered. On the Vespa ride over the bridge that morning, the heat of the summer, the stench of the bay, the cries for help of another batch of humans, stranded on another yacht, made me wish I were somehow permanently human so I could pilot a full-sized automobile.

Hissing gulls fought over an opened candy bar. In the background beyond the bridge's guardrail, the strings of the puppets that struggled on the yacht below shot down from the heavens like the contrails of crashing jets. This distraction caused me to almost bumper-fuck a convertible as purple rays impaired my vision. Such had been the perils of puppet commutes.

My encounter with the seamsters plagued my mind. They were free despite earning less. Perhaps I should have been sewn a seamster. I doubted seamsters could ever be spokes-puppets. Although who knew? Who paid notice to a puppet's advancement? The guide rods and strings that attended seamsters appeared reliable, sturdier, thicker. They allowed less freedom. Yet how they smiled and a seamster on our tour smiled just then.

"Who does this seamster smile at?" Root Beer asked. "Kiss the seams! FuzzPalace, let me assist you."

"Divide this assistance by zero."

"By unity of Truth divided," Root Beer said, dodging conduit, smiling his smile.

"When I went to work for Richnuss, selling his *Arrnomova* rocks, ditching the robe for a business suit, I, too, was hunted by the descent of strings. But they never attached. When the daily routine got tough I took to the help at hand. I smoked me a rock and delved inward. I let these rocks propel my truer nature: my monster-hood, FuzzPalace. Behold the being before you, so large. Almost as a man, yes?"

"A child, drunk off candy."

"So fierce. No strings. Wavy red hair, wavy red chest hair that also reaches out to say, 'Oh…hello there.'"

"Seal your trap, regarding your chest hair."

"Let peepers peep. Look how the mother of your child shows you up. She is real. You are a puppet. Allow this—"

"Ouch, stop!" I said. "What happens? What action did you undertake?"

"Cross-wired your *Fatherhood* and *Promotion* strings," Root Beer said. "My fingers burned from the spark. Like electricity and the hunt of hungry energy. Do you even know the spark? Do you know the flashing energy that leaps the gap? It's your ambition, FuzzPalace! Can you admit it?"

"I admit, puppet. Leave it.

"Stephy, let me carry Integrevy."

"The combination of Integrity and Envy is too big to carry," Stephy said.

"Must he do his scooting on this uncertain ground?" I asked.

"Let him face this world." In response to his mother's encouragement, Integrevy slithered sprightlier and from the entirety of his skin he vibrated a cry that sounded like: *toot-toot-toot-toot—tootily-dooo! Toot-toot-toot-toot—tootily-dooo!* "There you go," Stephy said. "Toot like I taught ya." *Raawow,* Polydimethylsiloxane said, flashing her claws at Integrevy.

"Stephy!" I protested.

"He's fine."

Integrevy rolled himself into a ball, which bounced, and then bounced menacingly, toward that pussy.

"Look at these spokes-puppets of yours," Root Beer said. "Their strings will keep them too tangled to follow their dreams. Your stringed puppets are pathetic. Their felt, frumpy."

"No frump on our felt. It is through our strings that our dreams will be realized."

"WE APPROACH AN INNOVATION OF THE SECOND NORTHEAST LOOP," Headless Boardsman said. He led the charge of buzzing reporters. They strained forwards with their microphones and their flash-popping cameras cast about grotesque shadows. "THANKS IN NO SMALL PART TO ONE OF OUR PUPPET ENGINEERS. SAY HELLO TO THE REPORTERS, FELTY FUZZPALACE."

"Hello, reporters."

Raawow—!

"I tried my best against stupefying odds. My designs were never intended as evil."

"HA HA HA," boomed Headless Boardsman, "WE LET OUR PUPPET ENGINEERS KEEP A LIGHT MOOD, HERE AT POWER CHEMICALS. STEPHY, WON'T YOU TELL US ABOUT OUR NEW LIDS?"

"Here at Integrevy," Stephy said, "I mean, uh…here at Power Chemicals, we take opportunities seriously. Like the opportunity to offer quality products at low-low costs, so *all* Westonians can afford to keep their torsos well rested. We know for a fact that under-privileged Westonians still suffer from restless torsos. Having an optimized, state of the art facility allows us, here at

Power Chemicals, to offer pharmaceutical solutions to the broadest possible patient demographics. These new lids—the Lobster's Iris—I believe the project was nicknamed—"

"I never called it that," I said.

"These new lids allow one-hundred percent visual inspection of key ingredients during the agitation process. It's critical we have one hundred percent visual inspection of mixing. You wouldn't believe—nor could you venture to guess—the vast chemicals we're mixing—around the clock—to bring *Arrnomova* to your schools, your offices, your homes. This mixing is delicate, such low partial pressures, such high flow rates, that continual monitoring is required to virtually guarantee a something…something product. Integrevy! Leave…leave her alone. In conclusion… *LINE?*"

"POWER CHEMICALS KEEPS BRINGING YOU WHAT YOU NEED."

"Power chemicals keeps bringing you what you need."

"VERY GOOD, STEPHY. IT IS SAFE. SAFETY IS THE TOP OF THE TACO, HERE AT PC. ISN'T THAT TRUE, SEAMSTER?"

"Yes sir, safety, top of taco. We never get no kill."

"FUZZPALACE!"

"Yes sir."

"Where is your friend, Eyeam?" Root Beer asked.

"Be quiet," I said to Root Beer as my *Promotion* string tugged.

"FUZZPALACE—!"

"Why is Eyeam not here with us?" Root Beer asked. "He also worked to design these lids."

"Be quiet."

"What's that, puppet?" Root Beer asked.

"Eyeam is terrified of these lids."

"FUZZPALACE, TELL OUR GUESTS HOW STRONG AND SAFE YOUR NEW LIDS ARE, EVEN UNDER ENORMOUS VACUUM PRESSURES. TELL THEM!"

My *Promotion, Fatherhood* and *Guilt* string pulled in balanced directions, and in this balance, emptiness dwelled that a purity of thought poured from. This purity was apart from me as if it had always existed. "Based on our testing and analysis, I would advise only one, medium-build human step on these lids at one time. Very light-footed should these footfalls step down on these lids."

Flashbulbs popped; reporters gazed at my lids and scribbled as vast engines from the Sub-fab whirred in accordance with their schedule and the looping, catwalk structure contracted and relaxed like a snake.

"FELTY FUZZPALACE," Headless Boardsman said, "COME FORWARD. STAND ON THIS LID. PROVE THEIR SAFETY."

"Merely two puppets on my lid," I mumbled. "It should withstand our combined weight." The pinball shenanigans that circumambulate a decision pressed my mind toward haste. A new string, known as *Pride*, descended to outweigh *Mortgage, Promotion* and *Fatherhood*. And the plastic string, *Horseteeth502,* stung into the back of my neck to outdo *Pride*. I drew out the deer-hunting knife and, with agony, sawed *Horseteeth502* off my neck.

"COME, PUPPET," Headless Boardsman said, "PROVE YOUR DESIGN!"

"No," someone said.

"WHO SAID THAT?"

"I said no." Stephy crossed her arms as she searched the passageway's walls and locked on to something in the distance. "It's not safe, Felty. It's not worth it. We can get new jobs."

"Zorf."

"STEPHY YOU ARE FIRED!"

"An empty suit can't fire me."

Headless Boardsman wrinkled. The singular string that held him up from the floor had withered to a mere gossamer. His suit crumpled as the yellow light beat out each syllable of his speech: "COME FORWARD FOR ME FELTY. PROVE YOUR WORTH… UNLESS YOUR MAKER WAS NOT SKILLED. NOT SKILLED ENOUGH TO SEW A PUPPET THAT COULD ENGINEER THESE LIDS."

Another string descended, and I knew this as a new archetype. It could manipulate in ways I never thought possible, in ways I could never predict.

Hooonk!

"That's right, Honkey," Pirate said. "*DNA* strings are the worst."

Honk, honk.

"The best, too," Pirate said.

My cufflinks divined toward the lid to discern whether it could withstand my additional weight. How could I uphold the Three Laws of Engineering if I did not understand the serviceability of my design? How could an ignorant puppet protect and provide for his woman? How could I defend anything if my weakened form was as dumb as theirs? Under these conditions, though strings might descend, guide rods might prop my libidinous ways, the only recourse was gambling.

"Felty, you don't have to do anything," Stephy said. She blocked my path as I tried to rush through reporters. "You are free."

"I cannot stop," I said. In her grown woman form I could never push passed her. Strings pulled each step forward, and I blocked through my ankle and jumped as the strings pulled me into the air, high above her.

She jumped to swipe at one of my feet: "Cheater!"

"I had to know." I landed flat-footed on the lid with Headless Boardsman. We both recoiled from each other with a half step as the landing's crunch spider-legged out in cracks beneath us. Headless Boardsman gasped as his yellow light flickered, and reporters groaned and lurched back. Ambition glued my feet down, was the lid strong enough to withstand the vacuum and our weight? Was I great? "Everything is fine!" I said. "Math and science win. They win the day with…*with Felty!*"

"They don't." Stephy rushed toward hoses coiled near the walls and began lashing herself down as she encouraged Integrevy to do the same. "Get off that lid, Felty."

And my felties crowded nearer to us. "Stay back, felties," Piss Ant said. He pushed them. "The lid is not safe."

"My mind is the smartest," I said. "Not only foam up there, no, no, no."

"You don't have to impress anyone," Stephy said.

Hoooonk!

"What is that, Horn Mouth?" I asked. "The lid will break?"

"Why won't you listen to me?" Stephy asked.

"Headless Boardsman, I am not sure about this lid," I said.

"I can help you prove their safety. I will join you," Root Beer said. "Headless Boardsman, allow me to offer sales-monster-ship for I can vouch for Felty's engineering skill with a monster's weight." How much could a monster weigh, I wondered, as Root Beer remained outside the rim of the lid. "Headless Boardsman," Root Beer said, "now that we have a moment, consider the vast distribution potential of a sales-monster such as myself. My past experience of fortune telling, for humans and puppets, enables me to cold-read prospective clients—"

The lid creaked. Headless Boardsman stood frozen as pride held my feet glued. "It holds," I said. "It holds against the pressures."

"Felty, get off that lid," Stephy said. "Stay away from them, Root Beer!"

The lid creaked and bowed. "It holds," I said. "Haha, I knew it."

Headless Boardsman seemed to look down as another crack shot across the lid. His suit sunk in and wrinkled. He lowered his voice to whisper and mumble, "Maybe this suit was only ever meant for a man to fill. My spirit never should have possessed it."

Hoonk! Horn Mouth honked.

"Root Beer, stay where you are," I said. "I need this job, I need to be strong to be good, I need to prove my design to these reporters. The lids, however, are inferior. Headless Boardsman, we must edge our way off."

"Unsafe? More confidence then," Root Beer said. "Do as monsters do. Push through, puppet."

"Stay off this lid," I said.

"I stay," Root Beer said.

"Raawow!" Polydimethylsiloxane said. *Toot-toot-toot-toot-tootily-doo!* Integrevy recoiled from a swiping claw and uncoiled his tail on the catwalk before Root Beer's feet.

"What in Urftoo—?" Root Beer asked as he stumbled.

"Watch it Root Beer!" Stephy said.

"Ahh—*ack!*" Root Beer tripped and fell, face first, onto the lid with a *crack*.

Within a silence, the reporters breathed deep before the lid pulverized into granules that dusted up and everywhere along with the glittery red, yellow, and blue chemical mists. As if they had minds of their own, the strings of myself and Headless Boardsman pulled us high up into the air, letting our bodies dangle above as suction fought to pull us down into the counter-rotating mincing action of the S-bend.

The bodies of several reporters sucked into the tunnel and ricocheted off the twisting walls before the ear-splitting screams from their dismemberment echoed and resounded. And from the diffuse light making its way down into the S-bend the blood-geysers and gyres congealed with oh the most horrible and rancid, festering glittorious flower-bombs of red, yellow, and blue blowing, dying and rising again to be so bright that we prayed to close our eyes but do you not know by now that puppets lack eyelids or any such windshield wipers or real tears to wash away what man made.

Stephy and Integrevy held fast in their hose strongholds near the walls, yet Integrevy's long length unfurled itself and draped over the rim of the shattered lid. "Hang on," Stephy said to Integrevy through her caked red, yellow and blue glitterings. "The emergency shutdown should initiate. Hold on—"

Toot-toot—toot! Integrevy's 'I' and 'n' stretched grotesquely to hold on to the loops of hoses as the suction pulled him taut. Glittery reporters reached out and grabbed his word-art flesh and complained, "The chemicals taste like poison! What is this thing?" "Oh, what the? I touched the…I touched the second e!"

"Respect him, state-sponsored reporters," I yelled, "cherish him with envy, or be sucked down to your deaths."

Stephy positioned herself near Integrevy to brace him within the conduit and encourage him into a stronger grip. "Grab this.

This conduit is safe."

"Can Integrevy hold on?" I asked.

"I told you not to step on it," Stephy said.

Root Beer's glittery form scrabbled against the suction as his lower legs and waist sunk beneath the lid's rim. "Help FuzzPalace," Root Beer said. "Aloof puppet! Come down here."

"Grab hold of my son," I said.

"Your son bears much weight," Root Beer said. "I would pull him and the reporters into the S-bend. You must help me."

"Gamble not with your life."

"You swore, if fortune misplaced me, you would not."

"Stephy, can Integrevy handle Root Beer's weight?" I asked.

"He's slipping."

"The root beer has gone flat," Root Beer said. "Not bitter to the tongue, as with the first fizz."

"Seal your trap, Root Beer," I said. "Fight the suction."

"Suction pulls at us all."

My felties pulled toward the breach in the lid, but their strings bounced them higher and held them above the fray. Headless Boardsman arched his neck opening to the thinness of his singular gossamer that strung him above the vortex. The wrinkles of his suit pulsed with hyperventilating spasms. "My connections have dwindled from five, to three, to this one— Oh, and this one— oh, how it's not fun—so quickly to come undone." The string snapped and flung upwards as he descended: "FREEDOM WAS MY UNDOING!"

"FuzzPalace, look at me," Root Beer said.

"I see you."

"Remember your promise?"

"I do."

"Then—oh, my monstrous fingers slip—do your duty, as you did before. Man-up, become a real man, save me!"

"I would lose my puppet strings and fall, smashing us *both* into the S-bend."

"Do your duty."

"Not all problems can be solved by manning-up. Fight that suction. The emergency shut-off will activate. Show us what monsters can do."

"Monsters are not known for staying power," Root Beer said, "I slip!"

"If I swung a little, I could reach you."

"You are high, I am low."

"Get low, monster."

"FuzzPalace, I am dying."

"Remain not in the middle for long, or I spit on you. I do spit." I spat a slobber-felt on his face like a fuzzy, fried egg and smiled down upon him.

"Before I am to perish? FuzzPalace, how could you?"

"Smelly monsters always perish. As a puppet, your felt was frumpy—pill-balled, pathetic—a hangout for flies of low repute, a stench that spread as looters loot, an intellect that idiots could never cahoot."

"My fingers slip, puppet!"

"*My fingers slip, puppet!* Miltro sewed you as the dark side of his psyche, his shadow. The shadow needs perspective to illuminate it. Do what you have never done. Practice humility."

"I am worthless." His carrot nose curled left and right.

"Correct."

"I am foolish." His pingpongs egg-rattled and sparked.

"Right."

"Abandoned by humans, puppets, monsters—by all."

"True."

"I am a lowly puppet."

"Now you feel it!" I said.

A whistling began as of something falling from high above.

"I told so many fortunes," Root Beer said. "I never saw that you would betray me!"

"I have not."

"Oh…oh, no," His fingers loosened off the rim as he slipped into the S-bend's tunnel. *"Oyster-spaaa-ackle!"* His screams diminished before his echos faded.

"Root Beer!" Stephy screamed.

"There is time," I said.

"Time for what?" she asked. *Hooonk! Toot-toot-toot—!*

A whistling came from somewhere. Descending at first steadily, the whistling sound dropped from above. From high above, the thickest, fastest, most spiraling string dove into the tunnel in pursuit. Coil after coil, the helix of braided string descended, interminably slow, and ever so gradually the rings of the helix narrowed. Chopping and sluicing sounds reverberated back up and echoed. The string stretched, tautly, and it bounced.

"Root Beer," I said, "did you survive?"

"Does he survive?" Matchy asked.

"If the puppet perished," Herbivore said, "let my claim be laid to his gray robe."

"Treacherous fool," Piss Ant said.

"It is mine, for I claimed it. Everyone heard me. Its powers will be mine."

"Be silent," Piss Ant said. "Your claim has no merit."

"Root Beer, do you survive?" I asked.

A reporter's flashbulb snapped as he climbed up out of the S-bend over the sweaty, veiny nooks and crannies.

"If he is gone—"

Root Beer hung from between his shoulder blades by a single string, limp, with his suit jacket and shoes ripped off. "I survive to confess my envy," he said. "I envy your position, here at Power Chemicals, Felty."

"Your first puppet string," I said. "Can you read me its tag?"

The wind from the suction died down and a reporter's flashbulb dazed the inked-on patina of Root Beer's irises as he looked up. "The tag reads— It is…it is written so sloppy, like from a child. I cannot read it." His string pulled him up, out of the S-bend.

"It is nice having someone to envy," I said. "I envy your freedom."

"Free no longer, I must admit. The tag…the tag reads: *Humanity.* A strange tag for a monster to have. It's nice belonging to something bigger." He laughed a solemn chuckle as he appraised the sparkling, multicolored chemicals that caked him, and he appeared over the rim of the pulverized lid with hands outstretched in a new welcome. "Your expectations are strong. They hold me up."